The Ninth Man

By

Bill Pennabaker

This is a work of fiction. Any similarities to real people or organizations are strictly coincidental. In order to add authenticity to the story, the names of certain real baseball teams, baseball players, Major League Baseball and Minor League Baseball have been used fictitiously. This does not imply knowledge of, or involvement by, those people or organizations.

ISBN: 1-4107-1857-3 (Electronic)
ISBN: 1-4107-1858-1 (Paperback)
ISBN: 1-4107-1862-X (Dust Jacket)
ISBN: 1-4107-1863-8 (Rocket Book)

Library of Congress Control Number: 2003090682

This book is printed on acid free paper.

Printed in the United States of America
Bloomington, IN

1stBooks – rev. 02/20/03

Acknowledgements

To my father, Bill Pennabaker. An un-hittable fast-pitch softball pitcher in his prime, when he got older, he was even better.

To my mother, Jane Pennabaker, who never missed one of her eight children's games.

To my lovely wife Marivic, from the Philippines, who although has only been in this country for a short time, has become a rabid Mariner's fan.

To Dave Niehauss, Ron Fairly, Rick Rizzs, and the rest of the Mariner's broadcast team, thank you for making watching and listening to Mariner's games a great experience.

To Drew Mahalic and the Oregon Baseball Campaign – I hope Portland gets it's Major League team – you deserve it. We in Seattle would love the immediate I-5 rivalry, which of course we would always win. ☺

To Susan Goodenow of Eisner-Sanderson, thank you for the insight into women's interest in baseball.

Thank you to the All-Star Book Review Team:

Mark Alfieri	Jillian Chandler	Al Eicholz
Young Forbush	Todd Freefield	Phil Heerwald
Mark Hinish	Dave Mathieson	Dave Nelson
Matt Nichols	Billie Jo Pennabaker	Jane Pennabaker
Ann Prestel	Eric Varness	Julie Varness

Special thanks to Al Eicholz, for being a great sounding board, and for having to endure listening to me talk about this project for the last year. Thanks Al!

Foreword

Like all the other baseball players for the Class A Richmond Tigers, Casey Collins followed a standard game day routine. A light meal a few hours before game time was followed by a short drive to the ballpark, a friendly nod to the lone security guard at the gate before parking, and the walk into the locker room.

Casey checked the line-up card posted on the manager's office door, although, like everyone else, already knew which name would be at the bottom:

1   Jones CF
2   Hernandez 2B
3   Miller 3B
4   Jackson DH
5   Thomas 1B
6   Murray LF
7   Daley C
8   Gonzalez SS
9   Collins RF

And like the other players, while dressing for the game Casey experienced a certain amount of pre-game excitement and jitters. It was *game day* after all, time to "step it up," as they say.

But Casey Collins did not participate in any of the traditional pre-game locker room antics. No snapping of the towels, cracking bad jokes, or any of the other usual banter among teammates. As a matter of fact, there *were* no other teammates in Casey Collins' special, private locker room.

Because unlike the eight other players in the starting line-up, the right fielder and the ninth man on the roster for the Class A Richmond Tigers, was a woman.

One

"I'll take Johnson," twelve year-old Dirk Thomas said, pointing to the red-haired, freckled-faced boy standing at the end of the line. Jerry Johnson nodded as he jogged over and stood behind Dirk. Dirk was the oldest of the boys and usually one of the two team captains.

The other captain today was Brian Smith, and he spoke up next. "I'll take Bobby," he said, as he pointed to a boy near the middle of the line, who grinned as he walked over and took his place behind Brian.

In a scene that is played out every summer on baseball fields all across America, a group of young boys stood in a semi-circle, waiting to be picked for one of the two teams being formed.

One by one, the two captains continued the selection process until all the boys in the line had been chosen. Each captain then turned around and surveyed his team, which is when Dirk Thomas said, "Hey, we're a man short."

This revelation immediately caused every single boy on each team to turn around and start pointing a finger at their teammates one by one while counting out loud until it was agreed that yes, in fact, Dirk's team was one player short.

Dirk looked over at Bobby Carter who was now standing over on Brian Smith's team. "Hey, Bobby," he said, "I thought your brother was coming today."

"Nah, he can't," Bobby replied. "He's grounded."

"Great," Dirk frowned, as he stood there with his hands on his hips. "Now what?"

"We can just close a field," Brian Smith volunteered, referring to a tactic often used when a team couldn't field a full nine players.

"Closing a field" meant that the player who was batting would pick one of the outfield positions and state that they would not hit the ball to that field; if they did, they were out. So, if a batter "closed" right field, the defensive team could put their

1

outfielders in left and center fields and not have to cover right field, allowing them to play with one player short. It wasn't as good as playing with a full team, but at least it allowed them to play.

"No, I hate doing that," Dirk said with disgust. "We need another player." He turned around and took a few steps towards the backstop, behind which were various small groups of kids milling around the bleachers and the surrounding play area.

"Hey," Dirk called out loudly. "We need a ninth man. Anybody want to play?"

Eight-year-old Casey Collins was sitting at one end of the bleachers, and had watched the entire selection process. She immediately leapt up, raised her hand and shouted, "I do!" She grabbed her glove and went running out around the backstop towards the infield.

"Great!" Dirk said as he started to turn back toward the group of players. That was, until he noticed the person who had volunteered. "Hey, wait a minute," he said, "you're a girl."

Casey slowed down and stopped a few feet in front of him, and looked up at him from under the bill of a baseball cap. "Yeah, so?" she asked defiantly.

"You can't play. I thought you were a boy. Thanks, anyway."

"I can play," she insisted. "Just give me a chance. I'll show you."

Dirk stood there with his hands on his hips, his glove dangling from one hand, as he looked her up and down. She was wearing sneakers, gray sweatpants, a baseball shirt with three-quarter-length sleeves and a baseball cap. Her sandy blonde hair was tied in a ponytail, which jutted out from the back of her cap.

"How old are you, anyway?" he asked.

"I'm nine," she lied, then added, "and a half. I'm telling you I can play. My dad's a professional baseball player. He trains me. Just let me play. I'll show you."

Dirk pushed his hat back on his head a few inches as he considered this for a moment. He knew there was a professional baseball player in town; he just didn't know he had

2

a daughter. He looked at Casey. She *was* dressed like a baseball player, and the fact that her dad was a professional impressed him. Besides, he really did hate to play with closed fields. "All right," he said reluctantly. "You can play. But don't blame us if you get hurt." He turned and headed back toward the other boys, who had all been watching intently.

"I won't," Casey promised as she tagged along after him.

"Hey, we've got a ninth," Dirk announced to the group. "She's a girl but I told her she could play. She's got her own glove."

There was a mixture of groans and laughter from the other boys. "Great," one of them said. "As long as she's on your team."

"Don't worry," Dirk countered, "We'll put her in right field. But you guys can't just hit it to her every time up. You have to play fair."

"Sure, no problem," another one chuckled. "You guys are in the field first."

None of them seemed concerned that all of this conversation took place right in front of Casey. In fact, they didn't even ask her name. It didn't bother Casey, as she was just happy to have a chance to play. As the two teams split up, she jogged out into right field as instructed and took her position.

At that age, teams would try to "hide" their weaker players in right field. The thinking was that since most of the boys batted right-handed, they would hit the ball to left or center fields, and that the right fielder wouldn't see that much action. At that age, they usually didn't.

So of course the first boy who came up to bat for the other team went out of his way to hit the ball to Casey in right field. He batted right-handed, but shuffled his feet around and contorted his body in an exaggerated motion so he could hit the ball to the opposite field. On the third pitch, he hit a fly ball to Casey, who positioned herself under it. It was a routine play but nobody on either team expected her to catch it.

Both the first baseman and the second baseman went running out to right field, expecting to have to chase down the ball after Casey missed it. When she made the catch easily and tossed the ball in to the surprised second baseman, he almost dropped the throw.

"Uh, nice catch," he muttered.

"Yeah, nice catch," echoed the first baseman. Neither of them were quite sure if it was luck or not.

"Lucky catch!" someone from the other team groaned, as they now had one out. This did not stop the second boy from also trying to hit the ball to Casey, but he feebly grounded out to the first baseman instead. The third batter tried the same thing, and did succeed in hitting a line drive over the first baseman's head for a hit. Again the first and second basemen went running out to cover for Casey, but again, it wasn't necessary.

She was in position to field the ball long before it got to her, and she scooped it up easily, throwing it over the second baseman's head directly to second base, where the shortstop was covering the bag. The batter had assumed he would get an easy double out of it and he didn't even slide as he approached second base. He was out by five feet, to his chagrin and his teammates'.

Laughter echoed from the opposing bench. "You got thrown out by a girl," one of them mocked as he trotted back to the bench.

"Hey, it was a good throw," he mumbled weakly in self-defense, avoiding the eyes of his teammates who ran by him on their way out to the field.

Casey jogged into the bench where most of her teammates were already assembled. They all looked at her surprisingly and a few even congratulated her on her plays in right field. Dirk Thomas came over and said, "Hey, nice playing out there. What's your name?"

"Casey," she replied. "Casey Collins." The other boys took Dirk's lead and came over and introduced themselves.

"You bat ninth, following Kyle," Dirk commanded as he walked over to the end of the bench, grabbed a bat and headed out to the batter's box.

Casey didn't get her turn to bat until early in the third inning, when she was the first batter up. She grabbed the lightest bat she could find and took her position in the batter's box. The boys from both teams watched curiously as she stepped up to the left side of the plate.

"Hey look, she's a lefty," the third baseman chirped, as he took a few steps closer to the plate.

Brian Smith, the captain for the other team, was playing shortstop, and he turned around and yelled to his outfield. "Hey, the girl's up, everybody move in," he ordered as he motioned with both hands for his teammates to move in closer to the infield.

The boys in the field were all chuckling as the infielders moved up to the edge of the infield grass, and the outfielders took positions only about 10 feet behind them, barely standing on the outfield grass.

"Okay, ready," Smith indicated to the pitcher, who nodded and prepared to go into his windup.

Casey had taken a few practice swings, and she stepped into the batter's box. Standing tall, she held the bat behind her and slightly over her head, waiting for the first pitch. She watched as it went right down the middle of the plate.

"Strike!" the catcher called out. Since there was no umpire in most pick-up games, the catcher typically called balls and strikes, and usually tried to be fair, since the opposing catcher would be calling the balls and strikes when his team was at bat.

"No batter. No batter. She can't hit!" came the chatter from around the infield.

"Come on Casey, get a hit!" came the supporting calls from her teammates.

Casey took a few more practice swings and waited for the second pitch. The pitcher wound up and delivered a pitch that was high and outside.

"Strike two!" the catcher called out.

Casey turned and looked at him. "That wasn't a strike," she complained. "It was high and outside."

5

"It was a strike," the catcher retorted with a smirk. "A guy would have hit it." He grunted as he threw the ball back to the pitcher.

"C'mon, she's afraid to swing the bat," the first baseman called over to the pitcher, who smiled and prepared to deliver the next pitch.

Casey, standing in the batter's box, moved her hands up a couple of inches on the bat, "choking up", as they called it, in order to make the bat feel a little lighter. As the pitcher wound up and delivered another pitch down the middle of the plate, she shifted her weight forward and swung hard at the pitch.

There was a loud *crack* as the bat connected with the ball, which went sailing over the surprised leftfielder's head. "Whoa!" he yelled as he turned around and sprinted after the ball, which had landed 10 feet behind him and was rolling towards the chain-link fence in the outfield.

Casey's team roared in delight at the comical scene taking place on the field. She was well on her way to first base as the left fielder and center fielder went running after the ball. The shortstop was running after the left fielder and yelling as he waved his hands frantically over his head.

"Hurry up! Get it! Throw me the ball!" he yelled in panic.

The left fielder went into a slide as he finally caught up with the ball. Turning around and standing up, he threw the ball to the shortstop, who had come out into the outfield to receive the ball. The shortstop caught the ball, turned and fired a perfect strike to the second baseman, who was covering second.

But Casey had already rounded second base and was halfway on her way to third. The second baseman caught the throw from the shortstop and hurriedly tried to throw it to third base, but by the time the ball got there, Casey had already executed a perfect slide, and was safe by ten feet.

Her teammates were hooting and hollering from their bench. "All right! Way to go! A triple!" they exclaimed in turn.

The shortstop turned to the second baseman, who was standing there with a stunned look on his face.

"Geez, she's fast," he muttered.

"Yeah," was the reply.

Casey scored on a base hit by the next batter. She ended up with 2 hits that day and had made a few more plays in the outfield. The boys had finally learned their lesson and stopped trying to hit it to her intentionally. The opposing outfielders also resumed their normal positions and no longer moved in when Casey came up to bat.

After the game had ended, the players were milling around, gathering up their equipment. Dirk Thomas grabbed his bat and glove and strolled over to Casey, who was dusting herself off and preparing to leave. He grabbed his hat by the bill and shifted it back on his head a little.

"Hey, Collins," he said. "We're playing again next Saturday, if you want to play."

It was the first of many on-field triumphs for Casey Collins, and it was a scenario that would repeat itself throughout her career. There was always the initial questioning of her ability, followed by her proving it on the field, then the eventual acceptance by the other players. She always seemed to be the ninth man, so to speak, but she had also always proved she was as good as, or better than, the other eight.

The question was, how long would this continue, and how far could it take her?

Two

Casey Collins was the only child of Rip and Sue Collins. Rip was a professional baseball player and Sue was a former high school track and field star, with the emphasis on track, excelling in the quarter mile.

Rip Collins spent eleven years in the minor leagues and was once even called up to the majors for a "Cup of Coffee", which was baseball lingo for a brief stay. Rip played center field with the Cincinnati Reds for a total of three weeks, got in to 16 games and went 9 for 52 for a grand batting average of .173. "The Ripper", as he was known, had good speed, a great arm and could hit a fastball out faster than it came in, but he could never quite adjust to the major league curve balls.

Once the major league pitchers figured that out, it was all they threw him, and he struck out 31 times in those 16 games. Originally called up to replace the starting center fielder who was injured, once that player returned, Rip was sent back down to the minors, where he languished for another three years.

He never made it back, and finally gave it up at the ripe old age of thirty-four. Four years later, he developed cancer of the mouth, which spread to his throat, and he died a year after that at the age of thirty-nine. Doctors said it was most likely caused by years of chewing tobacco, and although Sue was constantly trying to get him to quit, Rip continued chewing right until his death.

Casey was only thirteen at that time and was shattered by her father's death. She had lost more than her father; she lost her hero. From the time she was born, her father never showed his initial disappointment at not having a son, but, instead, fostered a loving relationship with his "little ballplayer". Rip refused to let Sue buy Casey any dolls and instead he bought her a glove, bat and ball set when she was only two years old. "Just because she's a girl doesn't mean she can't be a ballplayer," he said. And that was that.

Rip made it very clear to Sue that she had given birth to a baby ballplayer, and being the offspring of two athletes, Casey never really had any choice in the matter. Her natural athleticism was supplemented by her father's constant coaching and encouragement, which led to success on the field. In short, Casey Collins was destined to be a baseball player.

Rip started Casey off young, pitching to her in the living room with a Nerf ball until she started knocking over lamps and pictures, and until Sue finally kicked them out into the backyard. Then it was on to a Wiffle ball at age four and by age five, Rip had her hitting a youth league baseball with a real wooden bat.

Although Casey was naturally right-handed and threw that way, Rip forced her to bat left-handed from the very start. "The best sticks in baseball are usually left-handers," he used to say. Rip told her that the majority of pitchers would be right-handers, so she would be better able to see the ball when it left the pitcher's hand. He explained the natural advantage that left-handed batters had when running to first base because they are already a few steps closer when leaving the batter's box. Rip told her that with her natural speed plus batting left-handed, she could add 20 percentage points to her batting average. She didn't really know what a batting average was at that age, but it sure sounded important.

By the time Casey joined youth league baseball at the age of six, she was already far ahead of the boys. At that age, many of them were just getting their basic hand-eye coordination down, whereas Casey already had an established batting stance, as well as a strong knowledge of the game. She found it much too easy, and preferred playing with her father, who always pushed her to the limits of her abilities.

She continued to play through the youth leagues and joined her high school Junior Varsity men's team when she entered the ninth grade. There were initial objections from many different sources—the school district that was worried about her getting hurt, the boys that thought they were somehow lowering themselves by playing with a girl, and the parents that objected, out of principle, to a girl playing a boy's sport.

But Sue took up the challenge, and fought hard on Casey's behalf, going directly before the school board. "The term *baseball player* is not gender specific," Sue had said, "and neither is *athlete*, and my daughter can play as well as any boy in this town." Sue's insistence, combined with the population dynamics of a small town where they just didn't have that many boys going out for baseball anyway, convinced the Junior Varsity coach to give Casey a tryout one Saturday morning.

After hitting her a few fly balls in the outfield and having his son throw her some pitches, the coach was convinced, and let her on the team. Most of the boys on the team had played with her in pick-up games around the neighborhood at one time or another, and to them it was no big deal. It was just JV's after all.

Most of the opposing pitchers at that age did not know how to pitch to her. They mostly faced right-handers and were uncomfortable when a left-hander came up to the plate. As if that wasn't enough, when they saw that the left-hander coming up to the plate was female, it threw their concentration off. Casey led the team in walks, and with her natural speed, in stolen bases as well.

The next year, she tried out for and made the varsity team as a sixteen-year-old. The quality of pitching was better but it was nothing she couldn't handle. The following year, as a junior, she came in second for team MVP, next to Chip Miller, their senior starting pitcher who went 12 and 1 and made All-County. But he graduated in the spring and the next year, Casey's senior year, the MVP belonged to her.

She led her high school team in batting that year, hitting .428, and also led the team in stolen bases, with 29. Fully one-third of her base hits were infield hits, and it seemed that, as her father had indicated, her natural speed and left-handed approach at the plate had, in fact, given her that batting average lift.

Casey was also voted second string on the All-County team. There were many who thought she should have made first team, and it was suspected that the voters from around the league were still not that comfortable with the concept of a woman playing men's baseball. But her games had become a big event in her hometown of Richmond, Washington, and Casey had become somewhat of a local hero.

She had some college scouts attending her home games, and she even received two offers from small colleges in Washington State. She was tempted by the offers to play college baseball, but she had the feeling that they were more interested in her as a way to sell tickets and to generate positive publicity for their schools. Even though Sue pushed Casey to take one of the offers so she could get a college education, Casey was not ready to leave home, and so she declined.

She spent a year after high school hanging around town and playing baseball for a county league men's team, enjoying continued success. Even though Richmond was a relatively small town, they did have an independent minor league baseball team—the Class A Richmond Tigers. On Casey's second year after high school, the owner offered her a minor league contract. He had made it very clear that although he respected her ability, he also needed her local celebrity status to help sell tickets, and he offered her a salary of $16,500.

She was thrilled, and accepted. And so began the professional baseball career of Casey Collins.

Three

Seventeen years after the eight-year-old girl first proved she could play with the boys, the twenty-five-year-old woman walked through the door of her mother's restaurant. She was tall for a woman -– 5' 10 1/2" and lean at 136 pounds. Her sandy blonde hair was cut short to just below her ears, and she had a light sprinkle of freckles across the bridge of her nose, and a few on each cheek, under her light brown eyes.

Casey's athletic build, which she acquired from her parents, was honed by a lifetime of exercise, and she moved with the grace of a natural athlete. She was not beautiful, but she was attractive—with her father's strong jaw and a hint of her mother's cheekbones. Her freckles made her look younger than her 25 years, and gave her a tomboy-like appearance. The word most often used to describe her appearance, to her chagrin, was "cute". She thought that "cute" was great for a thirteen-year-old girl, but, for a grown woman, it wasn't completely flattering.

She was wearing blue jeans, sneakers and a pullover white cotton T-shirt, and had an athletic bag slung over one shoulder. A patron, seated at the counter eating a piece of pie and sipping some coffee, turned on the swivel bar stool to greet Casey as she entered.

"Hey, Casey, how are you doing?" he said. His name was Burt Drivers, and he was a truck driver for a local delivery service. The irony of his name and his occupation was a constant source of ribbing from his friends.

"I'm good, Burt, how are you?" Casey replied as she walked along the counter. "And how's the pie today?"

"It's great -– blueberry. My favorite. Hey, what were you yesterday, three for four?"

"Nah, the last one was a fielder's choice," she responded, as she continued her way through the restaurant. The counter was on her left, and there were ten tables, covered with red checkered tablecloths, positioned corner to corner, and arranged in two rows along the right side.

There were a few customers scattered among the tables, and most of them knew Casey. They waved their greetings as she came in the café. She gave a quick wave of acknowledgement and said a few "Hello's" in return.

Michael O'Brien was seated at the far end of the counter, and had a plate with a sandwich and some french fries in front of him. Michael was a retired postal carrier, and since he used to work for Uncle Sam, people called him Uncle Mike. He turned to greet Casey as she reached the end of the counter.

"Hey, Uncle Mike," Casey said as she put a hand on his shoulder. "How are you?"

"Good, Casey. And yourself?"

"I'm doing all right, thanks. So, did you see the game last night?"

"Of course," Uncle Mike responded. He was a huge baseball fan, and ever since he retired, had a lot of time on his hands. He attended every Richmond Tiger home game, and even a few road games, and unlike a lot of the more casual baseball fans, he knew a lot about baseball.

"What were you, two for four, last night?" he asked Casey as she stole a french fry off his plate.

"Yeah, fielder's choice on the last one," she answered, munching on the fry.

"I was thinking more about your first at bat," Uncle Mike said as he crossed his arms and looked at Casey. "If Kenny would have tagged up instead of running halfway, you'd have gotten a sacrifice fly and another RBI."

"Well," Casey said with a wink, "I'll send him over to talk to you before the next game." She stepped around the back of the counter and threw her bag in a corner behind the cash register.

Uncle Mike chuckled and went back to his sandwich, as Casey started to head for the double kitchen doors at the end of the counter.

"Casey, is that you?" Sue Collins said loudly as she came out of the kitchen. She was now forty-nine years old; her hair was still dark brown, but her figure had rounded a bit, more from working in the restaurant than anything else. With her high cheekbones and upright posture, it wasn't too hard to see that she used to be an athlete.

Sue was wiping her hands on a towel as she pushed through the swinging double doors. She was wearing her light blue apron that read *Tigers* on the front, which Casey had given her last Christmas.

"Yeah, Mom, it's me," Casey said as she went over to give her mother a kiss on the cheek. "Just stopped in for a quick bite."

"Well, you're in luck. I ran a pot roast special today and we still have some left. I'll fix you a plate with some mashed potatoes and gravy." She grabbed a clean plate from behind the counter and dished up a generous helping of food, setting it on the top of the counter for Casey.

"Mom, you know I don't like to eat too much meat, especially before a game."

"Nonsense," Sue said with a wave of her hand, "You need the protein to keep up your strength."

"Yeah, and I'm going to need that strength just to walk if I eat all of this. Mom!" Casey expressed in exasperation as she looked down at all the food on her plate.

But Sue would have none of it, and was already heading back into the kitchen. "Eat," she commanded as she pushed her way back through the swinging doors.

Casey started in on the plate of food, and glanced at the corner of the wall behind the cash register. It was known as "Casey's Corner", and it was plastered with news clippings and pictures of Casey throughout various stages of her career. Casey was uncomfortable having her pictures pasted all over the walls for everyone to see, but there was no use arguing with a proud mother, and she eventually got used to it.

Sue had opened the restaurant a year after Rip passed away. Although Rip never made a lot of money, he always kept his life insurance policy up-to-date, and Sue took that money and purchased a small restaurant off the main highway leading in and out of Richmond.

She couldn't always make it to Casey's games because of the restaurant, but she always listened to the game on the radio, and it was death to anyone who tried to change the dial when the Richmond Tigers were playing.

Having been married to one baseball player and having raised another one, Sue knew the game pretty well. She also knew most of the Tigers by name, although it was often hard because so many players came and went in the minors. Every now and then, Sue would bake some brownies or cookies and give them to Casey to distribute to the team. Casey always felt that her mother just wanted a family to cook for, and with her father gone and Casey on the road most of the time, the restaurant helped to fill that void.

Casey finished about half of her plate of food, and snuck the rest into a nearby garbage can while Sue was still back in the kitchen. After drinking a small glass of milk, she headed back into the kitchen to say goodbye.

Sue was stirring a big pot of soup on one of the stove tops, and looked up at Casey as she entered the kitchen. "How was everything?" she asked.

"Good, Mom. Thanks."

"Did you eat it all?"

"Well, most of it," Casey answered. A harmless white lie. She came over to give Sue a hug. "Look, Mom, I have to go. I'll see you at home later after the game, okay?"

Sue stopped stirring her soup and hugged Casey back, giving her a light peck on the check. "Okay, sweetheart, you take care, and have a great game tonight. I'll be listening."

"Thanks, Mom. I'll see you later. Love you." Casey turned to head out the door.

"I love you, too," Sue said, and then, right before Casey reached the door, called after her, "Are you sure you got enough to eat?"

"Yes, Mom, I'm sure," Casey said as she went through the door. *If it was up to Mom, I'd weigh 200 pounds*, she chuckled to herself.

Casey grabbed her athletic bag from behind the counter and made her way towards the front door, saying her goodbyes to every one on the way out. She checked her watch as she entered the parking lot, and it showed 4:30. She had plenty of time. It was only about a twenty-minute drive to the ball field, so she would still be there a couple of hours before game time.

Casey got into her car, a 1998 white Honda Civic, popped in a Sheryl Crow CD, and made the short drive to Tiger Stadium, as their stadium was affectionately known. She found a spot in the player's lot, parked her car, and headed inside towards the locker room facilities.

Four

Casey's "special locker room" was actually a converted small office with a single upright gym locker and a bench. The team had installed a bathroom and a small shower with a curtain, and this was where Casey headed before and after every home game. She had personalized it somewhat, with a picture of her father in his Cincinnati Reds uniform and her mom behind the counter in her restaurant.

Casey was almost finished dressing. She had one foot up on the bench and was bending over to lace up her spikes when she heard a knock on the door. The voice of Chuck Olson, the team manager, came through from the outside. Like most professional baseball managers, he was called "Skip", short for "Skipper", by his players.

"Casey, are you decent?" he asked through the door.

"One second, Skip," Casey said as she straightened up and finished buttoning up the front of her jersey. "Okay, come on in."

Olson pushed open the door and poked his head in. "Hey, I need to move you up to bat second tonight. We're facing Rivers and it's going to be tough to score against him. If Kenny gets on, we're going to need to bunt him along and play for the run. And you're my best bunter."

"No problem, boss. Happy to do it."

"Great. I knew I could count on you. See you on the field." Olson pulled his head back and closed the door behind him.

Casey had become a master bunter at the constant urging of her father. She recalled entire afternoons in the backyard dedicated strictly to bunting practice. Rip would throw her fastballs and curves, high and low, inside and outside, over and over again until she could lay down a perfect bunt in any situation.

She would practice the sacrifice bunt, where she would intentionally hit it to a fielder in such a way that he had to throw her out at first base, "sacrificing" herself so a runner already on base could advance to the next base.

Then she would switch to the "drag" bunt, where she would turn her entire body towards first base while holding out the bat and "dragging" the ball along with her down the first base line.

Over the years, she had developed quite a repertoire of different types of bunts, and it had served her well throughout her career. In addition to batting left-handed and having great speed, bunting was another way that Casey was able to compensate for not being as big and strong as the male players she competed against.

Through all those sessions in the backyard, she recalled Rip saying, *"Hey, if you're going to make it to the Bigs, you're going to need every edge you can get. And most of the so-called professional baseball players can't even lay down a decent bunt. If you can do it consistently, you've got an advantage over them. You compile enough advantages and you're in."*

Rip was always saying that—*"If you're going to make it to the Bigs"*—and he said it so often and with such conviction that Casey thought that he actually believed she could make it. At first, she didn't give it much consideration, but the further along she got in her career and the more success she had, the more she thought about it. It became her goal, and it was something she continued to strive for.

She finished lacing up her spikes, grabbed her glove and her bat, and headed out through the tunnel that connected the locker rooms to the field. The rest of the team was filtering out of the locker room, and their spikes made a clickety-click sound as they connected with the concrete floor. It was a sound that was all so familiar to Casey, and she loved it. It just smacked of baseball.

The other players greeted her as their paths merged heading into the tunnel.

"Hi, guys," Casey nodded to the group.

"Casey! Hey, Case! What's up, Case?" they greeted her in turn, with a few high fives thrown in.

Danny Jackson, the Tigers' third baseman, said "Hey, Case, can I borrow that bat of yours tonight? I'm in a major slump and I need help."

"I don't think so, Danny, you might just get some boy cooties on it, and I'd probably start growing a beard or something."

"What do you mean?" kidded Lyle Anderson, their left fielder. "He can't even grow a beard himself. Look at that stubble on his face. It looks like he just forgot to wash."

"Hey, at least I've got something on my face," Jackson countered. You look like you're twelve."

"Heh-heh, very funny," Anderson retorted.

Joel Lewis, their first baseman, spoke up. "Hey Case, I hear you're batting second tonight. What's up with that?"

"Skip wants me there to bunt in case Kenny over there closes his eyes and accidentally gets a hit."

Kenny Jones, their center fielder, feigned a frown, "Ouch, that hurt."

It was all part of the good-natured ribbing that was standard behavior among teammates. It was a way to keep everyone loose, and it helped to establish camaraderie among the players. Casey loved this interaction, and often wished she could share in the locker room antics that she knew took place among the other players. But due to her gender, some things just could not be, and she accepted it as part of her situation.

Most of the other players had accepted Casey as one of the guys. There were the exceptions, of course, but most of them respected her hard-nosed style of play, her constant hustle, and they were always amazed at her batting style. Very few of them ever felt threatened by her, since most of them were more worried about making it to the next level themselves.

Of course, a few of them had made some passes at Casey, but she made it clear she was not interested. She had tried dating another player once in high school, but when she wouldn't sleep with the guy on their first date, he went around telling everyone on the team that she did anyway, and it made things uncomfortable for the rest of the season. "I don't date baseball players," she would declare, and it usually ended there.

The players were now making their way out to the field and starting their pre-game warm-ups. The stadium was pretty typical for minor league baseball. It sat about 7,500 people, had bleachers that extended into the outfield along either baseline, and a modest press box behind home plate. The outfield fence looked like a collection of billboards filled with advertisements from local companies.

Casey walked up through the dugout and onto the field, crossing over the white chalk lines that separated fair territory from foul territory. This is where her transformation began— where she changed from a quiet, unassuming, polite young woman to a serious, aggressive, get-out-of-my-way-or-I'll-kick-your-ass professional baseball player. For Casey, it was like walking through some kind of magic portal, and it never ceased to exhilarate her.

She started by taking a lap around the entire field, and doing a couple of short sprints in the outfield. Even though she had been playing on the same field for years, she always checked the condition of the grass and the warning track before every game. It was just part of being prepared, and looking for any edge she could get.

The fans were starting to filter in, and a few of them called to Casey with choruses of "Hey, Casey, good luck tonight," and "Go get 'em, girl."

A few of the opposing players were checking her out, some looking to see how she handled the fly balls from batting practice and the rest just checking to see how she looked in her baseball pants. She was used to it by now. Although it was pretty much common knowledge around the league that the Tigers had a woman playing for them, there were always some players who had just signed contracts and were new to the league. They wanted to see what all the fuss was about. For Casey, it just went with the territory.

After both teams had taken their batting practice, the pre-game routine drew to an end, and each team made their way to their respective benches. They stowed their gloves and reassembled in front of their dugouts for the national anthem.

Once the anthem was finished, the hometown Tigers took the field and Casey ran out to her usual spot in right field. After a few warm-up tosses with the center fielder, the game was ready to start. Casey took the last throw from the center fielder and tossed the ball in towards the dugout, where the batboy retrieved it and placed it back in the ball rack, ready for the next inning. Casey took a few steps over to where she normally stood and assumed the ready position, hunched over with her hands on her knees.

"C'mon, Jesse," she yelled into the pitcher. "Good game now."

The other Tigers began their chatter in support of their pitcher.

"C'mon, Jess. C'mon, Babe."

"C'mon, Jess, you're the man now."

Jesse Palmer was from Mississippi, and his father was a Baptist preacher. This fact had earned him the nickname "The Preacher".

"C'mon, Preach, let's step it up now."

The leadoff batter for the visiting Daleyville Patriots, Johnny Patterson, stepped into the batter's box. "The Preacher" started him off with a fastball down the middle for a called strike one.

The chatter continued, as "The Preacher" wound up and delivered the next pitch. Wide and outside, for ball one. The following pitch was a curve ball that Patterson hit feebly back to the pitcher, who fielded it easily and threw the ball to first for out number one.

"'Atta boy, Preach," The Tigers all yelled, the infielders throwing the ball around to each other and holding up one finger over their heads to indicate that there was one out. It was critical that every player on the team always knew how many outs there were so that they could make the right play in the event that the ball was hit to them.

The second batter struck out and the third batter hit a routine fly ball to the left fielder. The Tigers all headed into the dugout, shouting encouragement to Jesse and high-fiving each other. "The Preacher" had good stuff tonight.

The visiting Patriots took the field and it was Richmond's turn to bat. Their leadoff hitter, Kenny Jones, stepped into the box as the public address announcer called out his name. "Leading off for the Richmond Tigers, the center fielder, Kenny Jones." There was a smattering of applause from the hometown fans as the opposing pitcher, Mitch Rivers, took the signs from the catcher.

Casey, batting second tonight, stepped into the on-deck circle. Grabbing her bat by the handle and holding it upside down with the fat end on the ground, she picked up the "doughnut" and placed in on her bat. The doughnut was a small, weighted metal ring that would fit over the small end of the bat and slide down to the fat part of the bat. The purpose of the doughnut was to make the bat heavier when the players were taking their practice swings, so that when it was their turn to bat and they removed the ring, their bat would feel lighter, in theory making it easier to hit the fastballs.

Casey watched closely as the pitcher wound up and delivered the first pitch. "Steee-rike!" the umpire called out as a fastball cracked into the catcher's mitt. Casey looked up at the scoreboard, where, like many ballparks these days, the Richmond scoreboard had a radar gun display which showed the miles per hour of each pitch. 91 MPH.

Not bad, she thought to herself as she continued to take her practice swings. Skip had told them during the pre-game briefing that that the opposing pitcher had good speed on his fastball, and it looked like it was true.

The pitcher wound up to deliver the second pitch. Another fastball, this one showing 92 mph on the radar gun. Jones swung late and fouled it off into the crowd along the first base line. The third pitch was also a fastball, and caught the inside corner of the plate. Jones watched it go by as the scoreboard showed 93 mph.

"Steee-rike three!" the umpire yelled, combining it with an emphatic motion of turning sideways, pushing one arm forward while pulling the other one to his chest. "Batter's out!"

Jones stood there for a moment, frozen, then headed sheepishly back to the dugout. "Be careful, he's quick," he muttered with a shake of his head as he passed Casey on his way back into the dugout. Casey, still in the on-deck circle, turned her bat upside down and pounded it into the ground, causing the metal doughnut to slip off. She nodded and made her way to the batter's box, pausing to take a couple of short, quick swings with the now lighter feeling bat.

"Now batting, the right fielder, Casey Collins," came the voice over the loudspeaker. A hearty cheer rose up from the crowd as they acknowledged their hometown hero, or this case, heroine. Casey walked up to the plate, clicking the bat on each of her spikes before she stepped into the batter's box. It was a little habit she had developed over the years and she repeated it every time she went to the plate.

Shouts of encouragement came from the crowd, "Come on, Casey, get a hit!" and "Let's go, Casey, you can do it!"

The inevitable chiding from the other team began. "Come on, she can't hit," the catcher yelled, emphasizing the word *she*.

"C'mon, Mitch, blow her away, man," from an infielder.

"Show her who's boss, Mitch," came in from outfield.

"C'mon, hummer, bring it to me now," the catcher called as he gave the pitcher the sign for the first pitch.

Casey was used to it, as she'd heard it all before. She blocked it out and surveyed the field before assuming her batting stance. She held her bat firmly, holding it high behind and over her head, then lowered it slightly so that her wrists were about chest level. If the ball came in above her wrists, it would be out of the strike zone, and she wouldn't swing. Likewise, if the pitch came in below her knees, she would lay off it. She watched the pitcher closely as she prepared for the first pitch.

Mitch Rivers wound up and threw a screaming fastball right down the middle of the plate. Casey watched it go by for a called strike one. She glanced at the scoreboard—93 miles an hour. Kenny was right. This guy was quick. She "choked up" up on her bat, moving both hands higher by a few inches, trying to make the bat seem shorter and easier to swing.

She resumed her stance and prepared for the second pitch. Another screamer right down the middle. This time Casey swung, and fouled the pitch off down the left side of the field toward the third base dugout. Strike two.

"C'mon, Mitch, she can't keep up with you. Set her down," someone called from the Patriots dugout.

"C'mon, Case, you can take him," the Tigers manager yelled from the dugout.

Casey backed one foot out of the batter's box and stared at the pitcher, as he glared back. *Think,* her dad's voice rang in the back of her head. *Think. What's this guy all about? He's a fastball pitcher and he's on his game tonight. He's a guy and he's never faced a woman before so he's going to try to blow me away with another fastball. An ego play all the way.*

She stepped back into the batter's box as the pitcher went through his windup and delivered. As he was preparing to release the ball, Casey shifted her weight from her back foot to her front foot and prepared to start her swing. If the pitch was going to be a strike, she would complete her swing, and if it was a ball she would "check" her swing, stopping it before her bat crossed over the plate.

With a fastball pitcher like this, there wasn't enough time to wait and see if the pitch was going to be a strike before starting her swing. The pitch would be by her before she was halfway into it. By starting her swing early, it enabled Casey to gain some forward momentum, and it was another way in which she compensated for the bigger, stronger pitchers she faced.

Sure enough, the next pitch was a fastball right down the middle of the plate. She stepped into the pitch and completed her swing, snapping her wrist forward as her bat connected with the ball. There was a loud *crack* as the ball sailed on a line drive over the third baseman's head and bounced ten feet behind him.

Being hit by a left-hander who was swinging a little late, the baseball had a lot of spin on it and was tailing off to the left as it hit the grass. It bounced and continued to skew to the left as it rolled into the outfield. The left fielder rushed up to field the ball as it headed toward the short wall along the third base line.

With the crack of the bat, Casey was on her way down the first base line. She glanced at the ball and saw it go over the third baseman's head as she neared first base.

"Look at two! Look at two!" the first base coach shouted, as he waved his left arm in a windmill fashion towards second base, indicating that Casey should take a wide turn around first base and possibly try for a double.

As she made her turn around first, Casey saw that the left fielder was just approaching the ball, which had skidded along the wall behind third base. She immediately made the commitment and put her head down, heading for second.

The left fielder reached the ball and bent over to pick it up while bracing his right foot against the bottom of the wall. He pushed off slightly as he raised up and fired the ball toward second base, where the second baseman was straddling the bag, waiting for the ball and eyeing Casey as she approached the bag.

Casey saw the throw and started to slide. She looked as if she was going to run straight into center field as she threw her feet out in front of her as her rear end hit the dirt. The throw came into the second baseman on one hop. In a single motion, he caught the ball in his glove and swept it over to where Casey was sliding in order to tag her. But his sweep went empty, as Casey actually slid by the bag, and, on her way past it, reached out and grabbed it with her left hand.

"SAFE!" the umpire called from his squat position two feet from the play.

A loud cheer rose up from the crowd as Casey called time-out so she could brush herself off. In her mind, she silently thanked Rip for all the sliding practice he made her take in the backyard. It was one more edge that she could chalk up to her father's coaching.

"Nice slide," the second baseman commented as he watched Casey brush herself off.

"Thanks," she replied as she took her position on the base.

"Nice hit, too," he smirked as he headed back to his position between second and first.

"Thanks again," she smiled as the umpire indicated that play was to resume.

One out and a runner on second. Casey looked at the pitcher, who glared back at her as if to say, *Who do you think you are, hitting me like that?* Casey smirked at him and took a few steps off of second base. She had learned long ago not to be intimated and wouldn't have any of it here. She looked over at the third base coach to check the signals, but they were only for the batter to swing away.

Rivers went into his stretch as he took his signal from the catcher. He swiveled his head a couple of times to check Casey at second base, and delivered his pitch to Danny Jackson, the Tigers number three hitter and third baseman. Again, it was a fastball right down the middle, and Jackson smacked it high and deep, but foul, down the left field line.

Casey had run halfway towards third base while watching the ball to see what would happen, and now she trotted back to second base, watching the pitcher's face closely. His expression told her that he was still a little shaken by her hit and by the fact that Jackson had been right on in timing his last fastball, and probably feeling lucky that he hadn't given up a two-run homer.

That means he's probably going to go to a breaking ball, she thought to herself. *And that will give me more time.* She took her lead off of second again as the pitcher went into his stretch. He glanced over at her once, and then started his move toward the plate. Casey waited for him to commit to throwing home, and took off towards third base, sprinting as fast as she could and glancing towards home plate.

Jackson saw her take off and swung at the pitch even though it was low and outside, in order to make the catcher wait for him to complete the swing before he could catch the ball and step forward to make the throw to third. Additionally, being a right-hand batter and fairly large, Jackson made no effort to get out of the catcher's way as he attempted to throw to third base.

Casey was already beginning her slide as the catcher was releasing the ball. The throw was high and Casey slid safely into the bag, popping up to her feet while standing on the bag. Again the hometown crowd cheered, as the Tigers now had a runner on third with only one out.

"Nice job, Case," the third base coach said with a shrug. He hadn't called for a steal, but he had learned quite a while ago that when Casey wanted to go, she went, and more often than not she made it. And now a sacrifice fly would get them a run.

Jackson, now knowing he didn't need a hit to let her score, concentrated on hitting the ball high and hard, which he did on the third pitch. Casey watched the towering fly ball drop into the center fielder's glove, and she tagged up and scored easily, giving the Richmond Tigers a one-run lead.

After the next batter struck out, it was the Tiger's turn to take the field. The players jogged out to their respective positions, with Casey taking hers in right field. After a few warm-up throws, it was time to play ball, as the number four hitter for the Daleyville Patriots stepped into the box. He was leading the league in home runs, and Chuck Olson yelled out to the outfielders, "Give him some room," indicating that they should back up a couple of steps.

On the second pitch, he hit a blazing line drive to right field, over Casey's head, and she immediately starting running backwards towards the fence. As she reached the end of the grass and hit the strip of dirt known as the warning track, she realized that the ball was going to hit the fence, and that she wouldn't be able to catch it on the fly.

She judged where she thought the ball was going to hit, and turned around to face the fence squarely. As the ball slammed off the fence and hit the ground, Casey caught in on the first bounce. She wheeled around and fired the ball to the second baseman, Luis Hernandez, who had run twenty feet into the outfield to take the relay throw from Casey. He, in turn, wheeled around and threw it to the shortstop covering second base. The base runner, who was thinking that he might be able to turn the hit into a triple, saw the relay throw come in to second, and cut his run short, sliding into second base for a double.

Jessie Palmer looked out at Casey from the pitcher's mound, and gave her a nod, acknowledging that her play had saved them from having a runner on third with no outs. He struck out the next batter, and got the following batter to fly out to left field. Daleyville now had two outs, with a runner on second. It looked like Richmond might get out of the inning without giving up a run, until the next batter hit a rocket shot into the gap in left center field. The base runner scored easily, and it was now tied 1-1. The following batter grounded out to the third baseman for the final out, but the damage had been done.

The two teams battled it out for the next seven innings, until it was 1-1 in the bottom of the ninth inning. After her initial hit back in the first inning, Casey had popped out in the fifth and grounded out in the seventh, making her 1 for 3 so far. She now stood on the on-deck circle as Kenny Jones prepared to step into the batter's box to lead off the inning for Richmond.

"C'mon, Kenny, we need you on, man," Casey said in encouragement.

Jones, who was 0 for 3 in the game so far, jumped on the very first pitch and hit a line drive right over the pitcher's head into short-center field for a single. The crowd cheered, as Richmond now had a man on first with no outs, and Casey stepped up to the plate. The hometown crowd knew by now that Casey was a great bunter, and they also knew that her job was to move the base runner down to second base and in to scoring position.

"Come on, Casey, get it down, now," a man yelled from the stands.

Casey took up her stance, briefly checking the third base coach for the signal, even though everyone in the stadium knew she was there to bunt. As the pitcher went into his windup, she moved her left hand halfway down towards the end of the bat, so that her hands were about eighteen inches apart. She also squared around to face the pitcher, so that she could have a better look at the ball coming in to the plate.

The ball came zinging right down the middle of the plate, but Casey let it go for a called strike one. A few people in the crowd groaned, wondering why Casey had let a perfect pitch go without executing the bunt. But Casey had done this intentionally so she could see how the opposing team would play it defensively. Just as Casey had several different types of bunts in her repertoire, the defensive team had several different ways in which they positioned themselves in order to field a bunt. There were almost as many strategies involved as there was skill.

In this case, Casey noticed that both the first and third basemen were charging in towards the plate, while the shortstop covered second base and the second baseman ran over to cover first. This told Casey where she was going to place her bunt.

She was back into her regular stance as the pitcher wound up and delivered the next pitch. Again, Casey squared around to bunt, and again the infielders positioned themselves as they had the play before, with every player in motion.

As the ball reached Casey, rather than just softly bunting it to one of the players and sacrificing herself, Casey moved the fat end of the bat forward sharply, "pushing" the ball firmly to where the second baseman had been playing. This wreaked havoc on the defense, as the second baseman was supposed to cover first base, and he had already started running in that direction. Casey's bunt forced him to skid to a stop and backtrack in order to field the ball.

The first baseman, seeing how the ball had been hit, now attempted to back peddle towards first base in order to cover the bag, as the pitcher, a little late, also ran over to cover it. But Casey was running forward at full speed, and raced past the scrambling first baseman on her way to the bag. By the time the second baseman fielded the ball and threw it to first base, Casey had already passed the bag, and Kenny Jones had slid safely into second base.

The crowd cheered wildly, as did the players and the coaches for the Richmond Tigers. Casey had taken a risk by trying for a base hit rather than the sure sacrifice bunt, but as they had seen from her before, it had been successful, and now they had runners on first and second with nobody out.

Now it was the third baseman Danny Jackson's turn to bat, and he was given the bunt signal. All he had to do now was lay down a decent sacrifice bunt and the Tigers would have runners on second and third with only one out. That would give them the opportunity to score the winning run off of a sacrifice fly or any kind of base hit.

But Danny Jackson was a power hitter and not called on to bunt often. As Rip Collins had said, many professional baseball players, especially the power hitters, had difficulty in laying down a good bunt. Jackson was a perfect example. Instead of squaring around to face the pitcher and spreading his hands apart on the bat, he half-turned towards the pitcher and tried to slap the ball lightly using his normal grip.

The ball went straight up in the air about ten feet, and the catcher ripped off his mask and prepared to make the catch. Both base coaches yelled "Back!" to Casey and to Kenny Jones, trying to let them know that Jackson had popped up. Casey had only taken a few steps toward second, and had been watching the ball, and she took three steps and dived safely back into first base.

But Kenny Jones had run halfway down to third base, and slipped a little as he tried to change directions. The catcher, already facing second base as he caught the pop-up, fired the ball down to second as the shortstop raced over to cover the bag. Jones was out by several feet, and the Patriots had an easy double play.

The crowd booed at the poor bunt attempt by Jackson, who slammed his bat into the ground, and walked back to the dugout in disgust. Now the Tigers had two outs and a runner on first. Normally, it would take at least two base hits to let Casey score, unless someone hit one into one of the outfield gaps, or a home run.

Casey decided that it was time to take matters into her own hands. As Joel Lewis, the number four hitter for Richmond, stepped up to the plate, she looked at him and patted the side of her left hip with one hand. It was a signal for him to give her a chance to steal second before he swung away. Lewis tugged at his belt as he stepped into the batter's box, acknowledging to Casey that he would give her the chance to steal second.

She took her lead off of first, watching the pitcher closely for a sign that he was going to throw home. The pitcher, remembering Casey's speed from the third inning, threw over to first base twice in an attempt to keep her closer to the bag. Both times Casey took one step and dove back into the bag safely.

Rising up from the dirt and brushing herself off, Casey again took her lead off of first. She assumed her ready position, hunched over slightly, facing the pitcher and placing one hand on each thigh. As the pitcher went into his stretch, she saw the signal she was looking for, which told her he was going to throw home, and she took off.

Using her left hand to provide an extra push off with her left leg, she turned and sprinted towards second. She was at full speed in a few strides, and turned her head once to look towards the catcher. The pitch had been in the dirt, and the catcher had some difficulty digging the ball out. He got a handle on the ball and stood up, prepared to throw down to second base. But he saw that Casey was already starting her slide, and decided to hold his throw.

The crowd cheered as now, suddenly, the game had changed. Casey was in scoring position and a base hit could allow her to score. Again, the pitcher glared at her in frustration from the mound. He looked at her once as he went into this stretch, remembering that Casey had stolen third off of him earlier. But he knew she probably wouldn't steal here, since with two outs there was no real advantage to her being on third as opposed to second, and he threw home.

It was a slider over the outside corner, and Lewis stepped into it as he swung, sending the ball over the first baseman's head. Casey was off with the crack of the bat, and was watching the third base coach intently as she approached the bag. He was waving his left arm wildly and yelling "Go Home! Go Home!"

The crowd was on its feet as Casey hit the inside of third base with her left foot, and made her way towards home plate.

The on-deck batter had come out of the on-deck circle to stand a few feet behind the catcher. His job was to tell Casey whether or not to slide, based on how close the play was going to be.

Casey saw that he was down on both knees and pushing his hands downward towards the ground—the sign to slide. Casey glanced briefly to the left side of the field and saw the ball coming in from the outfield. She went into her slide as the ball came in, bouncing once before the catcher caught it. He made a sweeping move with his glove to where Casey was sliding, but he was late by a good second. Casey was safe, and had just scored the winning run.

The crowd roared as the Richmond players rushed out of the dugout to greet Casey. They swarmed around her, giving her high fives and patting her on the back. Lewis, who just had the game-winning hit, stopped at first and came jogging in to join the celebration.

Casey raised her hand high as he approached. "Nice hit, big man," she said as he smacked her hand in recognition.

"Hey, it was all you, Babe," he responded. "Great hustle!"

The players finished congratulating each other, as Casey dusted herself off. Today's victory was due in large part to her efforts. She had scored both runs, and ended up going 2 for 4 with two stolen bases. Defensively, she had performed well, making some good plays in the outfield. It was when her team was on offense that she presented the most danger to opposing teams.

Her broad repertoire of bunts, combined with her great speed and base-stealing prowess, put constant pressure on the defense. Almost one-third of her hits for the season were bunts or other infield hits, and once again, her father had been proven correct about the game of baseball. You didn't have to be big and strong and hit 25 home runs in order to succeed. If you played intelligently, hustled, and took advantage of opportunities you could be every bit as effective as the big guys.

Casey finished dusting herself off. Her uniform was filthy at the front and back, a result of many slides and dives throughout the game. She felt like a little kid who just finished playing with her friends in the backyard, and thought to herself, *God I love this game.*

Five

Two divisions above Casey's Single A Richmond team, Triple A Sacramento was taking on visiting Portland. The pitcher for Sacramento, Ryan Miller, glared at the opposing batter, Jason Taylor, as he stepped into the batter's box. Taylor had hit a two-run home run off of him his last time up and a towering solo home run off of him in the first inning.

Taylor smirked at the pitcher and stepped into the box, digging his heels into the dirt about six inches from the plate. He took a few practice swings and then assumed his batting stance, waiting for the first pitch.

Miller continued glaring, and after pretending to take the sign from the catcher, wound up and threw a fastball as hard as he could, directly at Taylor's midsection. Taylor, realizing that he could not avoid the baseball heading right towards him, tucked his head and turned his shoulders away from the pitch, trying to shield himself from the ball. It plunked him right in the middle of the back with a resounding *thud*, causing Taylor to drop his bat and cringe in pain. The crowd let out a sympathetic "Oooh" at the sound of the baseball connecting with the middle of his back.

Taylor threw down his bat, turned towards the pitcher, and ran directly at him. The catcher threw off his mask and sprinted after Taylor. Still on the mound, Miller dropped his glove and assumed a defensive fighting stance. As Taylor approached the pitcher and was only a few feet away, the catcher dove and tackled him right at the edge of the dirt, causing Taylor, the catcher and the pitcher to tumble together in a heap on the mound.

The other players on the field rushed towards the mound. The crowd egged them on as the players from both benches raced out onto the field, all converging on and around the pitcher's mound. Players from the two teams were pushing and shoving each other, some actually throwing punches, while the umpires and the managers from to both teams were trying to separate the players and put a halt to the fighting.

It took them twenty minutes to get the teams separated and back to their respective dugouts. Miller and Taylor were both thrown out of the game, as well as the first baseman, who had rushed in and thrown a few punches. By the time Sacramento brought in a new pitcher and he went through his warm-up pitches, the game had already been delayed for 31 minutes.

It had been an ugly scene. More than just mere pushing and shoving among players, real punches were thrown and landed. One of the players was bleeding from a cut on his forehead and another player had to be helped off the field by his teammates, due to a badly sprained ankle. It was part of a disturbing trend that had been developing in the minor leagues, and had many people asking what was going to be done about the situation.

Six

Three days after the brawl between Sacramento and Portland, the current president of the Pacific Coast League, Huey Jacobs, paced in front of the group of sixteen team owners assembled in the hotel conference room. It was July 1, and the league was on a three-day break for the annual PCL All Star Game, which was being held this year in Spokane, Washington. Late last week, Jacobs had summoned the owners to Spokane for an emergency meeting.

Short and pudgy at 5'8" and 170 pounds, Jacobs had a round face that always seemed to be flushed, and people could never quite tell if he was upset or not. This morning, his face was even more red than usual, and in this case the redness was obviously a result of anger, which he showed visibly.

He slapped a copy of a report he had been holding in his hand on the table at the front of the room and said with disgust, "Look at this! Seven fights in the last month alone. Eighteen players ejected, five suspended and nine others placed on injured reserve as a result of injuries from fights. The papers are calling it "Base-Brawl". Last week, *ASN* called it "Friday night at the fights" and even the major league president called me to ask what I was going to do about it."

Leaning forward and placing both hands on the table, he continued, "Gentlemen, I'm telling you, this is going to stop. We are a family-oriented business and we will start conducting ourselves as professionals and not a bunch of soccer hooligans."

He pointed at Bud Harley, owner of the *Portland Power*, dressed in a suit and tie and sitting in the front row with his arms crossed. "You, Harley. Your guys are responsible for two of those fights in just the last week. What the hell was that all about?"

Harley uncrossed his arms, spread them outward and opened up his hands in defense, "Hey, Miller from Sacramento beaned my catcher the next time up after he hit a home run, and the next day some kid from Vancouver hit three of our players in one inning."

Sitting two rows behind Bud Harley, the Vancouver owner interjected. "Hey, we just signed the kid. He's young and he's wild."

Harley turned to face him, as he continued, "Well, my guys had enough and they rushed him. What did you expect them to do?"

The president walked around to the front of the table and pointed at Harley, "*I* expect your managers to keep them in the dugout where they belong, and if they have a problem with the way the game is being run, then they take it to the head umpire, and if that doesn't work, then you bring it me."

Another owner raised his hand and asked, "Have you talked with the umpires about this?"

"I have a meeting with Barry Mitchell tomorrow." Barry Mitchell was the head of minor league umpires. The president pointed a finger at the group for emphasis. "But it starts with you and your managers, and I expect you to control your players."

The owner of the Phoenix Vipers spoke up from the back of the room. "What can we do? You know the current trend among batters to crowd the plate, and the pitchers think *they* own the plate. People are going to get hit. That's part of baseball."

Jacobs was standing there with his hands on his hips. "Yeah, it's part of baseball, but turning it into an all-out free-for-all is not what this game is about. It's not what this *league* is about."

Bud Harley spoke again. "Okay, so what are we going to do about this?"

The president took a few steps back over to the table and picked up a stack of memos. He walked to the first person in each row and handed them a small stack so they could pass it along to others in the row. Returning to the front of the room, he held one of the memos in his hand as he faced the group.

"I'll tell you what we're going to do. Effective immediately, I am enacting the following measures." He emphatically raised his fingers in succession as he started to read from the memo.

"ONE," he stated firmly as he raised one finger. "Any player involved in any kind of fight, regardless of the reason and regardless of who instigated it, will automatically be suspended for one week.

"TWO," he continued, holding up a second finger. "That player will be fined the sum of one thousand dollars."

This caused some rumbling among the group. "One thousand dollars!" objected Ted Fryman, the owner of the Calgary Cowboys. "These kids don't have that kind of money."

Jacobs looked him straight in the eye. "Well, maybe now they'll get the idea that I'm serious about this. Of course, if you want to cover the fine yourself, that's your choice, but the fine *will* be levied, and that's final. Now, shall I continue?" He raised his eyebrows, challenging anyone to object. Fryman sulked back into his chair, and the rest of the room went silent.

"THREE," Jacobs read on, "The manager of the team involved in fighting will be fined the sum of two thousand five hundred dollars." Again, there was a murmur from the group and again Jacobs silenced them with a look.

He continued, "FOUR, any player involved in a fight a second time will be suspended for the rest of the season." He paused for emphasis.

"Finally, FIVE—and I'm serious about this gentlemen. If this fighting continues, I will suspend the season until further notice."

John Seybourne, owner of the Spokane Steam, jumped to his feet and said, "C'mon, Huey, don't you think that's a little extreme? I mean, we're trying to run a business here. Most of us are small market teams, and we're barely profitable as it is. Sometimes things just get out of hand."

"Not anymore they won't. I suggest you get your teams and your businesses under control, and let's get back to playing some baseball. Now, if you want to check the league charter, you will see I have full authority to implement these measures, and I am fully committed to enforcing them."

Another owner started to say something, but Jacobs waved his hand in dismissal. "It's already done," he stated, as he turned and stormed out of the room.

The owners were left sitting in their chairs, shaking their heads and looking around at each other. They all felt it was a bit of overreaction, and they wondered what had gotten the president so riled up.

What they didn't know was that since the beginning of the season, Huey Jacobs had been maneuvering for a front-office job up in the major leagues with the New York Mets. He knew his performance was being scrutinized this year, and that people were watching to see how he handled this situation.

He wasn't about to let a bunch of brawling hooligans jeopardize his future career. He would fine everybody, even the batboys, if that's what he had to do to keep the season under control.

Seven

Harold "Bud" Harley was not only a savvy businessman; he was a marketing genius. At age nineteen, he took the money his parents had given him for his college tuition and opened a used car lot. By the time he was twenty-five, it was the largest in the metropolitan Portland area.

No car dealer in America who had ever used gimmicks in an outlandish commercial had anything over Bud. He did it all — the crazy costumes, the pie-in-the face routines, the ads featuring scantily clad women, and of course, the corny tag lines – *"You can trust me, I'm your Bud. Bud Harley that is."*

His most famous commercial featured two men in white coats dragging a man in a straitjacket away from the car lot. The tag line was *"You'd have to be crazy not to buy a car from me!"* It didn't go over too well with the Psychiatric Association of Oregon, but it did gain him notoriety in the Portland area.

At age twenty-nine, he purchased a new car dealership from Mitzua (Mit-zoo-ah) Motors, an up-and-coming Japanese automobile maker that was interested in expanding into the Pacific Northwest. Five years later, there were three Mitzua Motors dealerships in the greater Portland area, and Bud Harley owned them all. At the request of the Mitzua management, he toned down his outrageous ads somewhat, but he was always looking for a new way to market his products.

He was the first to offer college seniors a year's free lease if they would agree to buy a car from Mitzua when they graduated. That and a few other creative campaigns earned Bud some acclaim not only within the Portland area but also within the Mitzua Corporation back in Japan. He was named Mitzua Motors' Dealer of the Year for two years in a row.

Bud's one great love, other than cars (and making money), was baseball. One of his favorite things to do was to travel north to Seattle to catch a weekend series with the Mariners. It was only a short three-hour drive, and he would put his luxury

Mitzua 5000 XE on cruise control, pop in a couple of jazz CD's, and relax. He had been traveling back and forth between Seattle and Portland for several years, but he always lamented the fact that Portland did not have a major league baseball team of their own.

Bud knew there were many people in Oregon who loved Major League Baseball, but those who didn't want to make the drive north to Seattle to watch the Mariners play, or take a longer trip south to watch the California teams play, were out of luck.

He was sure the city could support a major league team. There were over two million people in the Portland metropolitan area alone. Bud knew that they could also draw people from Eugene, Corvalis and Salem to the south, and from nearby Vancouver, Washington and maybe even Olympia, to the north.

At the age of thirty-six, Bud purchased the *Portland Warriors*, a Class AAA minor league baseball team, from the widow of the previous owner, who had passed away the year before. She had been struggling to keep the team profitable ever since her husband died, and she was anxious to sell the team. Bud immediately renamed the team *The Portland Power*, and the marketing genius went to work.

New uniforms, new marketing slogans – *"FEEL THE POWER"* and *"WATCH THE POWER SURGE"*, along with promotional tie-ins with his automobile dealerships gave the team new life. But alas, it was still only the minor leagues, and Bud was still harboring a dream to bring a major league baseball franchise to Portland. He began discussions with Major League Baseball about qualifying for a franchise when the league next expanded, or more likely, when another franchise was looking to relocate.

Bud presented the facts: Portland is the twenty-second-largest market in the U.S., and the biggest city in the country without a major league baseball franchise. Some of the teams that do have major league franchises are smaller than the Portland metropolitan area, and baseball viewership in the Portland area actually exceeded that of eight of the cities that did have an MLB franchise. Baseball and Portland seemed to be a perfect match.

But Bud had two problems in convincing MLB to award a new franchise to Portland. One problem was financing. Although Bud had been very successful, and had a net worth of over $40 million, he did not have the finances required to sustain a major league franchise.

His second problem was television viewership. No major league franchise could sustain itself without a substantial television contract, which could add several million dollars in additional revenue to the team. Even with the population from the major cities in Oregon and possibly a few from southern Washington State, he was only looking at around five million.

Bud realized that the answer to both problems was Mitzua Motors. Not only did they have deep pockets themselves, but like other large corporations in Japan, they were part of a larger business conglomerate, called a *Keiretsu*. One of the other members in their business conglomerate was TTV–Tokyo Television.   With estimated viewership at over 15 million people, they could far exceed any viewing audience that Bud would have reached in the greater Portland area.

With the recent success of Japanese baseball players in the major leagues, interest in baseball was on the rise in Japan. That fact, combined with Bud's reputation as a savvy businessman, convinced Mitzua Motors to become a silent partner in a bid to bring a major league baseball franchise to Portland.

There were only two pre-requisites required to secure Mitzua's backing. Bud had to agree to have at least one Japanese player on the roster at all times, and he had to demonstrate that he could generate enough local interest for baseball in and around the Portland area to fill a major league stadium.

The second condition was the one that had him most concerned. Last year had been wildly successful for the Power, as they had won their division for the third year in a row. He had even seen some kids scalping tickets outside the gate before one of the playoff games. *Amazing. Scalping tickets to a minor league baseball game*. It was clear that people in Portland were hungry for good baseball. His team's success had convinced him to take out a loan to add 15,000 new seats to the stadium, which was completed over the winter. This brought his stadium capacity up to 35,000, which was approaching major league standards.

But this year had been different. His team was struggling, currently in third place by six games. Their two best pitchers and their big home-run hitter from last year were all called up to the majors at the beginning of this season, and three of the nine players who the league president had mentioned were on the injured reserve list, were his.

A couple of weeks of bad weather early in the season combined with his team's mediocre performance had kept the crowds down. They tried some of the standard promotions and giveaways but nothing seemed to grab the attention of the fans, and now this whole fighting thing had cast a shadow over the whole season. Bud Harley saw his dream of bringing a major league franchise to Portland crumbling before him.

A few minutes after Huey Jacobs made his dramatic exit from the owners' meeting, Bud Harley walked out of the conference room, shaking his head. "I don't need this," he mumbled to himself as he made his way back to his hotel room.

Arriving at the room just as the phone was ringing, he hurriedly opened the door, ran over to the bedside table and picked up the receiver, throwing his keys on the bed. It was his manager, Butch Morris, calling with more bad news. Johnny Calvin, their star center fielder whom they thought only had a sprained ankle, had, in fact, fractured it. He was out indefinitely.

"Great," Bud said with exasperation into the receiver. "What are we going to do about it?"

Morris's voice came through from the other end of the line. "Well, we can move Johnson over from left field. He's got decent speed and he's been hitting the ball pretty well. We can move Jenkins from right to left."

43

"Who goes into right field?"

Morris paused on the other end as he thought about it. "Well, we can try Tucker in right, except he's really an infielder. We'll probably have to call someone up from Double A."

Great. Another new player, Bud thought to himself. Dealing with constantly changing rosters was part of life in the minor leagues, and Bud recognized that. But he was trying to field a winning team and he was trying to sell tickets. "Alright," he said as he let out a breath. "Call down to Salem and get us an outfielder. I'll be in tomorrow and we can talk."

Bud put down the phone and plopped back onto the bed, staring into space. *What else could possibly go wrong?* he mused to himself. No doubt about it, the Portland Power was in a funk. He had to do something to get the team back on track so he could sell enough tickets to pay for that big new stadium expansion, and to show major league baseball that he could fill the larger stadium.

Bud felt that if this year he didn't go deep into the playoffs, or maybe even win the league championship outright, his bid to bring a major league franchise to Portland was finished. He knew that the Sacramento organization was also lobbying Major League Baseball, and they had won the PCL championship the last three years, selling out most of their home games. Now, here they were, at the midway point of the season, and attendance for the Power games was already 40,000 fewer than last year's.

The marketing genius was running out of ideas.

He kicked off his shoes, put his feet up on the bed, and picked up the local newspaper from the nightstand. Leaning back against the headboard, he flipped to the sports section. He was scanning the headlines when a picture and a caption caught his eye. It was about a player for the Single A Richmond Tigers who had gone 2 for 4 with three stolen bases in the previous night's game against the Birmingham Eagles. The face smiling up from underneath the baseball cap belonged to Casey Collins.

Bud kicked his legs over the side of the bed, sitting upright as he read through the article, the marketing wheels starting to turn in his head. He jumped off the bed, grabbed his cell phone and pressed the speed dial button for his secretary back in Portland. "Get me everything you can on Casey Collins, right fielder for the Richmond Tigers," he ordered. "And call Coach Morris and tell him I want to see him in my office first thing tomorrow morning."

Eight

Butch Morris was the head manager for the Portland Power and he was the prototypical grizzled veteran manager. At fifty-two years of age, with mostly gray hair and a slight paunch, he had a gruff-looking face, and usually had at least a two day's worth of growth on his beard.

Butch was one of those people who didn't talk a lot, not because he was shy, by any means, but because if he thought he could explain something in three words instead of five, he did. He viewed an interview with the press as being equal to a dentist appointment, and only granted them on occasion.

Morris had an eye for talent and knew baseball inside and out. He was the undisputed leader of the team, and an authority figure for his players, commanding both fear and respect. Players did not cross Butch Morris; if they did, they were not around for very long.

The Kansas City Royals once considered Butch for a head manager's position, but in the end decided on another candidate. That was the only time he flirted with making it to the major leagues. He was now in his tenth year in the minors, and had worked for Bud Harley for six of those years. Butch generally considered owners to be a pain in the butt, but he also knew who wrote the checks. At least, Harley usually stayed out of the baseball side of the business.

Bud had told him of his plans to bring a major league franchise to Portland, and had said that Butch would be his head manager, providing he continued to do a good job at managing the Power. Bud made it clear that this meant more than just winning ballgames; it meant winning the championship.

Butch arrived in Bud Harley's office at 8:30 the next morning. He walked to the outer office where Bud's secretary was sitting, and he greeted her as he put his team jacket on the coat rack. "Hey, Sandy," he said, walking over to her desk, "how are you?"

"I'm fine, Coach, and yourself?"

"Well, other than losing half my team, I'm just great," he said sarcastically. Then nodding towards Bud's office door, "Is he in?"

"Yes. He said to send you right in as soon as you got here."

"All right, thanks," Butch said as he headed towards Bud's office door, which was slightly ajar. He rapped on the door as he opened it a little and poked his head in. "Bud?" he asked.

Bud was seated at his desk reading the morning newspaper. Always dressed in a suit and tie, he was the consummate businessman. His dark brown eyes were accented by his closely cropped black hair, which was receding slightly in front into a classic widow's peak. Bud was generally a cordial guy, but he could freeze people with a cold stare when he chose to.

He sprang up and walked around the desk to greet Morris and shake his hand. "Hey, Butch, how are you doing?" he asked warmly.

Butch looked a little perplexed, but responded, "Well, trying to keep a team on the field, which is getting harder by the moment. Why are you so cheery?"

Bud let out a short laugh and said, "Because, I think I've solved one of our personnel problems."

Butch looked at him warily, with his eyebrows furrowed. "Which one?"

Bud went over to his desk, picked up the newspaper with the article on Casey Collins, and handed it over to Morris. "Right field," he said.

Butch looked at it briefly, and as Bud had done the night before, read the headline of "Richmond Tiger Goes 2 for 4 with 3 Stolen Bases" before he looked at the picture, and then, realizing that it was a picture of a woman said, "Hey, wait minute. Casey Collins? Are you kidding me?"

"You've heard of her?"

"Of course I've heard of her. She plays for Richmond. But what's that got to with anything?" Bud just looked at Morris as he began to grasp what Bud was driving at.

"Aw, come on. We're in the middle of a pennant race here. We need someone who can help us win, not some circus sideshow." Morris threw the paper down on Bud's desk.

"What makes you think she can't help us win?"

"Look, I'm sure she's cute and wonderful and everything, and I'm glad that Richmond can say that they have a woman on their team. But this isn't Little League where you can hide somebody in right field. This is Triple A. These guys are one step away from the majors. Besides, isn't this a personnel decision that should be handled by Larson?" Al Larson was their director of player development.

"I've already talked to him."

"And he agreed?" Morris said with astonishment.

Bud, leaning against his desk, folded his arms and nodded his head. "Well, it took some convincing, but eventually, yeah, he agreed. We're offering her a direct three-month contract with the Portland Power, which will cover until the end of the season, so the broader organization has no exposure. At the end of the year, if she doesn't work out, we simply don't renew her contract. No harm, no foul."

"Unbelievable," Morris said with a wave of his arms. "Look, you want to sell tickets, I understand that. But we're in danger of losing the division. We're six games out of first place, just in case you haven't seen the standings."

"Of course, I've seen the standings. But I've also seen the attendance figures. We're not even filling to last year's capacity, let alone the expanded stadium." Bud pointed to Casey's picture in the newspaper. "This woman is going to help us sell tickets."

"That's great, but what about the pennant race? I don't need a baby-sitting job right now. I've got three kids of my own."

Bud put a hand on Butch's shoulder. "Look at it as a challenge. Besides, aren't two of your kids girls?"

"Yeah, so what?"

"Think how excited they'll be when they find out they can watch a woman playing on their daddy's baseball team."

"Great," Morris said with a shrug. "Why don't we just open a circus? I'm sure we could sell even more tickets then."

"Come on," Bud said encouragingly, as he handed Morris a file and escorted him out of his office. "It won't be so bad. Here's her file from Richmond. You might be pleasantly surprised."

"Yeah, right," Butch mumbled as he took the file and headed out the door, shaking his head.

Nine

That Sunday night, Casey was at home in her mother's house, sitting on the couch in a pair of gray sweat pants and a white T-shirt with a Washington State Cougars Football logo on the chest. She was watching the All Sports Network, or ASN, squeezing a tennis ball in her left hand while sipping on a Diet Coke from her right.

Casey often had some type of wrist strengthening device with her -- wrist weights, a tennis ball, a wrist flexor. Her father had stressed how important wrist strength was in hitting a baseball, and it was something she worked on constantly. She switched hands between the tennis ball and her soft drink, as she continued to watch television.

ASN had added a segment to their baseball coverage called *The Minor League Report*, and she was watching the two hosts, Alex Rivera and Dan Majors. Before going to commercial, Rivera said, "More fighting yet again in the minor leagues, up next when we return." The station broke and went to several commercials.

Sue Collins was in the kitchen doing some light cleaning. She yelled into the living room to Casey. "You want anything, sweetheart?"

"No thanks, Mom. I'm okay."

Sue finished wiping down the kitchen counter and entered the living room, joining Casey on the couch. "What are you watching, ASN?" she asked.

"Yeah, *The Minor League Report*," Casey responded as she continued to watch the television. "They're doing a special on the fights that have been happening in the minor leagues.

"I didn't think they covered the minors on national sports programs."

Casey switched the tennis ball over to her right hand, and looked over at her mom. "They don't usually, but they've been getting a lot of mileage out of some of the recent fights in Triple A, so they've been showing a few clips now and then."

"I didn't think they even had TV cameras at those games. They don't at your games, do they?"

"No, not at our games, and usually not much at all in the minors, but now and then a local station might cover a game, especially in the bigger market towns up in Triple A."

The commercials ended and Rivera came back on. "Welcome back. We're talking about the rising incidence of brawling in the minor leagues, and here's another incident from Thursday night." Then, mimicking an old-time announcer with a gravelly voice. "And now, back to the fights. Here's some action from Triple A's Portland Power, courtesy of KPTL TV in Portland, Oregon."

"Ding-ding-ding," Rivera said in a sing-song voice. "Here's round one from the first inning between the Portland Power and the Sacramento Sting. Power catcher Jason Taylor takes the pitch from Sacramento's Ryan Miller..." The camera shows Taylor swinging and connecting for a home run, as Rivera talks over the clip. "IT'S OUTTA HERE! A SOLO HOME RUN TO LEFT FIELD! Portland leads it one to nothing.

"We move to further action in round three. I mean inning three, or do I? Taylor at the plate again. Miller delivers..." The camera shows Taylor connecting again for another home run. "GONE! IT'S OUT OF HERE, AGAIN. This time a two-run blast to straight away center. Portland up three to nothing. Taylor takes his time rounding the bases, and gets a cold stare from Miller.

"Ding-ding-ding. Here we are now in round seven. Portland now leading three to two. Taylor at the plate again. Miller still on the mound. He winds up, delivers the pitch and KERPLUNK! HE NAILS HIM! RIGHT IN THE MIDDLE OF THE BACK! OUCH! THAT'S GOTTA HURT. Taylor rushes the mound. Both benches clear and chaos ensues. "IT'S A FREE-FOR-ALL!"

"Thirty-two minutes later, three players are ejected and two more have to be helped from the field. Judge's scorecards had the fight even." He turned to his co-host, "Dan, the minor leagues are out of control. It makes you wonder what they're doing about it at the league offices."

Majors looks over at Rivera and comments, "Well, you're right, Alex. It is out of control and someone needs to do something. Apparently, Huey Jacobs, the minor league president, has initiated some new measures. We're waiting to see what the nature of those measures is, and what effect they will have on this situation. But now, back to real baseball..."

"I don't know why they even show that nonsense," Sue said with disgust.

"Because it's news, Mom, and it sells."

"Well, I'm glad they're not doing that sort of thing in your league."

"Yeah, me too," Casey responded. She never told her mother about the time in Spokane when both benches cleared and Casey was stepped on in the melee, and that *that* was why she had the huge bruise on her foot when she came home, not due to a close play at the plate as she had told her mother. A harmless white lie; she didn't want her to worry.

The phone rang and Sue got off the couch to answer it. "Oh, hello, Chuck. I'm fine, thank you. And you? Good. Yes, she's right here. One moment, please." She cupped the phone and handed it outwards towards Casey, "It's for you, honey. Chuck Olson."

Casey rose from the couch and took the phone from Sue, who headed into the kitchen, not wanting to intrude on Casey's conversation. "Hey Skip, what's up?" Casey asked into the phone.

Olson spoke from the other end of the line, "Hey, I need you to come in to the office tomorrow. First thing, if you can."

"Okay," Casey responded warily. "What's up?"

"I don't know, exactly. I got a call from Doug Nelson's secretary and he wants us in his office tomorrow for some kind of big meeting. He wouldn't give me any specifics." Doug Nelson was the owner of the Richmond Tigers.

"Anyway, can you come in at nine?"

"Sure, I'll be there." Casey said goodbye and hung up the phone.

Sue was hovering around the kitchen, listening to the background conversation and heard Casey hang up the phone.

She walked back into the living room where Casey was standing with a puzzled look on her face. "What was that all about?" she asked.

"I'm not really sure," Casey answered. "Doug Nelson wants to see me in his office tomorrow. You don't think they're going to release me?" she asked with a concerned look on her face."

Sue waved her hand and scoffed. "Don't be ridiculous. You're doing great."

"I know, but…"

"Now dear, don't get yourself all riled up until you know what it's all about. I'm sure you'll find out tomorrow. Until then, there's nothing you can do about it. Why don't you just go upstairs and get a good night's sleep, and deal with it tomorrow?"

"Yeah, Mom, I guess you're right," Casey said with a frown. She switched off the TV, kissed her mother goodnight and headed up the stairs to her bedroom, still wearing a concerned look on her face.

Sue watched as Casey walked up the stairs. She had tried to console her daughter, but could see that she was still worried, and it caused Sue to worry as well. She knew how much playing baseball meant to Casey, and hoped that nothing was happening that would jeopardize her daughter's career.

Neither mother nor daughter could have known that rather than it being the end of her career, it was actually the start of a new and very exciting chapter in Casey Collins' life.

Ten

Casey didn't sleep very well that night, tossing and turning in her bed for several hours. Many thoughts were running through her mind, but the main one was whether or not the team was going to release her. She knew that she had no basis for that thought. As her mother had said, she was having a good year, as usual. But to be called in to the office like that usually meant that some type of move was going to be made, and it made her very uneasy. Although she tried to dismiss it, the thought gnawed at her until she finally nodded off around 3:00 A.M.

She was up at 7:30 A.M., which was early for Casey. With the Tigers playing mostly night games, oftentimes she didn't get home until midnight, so she usually slept in until around 9:00. She quickly showered and dressed in blue jeans, sneakers and a Tigers' baseball shirt, and went downstairs to the kitchen.

She skipped breakfast and had a Diet Coke instead, finishing it off on her way out to her car. As she was driving towards the team office, the thoughts that had kept her awake the previous night ran through her head again. This only added to her apprehension, and by the time she got to the parking lot at 8:20, she was a nervous wreck.

Since she was a little early, she decided to walk around the block a couple of times to try and settle down. It helped somewhat, but finally she decided to head in to the office at around 8:45 and wait inside for the meeting. She was surprised to see the lights in Doug Nelson's office already on, and she could hear some conversation coming from inside.

The door was slightly ajar, and she slowly walked over and knocked on it lightly.

A voice from inside said "Yes?" and Casey recognized Doug Nelson's voice. She pushed the door open slightly and stuck her head in.

"Hi, Mr. Nelson," she said. "You wanted to see me?"

"Yes, yes, come on in Casey," Nelson said as he came from behind his desk to greet her.

Casey opened the door fully, and saw that her manager, Chuck Olson was there, along with a man she didn't know. Both men were sitting in chairs facing Nelson's desk, and they rose to greet her.

"Hi, Skip," Casey said to Olson, who returned her greeting. She then turned to greet the stranger. He was about 5'10" tall, and impeccably dressed, wearing a dark blue suit with a pressed white shirt and a red tie, and his shiny black dress shoes reflected the office light. His dark brown eyes gave him a look of intensity, although he was smiling.

Doug Nelson positioned himself so that he was facing both Casey and the man in the suit, and he put a hand on the man's shoulder. "Casey, I'd like to introduce you to Bud Harley, owner of the Portland Power."

Casey wasn't sure why she was being introduced to this man, but she politely reached out her hand and said, "Hello, Mr. Harley, it's nice to meet you."

Bud reached out his hand and said, "Call me Bud, please, and the pleasure is all mine." He took notice of her strong grip, and looked her up and down. It wasn't a sexual appraisal; it was more like a racehorse owner evaluating a prized thoroughbred. He saw that Casey noticed he was looking at her, and stuttered, "Ah, sorry I wasn't looking at...I mean I wasn't..."

Casey had seen the look many times before. Men and women alike always gave her the once-over, wondering what it was about her that enabled her to play men's baseball. But baseball players were bought and sold, after all, and if Harley had given the once-over to a male player he was evaluating, nothing would be made of it. She gave a light laugh and a wave of the hand. "That's okay. I understand. I'm used to it."

"All right, well, anyway," Bud said, smoothing out his tie as a way of transition, "I'll get right to the point. The reason I'm here is that I want you to join the Portland Power."

The comment took Casey totally by surprise. She frowned slightly. "What do you mean, *join*?" she asked suspiciously.

Bud was a little confused by her question, believing that the meaning of his statement was obvious, and he stuttered again slightly, "Uh, I mean I want you to play for us – in right field."

Now it was Casey's turn to stutter, "For real? Why? I mean, are you sure?" she asked in rapid fire, feeling a mixture of excitement and anxiety.

Bud Harley, the consummate salesman, was good with people, and although he was a little slow, initially, in understanding her anxiety, he now understood it. He put both hands out in front of him as if pushing against the air. "Okay, look," he said with a smile, "First, let's all just relax and take a seat." Although everyone else took a seat, he remained standing, *the power position*.

After everyone else was seated, he looked at Casey and continued. "Casey, I understand this comes as a surprise to you. Let me assure you this is on the up and up. We need a right fielder, and we think you're a good fit. We'd like to give you the opportunity."

"But you're Triple A," Casey stated. "I'm Single A, from an independent team. Players don't usually jump like that, do they?"

"In special situations, they do. And this is a special situation."

Casey eyed him warily. "What kind of special situation?"

Bud held his hands in front of him and began to count off on his fingers, "Well, first of all, we've been decimated by injuries. We've got six people on injured reserve and four of them are outfielders. You may have seen our nice little clip on *ASN* last night. Not our finest moment."

Casey chuckled at the mention of the fight footage, as Bud continued. "Then, two nights later, our center fielder breaks his ankle. We've already moved some guys around from other positions, but the bottom line is, we need a right fielder, and we need one right away."

"But don't you have anyone in Double A?"

"Well, yeah we do, and, the truth is, we will probably call up one of them as a backup. But none of them are batting .337 and have nineteen stolen bases."

"And none of them are a woman."

"Well, none that we know of," he chuckled, then continued. "We've talked with Mr. Olson here. He says you're fast, you've got a good head on your shoulders and you don't make mistakes. Plus you're batting .337. That's pretty damn good in any league."

Casey nodded, then looked at him suspiciously. "Do you want me because you think I can play or do you want me so you can sell more tickets?"

Harley crossed his arms and looked at her as he continued. "Look, Casey, I'm not going to lie to you. This is a business and yeah, we need to sell tickets. I just spent ten million dollars on a stadium expansion, and yes, I believe we can generate some positive publicity around you. But I'm not about to jeopardize our team's position in the standings. The most important thing for us is to win the division. We're in third place now, six games out, and we intend to be in the pennant hunt. If I didn't think you could play, then I wouldn't be here."

If there was one thing Bud was good at, it was selling, and he shifted into his salesperson mode. "Besides, what do you really care? You're getting a chance to move up two levels and play Triple A ball. We're one step from the majors. As you said, not many players get that opportunity."

He paused as he patted his left breast pocket, then reached in and pulled out a check, which he handed over to Casey. "Oh, by the way, I forgot to mention one other thing. We're doubling your salary. You're now making thirty-two thousand dollars a year. We've pro-rated it out for the rest of the season, so this will bring you current. Here's a check for six thousand dollars. Your regular checks start next Friday."

Casey was stunned as she reached out and took the check. She stared at it in awe. Six thousand dollars! It was more money than she had seen at one time in her life. "Wow," was all she could manage to say.

Bud continued to press. "So, what do you say, are you in?"

Casey looked over at Doug Nelson, who had sat there in silence during the entire conversation. "You okay with this, boss?"

"Hey, it doesn't matter what I think. We're going to miss you around here for sure, but this is your shot, Casey. *Take it,*" he said emphatically.

Casey's head was still swimming. *Her shot?* Of course she dreamed of someday making it to the majors, but she was never really expecting *a shot.* She had been happy just to be playing baseball, and to be making over $16,000 while doing it was more than she had ever hoped for. Now, to double her salary and jump two levels! How could she refuse?

"All right," she said, rising to shake Bud's hand. "I'm in."

"Great," Bud said with a clap of his hands. "Now that that's settled, let's talk about some details." He walked behind Nelson's desk and picked up a short stack of typewritten pages that were stapled together. "Here's your itinerary," he said as he handed one to Casey.

"My itinerary?" she asked with raised eyebrows, impressed by how organized this all was, and by the fact that Bud had obviously assumed this was a done deal long before she had even accepted. He was a good salesman.

"Right," he continued, not even considering that anyone would take special notice of this. "Today is Monday. We need you to report to the team office in Portland by noon on Wednesday."

"Wednesday?" Casey asked with raised eyebrows.

Bud looked at her. "Yeah, why, is that a problem?"

"Uh, no, I guess not. I just thought there would be some time to think through this a little. I mean, we're playing Belleville on Wednesday night."

"No, you're not," Bud said with grin, as he pointed towards Chuck Olson. "*They're* playing Belleville on Wednesday. You are no longer a Richmond Tiger. Last night was your last game. You are now a member of the Portland Power."

He paused as he recognized Casey's discomfort. "Look, Casey," he said as he lowered his voice a little and tried to sound consoling. "I realize that all this must be a little overwhelming for you. That's to be expected. But trust me, we have it all worked out and we've made all the arrangements for you. When you get to Portland, just check in with my secretary and she'll take care of everything for you. Okay?"

"Okay," she said with a nod, as she stuck out her hand towards Bud. "Thank you. I mean, thank you very much for this opportunity."

"Think nothing of it. I have full confidence in you." He put his hand on her shoulder as he ushered her to the door. He shook her hand a final time and said "I'll see you in Portland."

Casey shook his hand and walked through the outer office past Doug Nelson's secretary, who had just arrived, not even remembering if she said goodbye or not, and headed out the door. Her head was swimming, and she was in a state of shock as she went through a range of emotions. First, excitement, then anxiety, then outright fear at the prospect of such a major move.

Wow, what just happened in there? Casey asked herself as she made her way back to her car. *Last night and this morning I was panicking that I might be released, and instead I'm going to Portland to play Triple A! I'm getting a raise, and I have six thousand dollars in my pocket.* She patted her back jeans pocket to make sure the check was really there, then pulled it out and looked at it, just to make doubly sure.

She got in her car and drove straight to her mother's restaurant, bursting through the door like a little girl coming home from school to show her mother her good report card. Sue was engaged in a conversation with one of the waitresses, but wrapped up the conversation as soon as she saw Casey come through the door. "...It only comes with mixed vegetables. Fries are fifty cents extra."

Sue saw the excitement on her daughter's face. *Maybe the meeting didn't go too badly*, she thought. But not wanting to jump to conclusions, she just put on a smile and greeted her daughter. "Hi, honey," she said, "How did it go?"

Casey was brimming with excitement, and didn't know how to start. She grabbed her mother's hand. "Mom, let's sit down first." She led her mother over to a nearby empty table, and they took a seat.

"What is it, dear?" Sue asked, starting to feel concern.

Casey's face broke into a big smile as she blurted out, "They want me to play for Portland, in Triple A."

"Triple A! Portland? Wow! How...?"

"That's what the meeting was all about. The owner from the Portland Power was there, and he said they need a right fielder, and they offered me the job. Mom, they're going to pay me thirty-two thousand dollars a year!" Casey pulled out the check Bud Harley had given her. "Look, they already gave me a check – six thousand dollars!

Sue took the check from Casey. "My God!" she exclaimed, as she looked at the check and then handed it back to Casey. She rose and gave her daughter a big hug. "This is amazing, Casey. I'm so proud of you!" Then she gave Casey a loving smack on the butt. "And you were worried about being released. I told you not to worry, didn't I? So, when do you have to leave?"

Casey pulled out the itinerary that Bud Harley had given her, and showed it to Sue, who looked it over, and said, "It doesn't look like you have a lot of time, do you?" Like any parent who was faced with one of her children moving away, she was feeling a mixture of pride at Casey taking the next step in her life, and sadness at losing her.

"No, I really don't," Casey said, also suddenly overcome with sadness at the prospect of leaving her mother. After all, she had lived with her for twenty-five years, and it had basically been just the two of them ever since Rip died twelve years earlier. "I have to leave on Wednesday morning. But don't worry, Mom, the season is half over, and I'll only be gone a few months. I'll call you every day."

Sue glanced down again at the itinerary, and raised her eyebrows as she looked at Casey. "Wow, look at this, a press conference!" she said, raising her eyebrows. "They're holding a press conference for you?" She pointed to a line at the bottom of the page:

Thursday, July 5th, 12:00 P.M. Press Conference. PP Corporate Office.

Casey took the paper back from Sue at looked at it. "Uh, yeah, I guess. I really hadn't noticed it before." A worried look came over her face, which Sue noticed.

"Oh don't worry about it," she said as she placed a hand over her daughter's hand. "I'm sure it's standard procedure."

Casey wasn't so sure. She didn't recall seeing any other press conferences when minor leaguers moved from one level to another, unless they were actually called up to the majors.

"I guess," Casey said as she folded the itinerary and put it in her back pocket. "Well, anyway, I've got a lot to do. What time are you going to be home?"

"I think, given the occasion, I'll probably leave a little early today. I should be home around six. You want to go out tonight and celebrate?"

"No, Mom, I just want to spend a quiet night at home with you. I'm going to head home and pack a few things, so I'll just see you there later. Love you." Casey kissed her mother on the cheek and waved goodbye to everyone on her way out the door.

Casey floated out the door, and she was still buzzing as she drove home, which was only about fifteen minutes from the restaurant. She prepared a mental checklist of everything she had to do before she left. *Let's see...I have to pack, obviously, which means I have to do laundry. I've got to clean out my locker at the stadium. I have to call my friends and tell them the news...What am I forgetting...? Oh yeah, one more thing. I have to call Jeff.*

Jeff Swanson was Casey's boyfriend since the middle of last year. He was a sales manager for a local sporting goods outfit, and they met when Casey had done a radio commercial for his company. Their relationship was fairly casual, although more so in Casey's mind than in Jeff's. With her playing baseball for half the year and traveling a lot with the Tigers, they didn't have that much time to spend together. They would catch an occasional movie or have some dinner, but it never really blossomed into a serious relationship.

They had only slept together twice, and Casey had resisted Jeff's efforts to take their relationship to another level by going on a vacation to Hawaii with him. It wasn't that she didn't like Jeff, she just wasn't in love with the guy. With her moving to another city, Casey figured that, maybe, the time was right to end the relationship and move on. She didn't want to string Jeff along, and she didn't want anything to distract her from concentrating on making it at the Triple A level.

Oh well, I'll deal with that later, Casey said to herself as she pulled into her driveway. She turned off the car and went inside, grabbing a Diet Coke from the refrigerator before heading up to her bedroom. As she entered, she paused and looked around the room she had lived in all her life. "Hey, guys," she said to the posters hanging on the walls.

Pete Rose, Tony Gwynn, and Ichiro Suzuki of the Seattle Mariners stared back at her from one wall. All left-handed batters, all great hitters. Masters of bat control, they were her role models for the way she played baseball.

The opposite wall had posters of some of the first women to play professional baseball—Dottie Stolze, Mildred "Babe" Didrikson, and "All The Way Faye" Dancer. Although they played in a separate women's league, they had shown long ago that women could play competitive baseball. Casey always marveled at the fact that they had to play in skirts, and she kept their pictures on her wall to remind her of how far women had come. They were part of her heritage.

Another wall belonged solely to her father. Rip was never in the big leagues long enough to have a poster made of him, but Sue had taken a photograph of him in his Cincinnati Reds uniform and had it blown up for Casey as a present.

Over her desk was the only non-baseball poster, which was a shot of a shirtless Jon Bon Jovi live in concert. The guy was a stud, after all.

Casey didn't plan on taking a lot of things with her to Portland. It was early July, and the Triple A season was already half over, so she would probably only be in Portland for a few months. She knew from the itinerary that the team had arranged a hotel room for her initially, and assumed that she would move into an apartment after that. The Power would be on the road half of the time anyway, so it just didn't make sense to take a lot of stuff.

By the time she did laundry and packed her things, Sue had arrived home from the restaurant. Casey filled her in with more details of her meeting with Bud Harley, and they talked over dinner about her new opportunity.

Sue and Casey were much more than mother and daughter; they were best friends. Casey had never even considered leaving home after she graduated high school, nor anytime since. She enjoyed having someone to talk to at home, and she liked working with her mother at the restaurant in the off-season.

When they were finished with dinner, Casey helped Sue clear the table, and as they were loading the dishes into the dishwasher, Sue said, "So, you just want to watch a movie or something? There's a good one at eight o'clock."

"Sure, Mom, that sounds good. But, first, I have to call Jeff." Casey left it right there, hoping that her mother wouldn't pry. But of course, she did.

"Oh, yeah, I forgot about Jeff in all of this. What are you going to do about him?"

Casey grabbed a dishcloth and started to wipe down the counter, while Sue was doing the same with the table. Although they were friends, Casey still felt a little uncomfortable discussing romantic issues with Sue. She knew that her mother wanted her to find someone to settle down with, but now just wasn't the time.

Without looking directly at her mother, Casey said, "I think I'm going to end it."

"You are? Why?"

"Well, I'm just not in love with him, Mom. I mean, he's a nice enough guy, but with me moving to Portland and everything, I just want to be able to focus on my new job. I think trying to maintain a long-distance relationship with Jeff would just be too distracting."

Sue had finished wiping down the table and walked over to where Casey was standing. "Well, that's sad, but I guess you know what you're doing. I was just hoping you would find someone on a more permanent basis, that's all. I just want you to be happy."

"I am happy, Mom. I mean look, I have this great opportunity, all of a sudden, to play Triple A ball; I got a big raise, and I'm moving to a new city. It's pretty exciting. And I will find somebody, someday. Just not now, all right?"

"All right, sweetheart," Sue said as she squeezed her daughter's hand. "You go make your phone call; I'll make some popcorn and we'll watch the movie."

"Sounds great, Mom," Casey said as she put the dishcloth down and started to walk out of the kitchen. "I'll be back down in twenty minutes."

Casey went upstairs to her bedroom and closed the door. She sat on the side of the bed, picked up the phone and dialed Jeff's number, waiting for him to answer.

He picked up after the second ring. "Hello?"

"Hello, Jeff, it's me."

"Hey, Casey! How ya doing? What's up?"

"Well, I need to talk to you. You probably haven't heard, but I've been called up to play Triple A ball."

"Wow, Triple A! That's great. Congratulations. Where?"

"Portland. The Portland Power."

"Portland? Hmm. When do you have to leave?"

"Wednesday morning."

Jeff thought for a moment. "Wow, that's fast. Do you want me to drive you?"

"No, thanks." Casey fumbled for a few seconds, trying to think of the right words to say. "Uh, look Jeff. This is a huge opportunity for me and I really need to focus on doing well, and, uh, I'll be away for several months anyway, and…"

Jeff's voice rose a little as he started to grasp what Casey was driving at. "Are you dumping me?"

"Well, it's not that I'm dumping you, exactly. I just think I need to move on, and…"

"So you *are* dumping me. What, now that you've made the big time, it's time to leave small-town Jeff behind, is that it?"

"No, it's nothing like that. First of all, I wouldn't call Triple A the big time. Secondly…"

"What, have you already met one of the players from your new team? Is that it?"

"Look, Jeff, I haven't met any of them yet, and secondly, I don't date baseball players. I've told you that. It's just time for me to move on."

"Fine." Jeff slammed down the phone, leaving Casey on the line with no connection. She placed the phone back on its receiver. That didn't go very well, but how good could a conversation like that go? She felt bad about hurting Jeff, but felt better knowing that that chapter was closed and she could move on with her new life, whatever it was to be.

Eleven

Casey spent most of the next day running errands and preparing for her trip. One of the first things she did was to cash her $6,000 check. Then she drove to Appliance World and paid cash for a top-of-the-line DCS Convection Oven for her mother's restaurant. Sue and Casey had been there several weeks ago to look at the new oven, but Sue had decided that it wasn't in her budget. Now, it didn't have to be. The salesman told Casey it would be delivered the following week, and it made her tingle with excitement knowing that it was just going to show up at the restaurant and would be a big surprise for Sue.

At noon, she headed over to MacHales, a mixed-theme restaurant located in downtown Richmond. Casey had called some of her friends from high school and invited them to lunch. "The Girls" had been excited to hear Casey's news, and they were already seated at the table when Casey arrived.

Bobbi Bailey and Sharon Thomas had been Casey's friends since junior high school, when they had asked Casey to play on their women's softball team one summer. Casey joined the team, and had a lot of fun, but found it much too easy. She batted 627, and played center field. The other teams couldn't get anything by her in the outfield, and they could not stop her on the base paths. She felt like if she wanted to, she could just slap the ball over the infielder's heads all day long, and never make an out. It was only when she was playing around and trying to do different things that she actually got out, but she was always careful to experiment only during non-critical situations.

Sharon and Bobbi were disappointed when Casey didn't join the team the next year, but reluctantly, they tried to understand. Although they were great athletes themselves, they could see that Casey was at a different level, that she had to challenge herself, and for her, that meant trying out for the men's team.

They supported her in her efforts, went to as many of her games as possible, and they remained friends ever since.

Sharon and Bobbi had both gained some weight since their high school days, and were now looking a little rounded. They were seated at the table with two other women.

Kelly Smart was the only one of Casey's close friends that was married, and she brought her two-year-old son along with her to the restaurant. She had been dating her boyfriend Brad all through high school, and when he enrolled in dental school, he asked her marry him. A year later, Tyler was born. Kelly also had a pretty good jump shot back when she was in high school, but did not really have enough talent to make anything out of it. These days, she was busy just trying to keep up with little Tyler.

Julie Rubieri was Casey's best friend from high school, and in Casey's opinion, the smartest human on the planet. She was currently studying economics at the University of Washington in Seattle, but she also studied forensic science as a hobby. *Excuse me, forensic science as a hobby?* Julie was taking the summer semester off to visit her parents, and as she said, get back to a small-town atmosphere for a while. In addition to Julie's stunning good looks, Casey figured her I.Q. had to be somewhere around 450. Talk about having it all.

The girls were seated around a circular table, next to a window on the far side of the restaurant, with little Tyler in his high chair next to Kelly, when Casey entered the room. Julie gave her a wave as Casey saw her and made her way to the table.

A couple of men seated at a table near the front watched Casey as she moved through the room, lithely maneuvering around the tables on her way to the far side of the restaurant. Although she moved with grace, it wasn't the fake, upright, head-and-shoulders-thrown-back kind of walk that models practiced over and over again.

It was more like a wild cheetah walking across the prairie with casual disinterest until it saw some prey, and suddenly it was sprinting at 60 miles an hour with seeming effortlessness. Watching Casey walk through the room, it was obvious she was an athlete, and it wasn't hard to picture her sprinting down the track with a baton in her hand, stealing the ball from a dribbling point guard, or running down fly balls in the outfield.

Casey attracted attention from men, but it wasn't as much a pure physical attraction focused on certain body parts, as was so often the case between men and women. Although her build did seem to be a perfect mix between muscularity and femininity, it was something else. It was more a matter of curiosity watching someone who moved with a fluidity and a confidence that said she has some kind of a special gift—and wanting to get close to it. It didn't hurt that she was cute, as long as you didn't call her that to her face.

Casey approached her friends, as they rose to greet her. "Hi, guys," she said.

"Hey, girl, hey, girl," Sharon and Bobbi chimed, while Julie pulled out a chair for Casey and said, "Hey, make room for the bigshot."

"Funny," Casey retorted as she gave Julie a light shove, and then went around to the high chair to give Tyler a kiss on the cheek. "Hey, little man, how're ya doing?" Tyler smiled as he held up a half-eaten breadstick in his hand.

"He's doing great," answered Kelly, as Tyler muttered something incomprehensible. "Just happy to see his Aunt Casey."

"Wow, he gets bigger every time I see him," Casey said, then asked, "So, how are you guys doing?"

Julie answered first. "How are *we* doing? How are *you* doing? You must be so excited. I can't believe you're moving up to that other league. What is it again, American or National?"

Bobbi and Sharon laughed, as Casey took her seat, and smiled. Julie didn't know too much about baseball, or sports in general for that matter, but when you had an I.Q. of 675, you didn't have to. "No, that's only for the major leagues. This is still the minors; it's just called Triple A, instead of Single A."

"But then, it's the majors, right?"

"Well, yeah, if you make it that far."

"Hey, you can make it," Sharon said.

"Yeah, we always knew you had talent," chipped in Bobbi, "now it looks like someone else is recognizing it. How are you feeling?"

Casey had one hand resting on the table, and the other on her leg. She spread her hands open and said, "Well, you know, excited of course. I've been flying high ever since yesterday morning when I found out. But, also a little nervous. It's a pretty big step for me."

"Yeah, but you can do it, if anyone can," Bobbi said. "You were always a whole other level above all of us. It was just a matter of time before you made it."

"Well, I haven't made it yet. Still a long way to go."

The waiter came and took their orders, then Kelly asked, "So, you're leaving tomorrow?" as she helped little Tyler take a drink of water from a glass.

"Yeah, I've got a lot to do. I've been running around doing errands and stuff, but I wanted to make sure I said goodbye to you guys before I left."

Julie asked, "So how does Jeff feel about all of this? I mean, he must be happy to see you get this opportunity and everything, but also probably a little sad to see you go."

Casey crossed her arms, frowned and said, "Well, speaking of Jeff..."

Julie cut in. "Oh, come on, you didn't..."

"You nuked him?" Kelly interrupted.

Casey laughed. "Well, I wasn't going to put it like that, but, yeah, I broke it off last night. There's just too much going on right now for me to try to maintain a relationship. I just want to get to Portland and concentrate on playing baseball."

"Well then, can I have him?" Julie asked with a sly smile, causing everyone to laugh. They all knew she could easily get any man she wanted.

Sharon had her hands on the table, and Bobbi leaned forward and placed one of her hands over Sharon's, as she looked at Casey. "Hey, we're still waiting for you to come over to our side."

Everyone laughed again, as Bobbi continued the joke. "Yeah, are you sure we can't make you an offer? We have a pretty good team too, you know."

Casey waved a hand as she deadpanned. "Nah, then I'd have to start wearing men's suits and ties and stuff. It's just not for me." More laughter, from the group of longtime friends who were completely comfortable with each other.

The waiter delivered the food, and they continued the chitchat while they ate. When everyone was finished, Casey asked for the check, and insisted on taking care of it. After accepting more ribbing about being a bigshot, Casey rose and prepared to leave.

"Hey, guys, thanks a lot for coming. It was great to see you, and I'll miss you all. Maybe you can make a road trip some time and come see one of my games."

After receiving promises of a visit to Portland, Casey said her goodbyes and made her way out of the restaurant. As she was almost out the front door, a male voice spoke to her from the lobby. "Excuse me, Casey?"

Casey turned to see a man in a blue business suit. He was tall, pretty good-looking, with light brown hair parted down the middle. "Yes?" she responded.

The man stuck out his hand as he walked over to Casey. "Hi, Jim Haffner."

Casey wondered what this was about as she shook his hand. "Nice to meet you."

The man continued, "Well, you don't know me, obviously, but I've seen you play a couple of times. Anyway, I saw you come in earlier, and I think you're pretty cute, and I just thought I'd ask you if you wanted to have dinner or something?"

There was the "cute" word again. What was she, twelve? Why didn't they ever say pretty, or beautiful or sexy or anything but cute? Damn freckles. Casey smiled, "Well, that's really nice, and I appreciate the offer, but I'm seeing someone right now, and actually I'm moving to Portland tomorrow."

"Oh, well, sorry. I didn't know," the man said awkwardly. Shot down. "Okay, well, maybe I'll see you around sometime."

"Yeah, maybe," Casey said as she turned and headed out of the restaurant.

Casey had one more important thing she had to do before she left town. She had to say goodbye to her old team, and she was very nervous about it. The words *old team* sounded so strange to her, even though she was just saying them in her head. Less than twenty-four hours ago, they were *her* team, *her* Richmond Tigers, and now they were just *the* Richmond Tigers. *The team I used to play for. Weird.*

She knew it was going to be uncomfortable but she couldn't just leave town without saying goodbye. She had played for the Tigers for over five years, and even though a lot of the players came and went, there were a few like her that had been around for a while. They were her teammates and her friends.

Later that afternoon, as she drove to Tiger Stadium, her nervousness grew as those thoughts played in her mind. She got to the parking lot and parked her car, telling herself she just had to deal with it.

She walked up to the main gate, where Dave, the security guard, was sitting inside the glass booth, skimming through a newspaper. He greeted her when she approached. "Hi Casey," he said with surprise. "You're a little late, aren't you?"

"Well," Casey said, "I'm not playing tonight. I just came to get my stuff and to say goodbye." She hesitated, then continued, "I'm getting moved up." It sounded strange when she said it. She half expected the security guard to leap out of his chair and point at her and scream "Fraud!" But instead he put down his paper and a big smile came over his face.

"You got promoted? Hey, that's great! Double A. Congratulations."

"Uh, no," she said awkwardly, almost apologetically, afraid to look him in the eye, "Triple A. I'm going to Portland."

"Portland? Wow! Triple A!" the security guard expressed amazement. "That's quite a jump. Good for you! I guess we won't be seeing you around here much.

"I guess not."

Bill Pennabaker

"Well, good luck to you."

"Thanks, Dave," she said as she turned and headed towards the players' locker room.

The Tigers were playing the first of a three-game series with Belleville, and the players were in the locker room dressing. She knew that Chuck Olson would have already told them about her situation, and she had asked him if she could have a few minutes with them after they finished dressing.

She was nervously pacing around outside the locker room when Olson came out. "Hi, Skip," she said, not really sure what else to say.

"I think that's ex-Skip now," he said with a smile.

"Did you tell them?" she asked.

"Yeah, they know. They're waiting for you." He held open the door to the locker room and motioned for her to go in.

Casey entered to find twenty-four guys staring at her. "Casey!" "Hey Case!" What's up, Case?" they greeted her as she entered.

"Hi, guys," she said as she looked apprehensively at the group. "I guess you've heard?"

"Of course, we have," answered Rob Bailey, the catcher. He walked over and shook her hand. "Congratulations."

"Yeah, congratulations," echoed Luis Hernandez, their second baseman.

One by one they offered their congratulations, but as Casey shook their hands, and looked around the room, she noticed something in the body language of some of the players. She had the distinct feeling that some of them were not sincere, even the ones that she had gotten to know pretty well the last couple of years. Some of the players didn't even move, and Joe Murray, their left fielder, actually turned his back on her.

At first, she couldn't quite put her finger on it, but then she realized what it was. *Resentment.* It was as if some of them were saying, *Yeah, congratulations, but I should have gotten the call, not you.* And she guessed what the next thought in their minds probably was. *But you got the call just because you're a woman.*

72

Casey could see it in their eyes, and she suddenly felt very odd, like an outsider. It was as if all the progress she had made over the last five years with her teammates had vanished. She suddenly needed to get out of there as fast as she could, and she hurriedly made some parting comments and exited out the locker room door.

As the door closed behind her, she felt flushed, and walked over to a water fountain along one wall. She actually braced herself on it slightly as she took a drink of water. She still saw the looks on the players' faces in her mind, when her thoughts were interrupted by Chuck Olson, who had walked over to where she was standing.

"Are you all right, Casey?" he asked.

Casey raised her head up from the fountain and tried to compose herself. "Oh, yeah, boss. I'm fine. Thanks."

The manager reached out with both arms and gave her a light hug. "I'm going to miss you, you know," he said as he gave her a pat on the back.

"I'm going to miss you too, Skip. I owe you so much."

"Nonsense," he said as they separated. "It's me who owes you. You made me look good. I sure am going to miss watching you play. You've got real heart, kid, and you're going to do great up there."

"Thanks, Skip. I appreciate it." Casey said, somewhat awkwardly. "Well, I guess I should be going. See you boss."

"Good luck, Casey, knock 'em dead," he said as he turned and headed back into the locker room to be with the team.

Casey continued on over to her private locker room and went inside. She had found an empty cardboard equipment box by the back door, and she went over to her locker, opened the door and starting filling up the box with her things. She removed her glove, her bat, spikes and some clothes. Lastly, she removed a 5-by-10 picture of her father in his Cincinnati Reds uniform, and carefully placed it on the top of the items in the box. "C'mon Dad, we're moving up," she said with a grin.

She grabbed the cardboard box and started out, pausing in the doorway to look around one last time. As she did, a sense of nostalgia came over her. This had been her private domain

Bill Pennabaker

for the last five and a half years. She had a lot of good times here, and she had matured as a ballplayer. After one last look, she turned and closed the door on her career as a Richmond Tiger.

Twelve

Casey was up early on Wednesday morning. It was a four-hour drive to Portland from Richmond, and Bud Harley had instructed her to be at the Power offices by noon. Allowing for a couple of hours of cushion, she had told her mother that she wanted to be on the road by six o'clock. Sue rose early so that she could fix Casey a going-away breakfast, and as usual, the doting mother overdid it a little. Eggs, bacon, hash brown potatoes, plus pancakes, milk and orange juice, and Casey was assured of leaving on a full stomach.

After a few hugs and a tearful goodbye, with Casey assuring her mother she would call as soon as she got to Portland, Casey was on the road to the next phase of her life.

As she headed southwest out of Richmond, she picked up I84 West, which would take her right into downtown Portland. It was a little over 200 miles, and if she averaged 50 miles per hour, she would make it in plenty of time. As she made the drive along the Columbia River on her way to Portland, one hand on the wheel and the other squeezing her wrist flexor, she reflected on her life, and what brought her to this moment.

She tried to remember exactly when it was that she first realized she was addicted to baseball. It wasn't during her very early childhood, those days of playing Nerf ball in the living room with her father. In fact, she barely remembered that, but Sue had told her the story of her knocking over the lamps so many times that she felt like she did actually remember it.

It probably wasn't even when she got her first wooden bat and a real leather glove, when she and Rip progressed to playing in the backyard. That was just plain fun, having the full attention of her father, a professional baseball player, pushing her to see how hard he could throw the ball to her, and how hard she could hit it back. She remembered the satisfaction she felt when Rip would call in to her from the makeshift pitching mound, "Okay, kid, here comes a really hard one," and the proud smile he got when she stepped into it and cracked it right back at him, as he pretended to be knocked off the mound by the strength of her hit. And Casey would sneak a look over her shoulder towards the kitchen window to see if her mother was watching – and she always was.

No, that was just part of growing up in America, playing ball with your dad in the backyard. Granted, it was usually the boys who were doing it while the girls were playing elsewhere, but Casey never knew any differently. And Rip and Casey's brand of ball always seemed to be a lot more serious, like a constant challenge to see how far Rip could push her and how quickly Casey could rise to the challenge.

Casey smiled as she recalled those days with fond memories, and then concluded that she had become officially addicted to baseball that one spring when she was eleven years old.

It was one of those springs where a premature bout of warm weather early in March had everyone thinking that spring had arrived and that summer couldn't be far behind. For Casey, it meant it was time to head to the backyard, or to the local ball field, to play with her dad. She remembered dragging Rip out to the field that one day in March, even though he told her that the ground would still be soaking wet from the melting snow, and over Sue's admonitions that she would "catch her death" this early in the year.

But out they went, to the field that was riddled with puddles, the one around home plate so large that Casey had to stand almost up against the backstop. Rip was on the mound, wearing a windbreaker that flapped in the occasional gust that would kick up, chilling both of their bones and reminding them that it was, in fact, still early March.

The first few times that Casey connected with the ball, it stung her hands, and it hurt so much that she dropped her bat. But it was a good hurt, a hurt that said, "Yeah, it hurts today, but it'll hurt a little less tomorrow, and a little less the day after that, 'cause it's springtime, baby, it's getting warmer, and summer's on its way." Surely it would be just a matter of time before the puddles vanished, the kids came out, and it would be time to play ball.

Then the snow storm hit – a big one—dropping over three feet of snow on Richmond, Washington, and causing three straight weeks of near-zero temperatures. School was canceled for the first time in three years, and Casey found herself at home in her living room, staring out the big picture window, wondering if she would ever see warm weather again.

She couldn't remember when she had ever been so depressed. Not when she had first struck out in a real game and had gone crying to her father, not when she was hoping for a new bicycle for Christmas and didn't get one, not when her mother told her that she was still too young to have her own phone in her room.

Those two brief days of being on the field had gotten her juices flowing. She was already going over in her mind some of the new moves that Rip had showed her in their basement over the Christmas break. A new way to hook slide to avoid a tag, a way to slap the ball hard directly into the ground for an infield hit, and a way to decoy a base runner into thinking you were going to catch the ball, when, in fact, it was hit over your head. She couldn't wait to try them out.

But she did have to wait, because the weather man said so. Casey remembered moping around the house during that streak of bad weather, watching all the news she could on how that year's major league spring training was progressing, seeing the warm weather and wondering why they couldn't just live in one of those cities instead. Her depression had gotten so bad that her mother had to have a talk with her, telling her to snap out of it and that warm weather would eventually arrive, and she would have the entire summer to play.

That's when Casey realized she was addicted to baseball, and suddenly she knew what she wanted to do with her life. It was when she changed from saying "Yeah right, Dad," when Rip would tell her she could to make it to the "Bigs", to saying "Do you really think I could do it?" From that point on, it became her mission in life.

Even two years later, when her father died, Casey tried to walk away from baseball, but couldn't. She remembered feeling betrayed that her father left her, like it was somehow his choice. She threw her glove in the garbage can, and swore she would never play baseball again. That lasted until she was in the car one day with her mother, on their way to the grocery store—or so Sue had told her. Somehow, Sue had "accidentally" taken a wrong turn, which mysteriously took them to the local ball field, where she pulled in under the guise of turning around. Casey's face was pressed up against the window, watching the kids playing ball on the field.

"Why don't you go join them, sweetheart?" Sue asked.

"I can't, Mom," Casey said, with tears running down her cheek. "I threw my glove away."

"Well, why don't you go look in the trunk?" Sue smiled and patted her daughter on the leg, then watched as Casey went around to the trunk of the car, found the glove that Sue had retrieved from the garbage can, and went sprinting out to join the other kids, calling "Thanks, Mom" over her shoulder.

And now here she was, crossing over the Washington/Oregon border, on her way to play Triple A baseball. Not quite the Big Leagues, but still a big step for the girl from a small town in eastern Washington. As she sped along the highway on her way to Portland, Casey moved from the past to the present, and she started to make the mental transition from the Single A Tigers in Richmond, Washington to the Triple A Power in Portland, Oregon.

As she whizzed by the road sign that said PORTLAND, 110, several thoughts went through her mind. *How much better are they in Triple A than Single A? Can I play at that level? What will my new teammates be like? How will they react to me? Will they accept me? Is this a legitimate opportunity or merely a publicity stunt? Thirty-two thousand dollars to play baseball!*

She recalled Bud Harley's words:

"If I didn't believe you could help us, I wouldn't be here."

"Well, yeah, we do need to sell tickets."

"You're no longer a Richmond Tiger."

One topic that kept popping back in to her mind was the press conference. It smelled to her of a circus, and she wasn't all that comfortable in those types of situations to begin with.

She remembered a presentation she had to make in front of one of her high school classes, and she had been so nervous that her hands were sweating, and she was grabbing the podium so hard that her knuckles turned white. Although since then she had been through many interviews with reporters at the various ballparks she played at, she somehow felt this was going to be a completely different situation.

Casey wasn't fooling herself; she knew that a large part of the reason she was getting this opportunity was because she was a woman, and no matter how much Bud Harley had tried to minimize it during their conversation, she knew it was there. She just didn't want it to take precedence over her real objective, which was to find out how good she really was, and how far she could go.

I guess I'll just have to deal with it, like everything else, she resolved to herself. She referred to the directions that were provided on page three of her itinerary. It contained a small breakout map of the Portland area, and directions to the *Portland Power* corporate office, which was on the outskirts of downtown Portland.

As she came off of I-84, she picked up I-5 South, and got her first real look at the city of Portland. She immediately moved over into the slow lane so she could take in the view, and also to occasionally glance at her map.

Wow, this is pretty, she thought to herself and she stared at the city on her right. She saw how it was nestled between the Willamette River, which curled around the city, and the surrounding hillsides, all of which looked very green. Looking across the Willamette, she saw the glistening buildings of the downtown district, which was set back from the river behind several waterfront parks and walkways. A ferry was gliding through the river, making its way from north to south, no doubt one of the many river cruises available as part of Portland's bustling tourism industry.

Casey liked the city immediately. It just looked friendly. She did get lost a couple of times, but eventually found her way to the Power Team offices, located in an office park in a section of town out by Union Station. They were in a four-story steel-

and-glass office building that would have looked like any other office building were it not for the plaque on the outside wall that read, *Home of the Portland Power*. Casey went inside and checked the listing of companies on the wall by the elevators. The Power offices were on the third floor. She pressed the UP button, waited for the elevators to open, and entered.

When the elevator arrived at the third floor, the doors opened up to a small lobby, which contained a large wooden desk. The desk had been engraved with the Power logo, a jagged yellow lightning bolt. Karen Jones was the receptionist and saw Casey approach. "Hello, may I help you?" she asked with a smile.

"Yes, I'm here to see Anne Ross, please," Casey replied.

"And your name?"

"Casey Collins."

The receptionist raised her eyebrows. "Oh, yes, Casey, we've been expecting you. We're all so excited to have you here! Welcome to Portland."

"Thank you," Casey said in return. "I'm happy to be here."

"Hold on one moment while I ring up Anne." She scanned through a laminated list that was taped to the top of her desk and found Anne Ross's extension. "Here we go," she said as she found the number and dialed.

After a few moments, there was a click at the other end. "Hello, Anne? This is Karen. Casey Collins is here in the lobby…Okay, great, I'll tell her…Bye."

Karen hung up the phone and said, "She'll be right with you. You can take a seat over there if you like." She pointed towards a leather couch against the far wall.

"Thanks," Casey said as she went over to the couch. There was a framed team photo of the Power on the wall above the couch, and Casey studied it for a few minutes. She noticed that it was last year's team picture, and she wondered how many of those in the 2002 picture were still on the team.

There were several magazines spread out on the glass-top coffee table next to the couch and Casey picked up a copy of *The Sporting News*. She took a seat and was sitting with her legs crossed, skimming through the magazine, when the hallway door opened and a smartly dressed woman walked through.

She was wearing dark shoes, navy blue slacks and a matching jacket, with a white blouse underneath. She was 5'8" tall, with short brown hair, brown eyes, and appeared to be about 28 years old. Casey looked up as the woman walked over to where she was sitting, held out her hand and smiled.

"Hi, I'm Anne Ross, the marketing coordinator for the Power. You must be Casey."

Casey placed the magazine back on the coffee table and rose to take Anne's hand. "Yes, hello, it's nice to meet you."

Anne looked up at Casey, who was a couple of inches taller and about fifteen pounds heavier. "Believe me, the pleasure's all mine. We are *so* excited to have you here." Then, noticing Casey's strong grip, she said, "Wow, you're strong. And tall, too."

She looked at Casey from head to toe. *There was that initial appraisal.* Everyone who met her wanted to get a good look at the woman who played men's baseball.

"Yeah, I guess so," she said with a shrug.

"I'm sorry," Anne blushed, putting a hand over her mouth. "That was rude of me. It's just that I've never met a woman baseball player before, and you're already somewhat famous around here. I'm sure there will be a lot more people who will want to meet you."

"It's all right," Casey said with a wave of her hand. "I'm used to it by now."

"I'll bet you are. Anyway, Mr. Harley asked me to show you around and to help you get settled in. How did you arrive here?"

"I drove. It was only a few hours. I'm in the front lot."

"Great. I'll tell you what. We've got you set up at the Portlander Hotel. Why don't you follow me over there? We'll get you checked in, then I'll show you around the city for a couple of hours. I have a blue Camry, and I'll pull around front and wait for you."

"Okay, I'm in the white Honda Civic."

After they got Casey checked in to her hotel, they both got back in Anne's Camry, and she began showing Casey around the city. "Thanks for doing this," Casey said, "this is great."

"No problem, I'm happy to do it. So, have you ever been to Portland before?"

"No, I haven't. I've been to Seattle a few times, but never to Portland."

"Well, you'll love it here. There's all kinds of things to do. Great restaurants, shopping, night clubs, lots of parks." Anne motioned with her hand to indicate the Willamette River. "You can see all the people out along the waterfront."

"It sounds great, but I'm not sure I'll have much time for a lot of that. We've got a pretty full schedule of games."

"Oh, right, of course," Anne laughed. "Well, you must be pretty excited, huh?"

Casey warmed to Anne immediately, and was impressed with how easygoing she was. "Oh, yeah, I'm very excited. It's a huge opportunity for me. Of course, I'm a little nervous too. It's a pretty big step."

"Yeah, I'll bet. I can't imagine how you can even play with guys in the first place. It's pretty amazing to me."

Casey shrugged, as she looked out the window. "I don't know. I never really looked at it like that. I just see myself as a baseball player, and the guys as other baseball players whom I compete with, and I try to focus on my game."

"Well, anyway, everyone's pretty excited to have you here."

"Really?"

"Sure. Ever since Sandy—that's Bud Harley's secretary—let it out that you were coming to Portland, there's been an extra level of excitement in the office."

"Why's that?"

"Well, part of it is just the women rooting for one of our own to make it, of course, but the stakes are actually higher than that."

"What do you mean?"

"Well, Bud Harley has made no secret of the fact that he's trying to bring a major league franchise to Portland, and we're all pulling for him. We love our baseball here in Portland, and we're tired of being forced to be Mariners fans just because we're in the same geographical quadrant. We're desperate to win the championship this year, and to show Major League Baseball that we can fill a stadium."

Casey pondered this for a few seconds, then turned to face Anne more squarely. "Okay, so let me ask you a question. Do you think Bud Harley brought me here to help him win games, or am I just part of some marketing ploy?

Anne laughed again as she waved her hand. "Hey, let me tell you, everything Bud Harley does is a marketing ploy. That's just the way he is. But he's also smart, and he's pretty fair. He wouldn't have brought you here if he didn't think you could play."

"So, you don't think he brought me here just to sell more tickets?"

Ann tilted her head slightly as she kept her eye on the road. "I can't answer that. To be honest with you, I'm sure that's part of it. I'm sure we'll market the hell out of the fact that a woman is joining the team. Like I said, that's just Bud, and it's also good marketing. But also, like I said, he is smart. He knows that it would probably do the team more harm than good if he brought you in just for publicity's sake, and then it turned out you couldn't play. Believe me, he probably knows your stats inside and out, and from what I've heard, they're pretty good. I know he wouldn't have brought you here if he didn't think you could help the team."

"Great, but I wanted to get my shot based on my performance, not as part of some circus act."

"Hey, who cares how you get your shot? The important thing is that you're getting it, and it's what you do with your shot that really matters, right? Look at me, for example. I got this job mainly because my uncle had worked with Bud Harley before. But I don't care. I've done a great job since I've been in this position, everyone knows it, and that's all that matters. Nobody says, "Hey Anne, great marketing job on the Vancouver series, although you did get this job because your uncle knew Bud."

"Yeah, I guess you're right. That's how I should look at it. Good advice."

"Okay, then, why don't we grab some lunch?"

Casey liked Anne already. She was outgoing and friendly, and at 28 years old, a little more mature than Casey. Casey appreciated Anne's candor, and she developed an immediate respect for her opinions. When they stopped for lunch, Anne had taken the time to go over the Power roster player by player, so that Casey could come up to speed faster with her new teammates. Casey was impressed with how much Anne knew about each player, and the workings of the entire organization. She could tell they were going to be good friends.

After lunch, they got back in Anne's car, and they continued the tour. Casey took it all in as they drove through downtown, then the business district, and finally out to the Portland Power stadium, where Anne pulled to a stop. "Here's your new home," she said.

Casey noticed a sense of pride in Anne as she motioned to the stadium. Looking at the structure, Casey was immediately impressed by the size. It was easily three times as big as anything she had played in, and it looked almost as big as a major league stadium.

In front of the main entrance was a double-life-sized bronze sculpture of a baseball player. The sculpture had been done by a local artist, and had been nicknamed *Mac* by the Power staff. Mac was named after John Macintosh, the first center fielder to play for the Power. He had gone on to have success in the majors, starting in center field for the then-named California Angels. Mac was posed as if he was running back towards the outfield fence ready to catch a fly ball. He was looking back over his left shoulder at the ball and he had his glove raised in preparation to make the catch.

Casey paused a few moments to look at Mac, amazed at how life-like it looked. The sculptor had done a good job. They didn't actually go into the stadium then, Anne telling Casey that she'd have plenty of time to see her new surroundings later. After a few minutes, they got back in the car, as Anne continued the tour of Portland, on the way back to Casey's hotel.

They chatted along the way about family, hobbies, boyfriends, etc. Anne wanted to know what it was like playing on a team with all men, and they laughed when Casey talked about the locker room situations and traveling and all the challenges it raised.

Like most women that Casey talked to, Anne thought it would be great to be on a team with 23 young guys, but Casey explained that being on a baseball team with them was not like being on a date. It was, she explained, more like having 23 brothers. She explained that, as a matter of fact, she didn't date baseball players.

"Are you kidding?" Anne exclaimed. "With that big of a talent pool around and you're not going to at least take a dip?" They both laughed, as Anne pulled back into the hotel parking lot, and dropped Casey off, giving her her phone number and telling her she could call her anytime.

Later that night, Casey was sitting at the desk in her hotel room and sipping on a Diet Coke. She pulled out the notes she had made about the Power players during lunch, and she reviewed the roster that Anne had given her:

STARTING LINE-UP

First Base: Eric "Crush" Davis. At 6'4" and 245 pounds, Eric was a hulk of a man. A left-handed thrower and batter, he got his nickname from the towering home runs he would hit over the right field wall. He was good defensively as well, and was expected to be called up either as a first baseman or as a designated hitter. He was second on the team in home runs, with 16.

Second Base: Bobby Turner. The 23-year-old from Texas, currently batting .275. A solid fielder who was great at turning the double play, the main thing keeping him from being called

85

up was the fact that the Major League second baseman ahead of him was a Gold Glove All-Star who was batting .315.

Shortstop: Julio Perez. The 24-year-old from Puerto Rico was very quick, with a sure glove and a great arm. Currently, he was only batting .215, which was what was keeping him from moving up to the majors. Julio was a hard worker, and always took extra batting practice to try and get his batting average up.

Third Base: Scott Wilson, a 24-year-old from Oklahoma State. Good with the glove and solid at the plate, but was prone to wild throws over to first. Scott was nicknamed "Stud" by his teammates because he was always picking up women at the local bars when the team was on the road. Anne described him as "gorgeous."

Catcher: Jason Taylor. Short and stocky at 5'10" and 195 pounds, he had earned the nickname "Grunt" for the way he pounced around in the dirt after wild pitches. With a square jaw and a pug nose, "Grunt" was very adept at springing up from his catcher's stance to throw out base runners who were attempting to steal. He also had a good eye at the plate, and was batting .275. The coaching staff wanted him to get a little more experience at handling different types of pitchers, but it was expected that he would soon find his way into the majors. He was always getting in fights, and had initiated the last brawl that the Power was involved in.

Center field: James Johnson. Johnson has started for the Power for the last three years, and was known for always wearing a big smile on his face. Originally the Power's left fielder, he was moved over to center field when the previous player broke his ankle. Currently batting .278, he had great speed and always got a good jump on the ball in the outfield, but didn't have a great arm. Players rounding third or tagging on fly balls would test his arm, often with success.

Left field: Darnell Jenkins. Played college baseball at UCLA. Somewhat aloof, Jenkins's favorite movie was *Shaft*, and he often dressed like the character. He was 6'1" and 190 pounds, with a great arm and a lot of power at the plate. He led the team in doubles, and was third in home runs, with 12.

Designated Hitter: Juan Garcia. From Los Lumas, Mexico, Juan was the son of a migrant farm worker. He was first noticed by a scout watching a high school game, who saw that when Juan came up to the plate, the opposing outfielders moved back and stood on the warning track. With a huge barrel chest, he was nicknamed "El Torro", or *The Bull*. The Bull did not speak very good English, and often limited his comments to one- or two-word sentences.

Two years ago, the radio announcer for the Portland Power, Stan Marx, was calling a game when El Torro hit a towering home run to center field. When the ball went over the fence, Marx yelled *"Hasta la baseball, baby!"* Although the phrase didn't directly translate to anything in Spanish, the phrase stuck and became Stan Marx's trademark homerun call.

STARTING PITCHING STAFF

Dale Roberts. A right-handed pitcher, he had a great fastball which averaged 95 miles an hour, and a wicked slider to match. His biggest problem was that he would often let his ego take control on the mound and he would try to just blow his fastball by batters, rather than try to place the ball or mix up his pitches.

Roberts was actually called up to the majors for a month last season, but his arrogance in trying to blow his fastball past batters didn't work against the major league hitters, and after compiling an ERA of 7.85, he was sent back down to Portland.

Roberts was insulted that he would be sent back down to the minors, and acted like it was beneath him. In his mind, he was he was "just down getting some extra work." He walked around with his head thrown back in a gesture of superiority, leading one of the players to nickname him "Turk", to which the other players quickly added "The Jerk."

He always made it a point to tell everyone, "Hey, I've won in the majors." What he didn't tell everyone was that the one game he won his team scored eight runs and they won 8-7. He was not well liked, and his other nickname was *Seven Eighty Five*, a reference to his less-than-stalwart earned run average.

Dillon James. A left-handed junk ball pitcher, he threw mostly curves, sliders and off-speed pitches. His fastball was marginal at 89 miles an hour, and his main strategy was to keep batters off balance.

Carlos Rodriguez. A right-handed pitcher, he had a fastball, slider and a curve, but had problems getting his curve ball over for strikes. The pitching staff was working with him on his control, and if he could throw his curve ball over consistently, he would be pitching in the majors soon.

TJ Morrison. A left-handed pitcher, he had a good fastball, curve and a slider. He had a tendency to get lazy when he got ahead in the count, and would often "groove" a fastball right down the middle in an attempt to get the batter out, which often led to the opposing batter hitting a home run. In fact, this year TJ led the team in home runs given up.

RELIEF PITCHERS

Derek Rogers. A right-hander, Derek was mainly a fastball pitcher, but he was developing a decent change-up with the help of the pitching staff. His main problem, currently, was in trying to disguise the change-up so that the batters could not tell from his motion which pitch was coming.

Warren B. Coleman, Jr. Warren was a left-handed fireball pitcher who served as the middle reliever for the Power. He would come in to pitch whenever a starting pitcher could not make it to the later innings.

Michael "Mooch" Moran. A right-handed pitcher, Moran was the Power's closer, and one of many quirky relievers that had colored the league over the years. He was wiry at 6'2", 180 pounds, and could never seem to keep his baseball hat on straight. It wasn't that he wore it a certain way out of style, it was just that when he was going through his between-pitch routine, he would always take off his hat and place it back on his head. He just never seemed to be able to put it on the same way twice.

When Mooch was on the mound, he would always glare menacingly at the batters, but with the way his cap was always on crooked, it ended up just looking comical. Mooch only had two pitches – a fastball and a slider, but when your fastball has been clocked at over 98 miles an hour, and the slider not far behind that, it was enough to get you to the majors.

He was nicknamed Mooch because when he first arrived in Portland, he was always borrowing chewing tobacco from his teammates. Not long after that, word had gotten out to the *Power* fans that his nickname was Mooch. Whenever he would enter the game, coming in through a door in the left field fence, they would all stand on their feet and yell *Mooooch!* such that it sounded like a chorus of "Boos", but in reality was a cheer for their hometown player, who had become the fans' favorite.

But Mooch was often wild and inconsistent, and the majors were waiting for him to get better control before they move him up. A Grateful Dead fan, he loved the line, "Hey, man, the Dead live."

After Casey reviewed the roster, she opened a copy of the local newspaper, the *Portland Times*, and looked up the league standings on the sports page.

PACIFIC COAST LEAGUE STANDINGS

NORTHERN DIVISION	W	L	PCT.	Games Behind
Calgary Cowboys	38	32	.543	----
Vancouver Lions	35	35	.500	3
Portland Power	32	38	.457	6
Spokane Steam	30	39	.435	7 1/2

Bill Pennabaker

SOUTHERN DIVISION	W	L	PCT.	Games Behind
Sacramento Sting	40	30	.571	----
Phoenix Vipers	35	35	.500	5
Las Vegas Gamblers	33	38	.465	7 1/2
Fresno Bears	30	39	.429	10 1/2

CENTRAL DIVISION	W	L	PCT.	Games Behind
Salt Lake Racers	38	32	.543	----
Omaha Chiefs	37	33	.529	1
Colorado Pioneers	36	34	.514	2
Iowa Blizzard	35	35	.500	5

EASTERN DIVISION	W	L	PCT.	Games Behind
Memphis Hawks	39	31	.557	----
Orlando Sharks	39	31	.557	----
Oklahoma Thunder	35	35	.500	4
Birmingham Bulls	34	35	.478	5 1/2

The *Portland Power* was in the Class AAA Pacific Coast League (PCL) of Minor League baseball. There were four divisions—*Northern, Southern, Central and Eastern*, with Portland in the Northern. Each division had four teams, for a total of 16 teams in the league. At the end of a 144-game regular season, the winner of the Northern division played the winner of the Eastern division in a best-of-five semifinal series, while the winner of the Central division played the winner of the Southern division in the other semifinal series.

The winner of the two divisional playoff series went on to play in the Pacific Coast League Championship, which was won the last three years in a row by the Sacramento Sting of the Southern division.

They were a little over halfway through the season, and the Portland Power was currently six games out of first place. It seemed like their first order of business was to overtake Vancouver and Calgary in order to get to the divisional playoffs.

Casey noticed that Sacramento, whom Anne had mentioned had become the Power's nemesis and rival, was already steaming towards another divisional pennant. Anne had told her that Sacramento was also lobbying Major League Baseball for a franchise, which added to the sense of rivalry between the two cities.

Feeling like she had a little better understanding of her new environment, Casey put down the newspaper and her notes, and got ready for bed. After calling her mother to let her know that she had arrived safely, she watched a half hour of *the All Sports Network* and fell asleep.

Thirteen

Casey woke up around nine o'clock the following morning. She was used to staying in hotel rooms from her travels with the Richmond Tigers, so she ordered room service, grabbed the morning newspaper from outside her door, and flipped on the television to the local news. She wanted to get acclimated to Portland as much as possible, so she also read the local entertainment guide and the map of Portland which was included as a fold-out inside.

After finishing breakfast, Casey glanced at her watch. It was ten o'clock, and the press conference was two hours away. Anne had told her to be there an hour early so they could give her a briefing, so it was time to hit the shower.

Feeling a little nervous, Casey pondered what to wear. It was obviously a business situation, but she was also a ballplayer. She couldn't wear jeans and a baseball shirt -- that would be way too casual. She couldn't wear a dress. That would be too corny. Might as well just wear a shawl and carry an umbrella while she's at it. She decided to go with business casual – black slacks and black heels, a white button-down blouse, and a maroon jacket to wear over the top.

Satisfied that she looked presentable, Casey drove to the team office and arrived a little before eleven. Bud Harley's secretary, Sandy, was at her desk outside his office, and she greeted her warmly.

She motioned her into Bud's office, where, upon seeing her, Bud rose from his desk and came over to greet her. As usual, he was wearing a suit and tie. "There she is," he said warmly as he reached out to shake her hand. "Glad to see you made it. Welcome to Portland. Are we taking care of you all right?"

"Hi, Mr. Harley," she said, taking his hand. Then in response to his question, "Yes, everyone's been great. Anne showed me around and got me settled in over at the Portlander."

"Good. Before we get started, I'd like to introduce you to someone." Bud gestured to the side of the office where Butch

Morris had been sitting quietly. Casey hadn't even noticed he was there.

Bud continued, "Casey, this is Butch Morris, our head manager." Morris stood up and came over to greet her, and Casey held out her hand.

"Hi, Mr. Morris, nice to meet you," Casey said awkwardly. She had been so worried about the press conference that she almost forgot that she had a new boss. Now, suddenly here he was, standing in front of her. Unlike Bud Harley's well-styled business suit, Morris was wearing gray slacks, an open-collar blue shirt, and a plaid yellow-and-black sports jacket.

Morris took her hand, and stared at it as he felt the strength of her grip. "Hi. Good to meet you." Unlike others who gave Casey the initial physical appraisal and then apologized, Morris looked her up and down without feeling the slightest bit embarrassed.

He crossed his arms as he stared at her, and Casey shifted uncomfortably under his gaze. What are you, five-ten?" he asked.

"And a half."

"One forty?"

"One thirty-six, actually."

"Lefty, right?"

"Actually, I bat left-handed, but I throw right-handed."

"Hmm," Morris grunted in acknowledgement. "Bud says you're pretty fast on the base paths."

Casey shrugged. "I do all right."

The interview continued. "How fast are you down to first?"

"I've been clocked at three point nine seconds."

"Three point nine!" Morris exclaimed in amazement, as Bud Harley beamed. That was only slightly behind Ichiro Susuki, the speedy right fielder of the Seattle Mariners.

"You're file says you have nineteen stolen bases. How many attempts?"

"Nineteen."

Morris raised his eyebrows as Bud cut in. "All right," he said, "you two will have plenty of time to get acquainted later.

Right now, we need to focus on the press conference. Butch, you're welcome to stay, or join us in thirty minutes."

Morris responded, "Actually, I have a few phone calls to make. I'll be back." He nodded to the two and then left the room.

Bud looked at Casey, who wasn't sure what to make of her new boss. "Don't worry," he said with a chuckle. "Butch is a little blunt sometimes. But he's a good manager. He's done a great job in keeping the team together this year."

Then he walked over to his desk and grabbed a jersey and a baseball hat off of the corner. "Hey, before I forget, I have a few things for you." He unfolded the jersey and held it up for her to see. It was a traditional button-down baseball jersey with the *Power* logo on the front. He turned it around so she could see the back. It had the number "9" on the back, and her name, *"Collins"* stenciled across the top of the jersey. "Well, what do you think?" he asked.

"It looks great," she said. "Should I put it on now?"

"No. Wait for the conference. After I introduce you, I'll hand you the jersey and you'll put it on in front of everyone. It shouldn't be a problem. It's a button down so just put it on over your blouse. We can leave them here for now," Bud said as he placed the uniform and the hat back on the corner of his desk.

Then, with a slight nod of his head, Bud indicated a door off to the side of his office, which Casey hadn't noticed before. He motioned for her to follow with a wave of his hand. "Why don't we check out the conference room so you can see where we'll be?" He walked over to the door, opened it and went through. Casey followed him through the door and saw that it opened up into a another room.

"Wow, this is convenient," she commented, as she looked around the room.

At the front of the room, in the center, was a wooden podium, complete with a microphone, and a six-foot-long table on either side. Each table had a few office-style chairs with wheels on the bottom, spread along the length, facing the rest of the room. There were 5 rows of folding chairs with about 8 chairs in each row, or seating for about 40 people, facing the podium.

"We use this room for staff meetings and such, and of course, for press conferences as well," Bud said as he waved his hand across the room.

"How often do you have press conferences?" Casey asked suspiciously.

"Now and then," he smiled, basically avoiding her question. Then he continued the briefing. "Okay, here's how it works. I'll be behind the podium and you and coach will be seated to my left. I'll open up the conference; make a few comments welcoming the press, etcetera, etcetera, and then I'll introduce you.

"You walk up to the podium, shake my hand, and take the uniform and hat from me. You put them on and then let them take some pictures. Pretty standard stuff."

"Standard for you, you mean," she said with a worried look. "Will there be a lot of questions?"

"I'm sure there will be," he said. "But don't worry. Just answer honestly, and if you're not comfortable with something just say, 'No comment'. Okay?"

"Okay," she said. "So, do we wait in here or what?"

"No," he said with a shake of his head. "We wait in my office until the press is assembled." He pointed to a set of double doors at the rear of the room. "They enter through those doors there, and once they're all set up, we make our grand entrance. Any questions?" he asked.

Casey shrugged. "No, I guess not."

"Good. Why don't we wait in my office then, and Anne will let us know when everybody's here? They should probably start filing in soon." He walked back through the door into his office as Casey followed.

"You want something to drink?" he asked.

"Actually, I could use some water," Casey replied.

"No problem," Bud said. He went over to a small refrigerator that was against the wall behind his desk, bent over and grabbed a bottle of Perrier. He opened it using a small opener in the door of the refrigerator, and handed it to her.

"Thanks," she said. "I guess I'm a little dry." She took a long drink.

Bud noticed Casey wiping her hands on her pants and sensed her nervousness. "Don't worry," he said. "This isn't Watergate or anything. Just relax and be yourself. We've still got about twenty minutes, okay?"

"Okay," she said, not quite so confidently.

They chatted for several minutes as he asked her questions about her family and her background, trying to put her at ease. It worked somewhat, as Casey started to feel a little more comfortable. They were talking about her mom's restaurant when there was a knock on Bud's main office door.

Anne Ross poked her head through and said, "They're ready for you, boss." Butch Morris was behind her, and rejoined them in the office.

"Thanks, Anne," Bud said, as he rose up and grabbed his suit jacket which he had slumped over his chair. "You ready?" he asked, putting his jacket on.

"As ready as I'll ever be," she answered as she stood up and took a last swig of her bottled water. She glanced over at Butch Morris, who seemed apathetic about the whole thing. Casey assumed he had been through this many times before, unlike herself.

"Attagirl," Bud said with a wink as he motioned for her to follow him into the conference room.

He opened the door to the conference room and entered with a broad smile on his face. There were about twenty members of the local press gathered in the room, and they were engaged in small conversations among themselves. He waved and nodded to a few of them as the conversations gradually subsided.

There were representatives from the three local television stations in the greater Portland area, KTOP, KOTV, KIXX, two radio stations, KPOR and KSPT, and from the one major newspaper, the *Portland Times*.

At first they hadn't been all that motivated to drag their equipment over to the Power office for an announcement of another new minor league baseball player. But when Anne mentioned that it was a woman, their interest was immediately piqued.

The first thing Casey noticed when she walked into the room, other than the people, was the row of television cameras set up along the back of the room. She hadn't quite expected that, even though Bud had mentioned that there would be representatives from the local television stations at the conference. She just hadn't made the connection in her mind, and it was a little unsettling.

Bud walked up to the podium with Butch Morris following right behind him and Casey bringing up the rear. Morris walked by the podium and took the second seat closest to the podium, motioning for Casey to take the closest seat.

Casey took her seat, and immediately felt all the eyes in the room looking at her. Fortunately, there was a pitcher of water and a couple of glasses at the table in front of her, and she took one glass and filled it up with water, taking a nervous sip as she waited for the conference to begin.

Bud was at the podium and had his hands placed on either side of the wooden structure. He adjusted the microphone slightly as he started to speak, as much to get everyone's attention as anything else. "Good morning, everyone," he said loudly. "Thank you all for coming. Vince, glad to see you could make it out from behind your desk to be with us today," he joked as a way to insert some humor into his opening.

Vince Daley, the senior sports reporter for the *Portland Times*, was seated in the front row. He nodded in recognition and joked back, "Hey, I have to get some exercise somehow."

There were a few more chuckles, and then the room quieted down as Bud continued. "As you know, we invited you all here today so they we could introduce you to the newest addition to the *Power* family. And so, without further ado, I am pleased to present the new right fielder for the Portland Power, Casey Collins. Casey," he said, as he motioned to Casey to join him at the podium.

There was a smattering of light applause as Casey rose and joined him at the podium. Bud shook her hand and briefly held up her new jersey for the audience to see, before handing it to her. Cameras flashed as Casey, a full inch taller than Bud, took the jersey from him and put it on, buttoning up the front before taking the baseball cap from Bud and also putting it on. She stood there smiling beside Bud for a few minutes while the cameras flashed. They did a few different poses such as shaking hands, putting one arm around each other, etc.

Then Bud said into the microphone, "Okay, we'll open it up for questions now."

Immediately, hands went up into the air. "Yes, Vince," he said, acknowledging the senior reporter.

Vince remained seated with his legs crossed and his notebook on his lap. "Yes, Bud," he started. "I understand that Miss Collins came from Richmond, which is Single A. Isn't it unusual for a player to jump two levels like this? Can you take us through your decision process?"

"It's not that unusual," Bud countered. "It's been done before. The thing is, we need a right fielder. We looked over our available personnel and decided that Casey would be the best fit for us at this time."

A reporter from the television station, KTTV stood up and asked. "Who made this decision, Bud, was it you or the manager?"

"We made this decision together," the owner responded.

"Is this a publicity stunt to sell more tickets, bringing in a woman to play on a men's team?" a reporter from radio station KSPT asked.

"Absolutely not," Bud said emphatically, looking directly at the reporter who had asked the question. "Look, as Casey's mother once said, the term *baseball player* is not gender specific. Casey Collins is a good athlete and a good baseball player. She was batting .337 in Richmond, with nineteen stolen bases. She has demonstrated that she can play, and we decided it was time to give her a shot."

Casey was impressed. She had only told Bud about Sue's famous line fifteen minutes earlier when they were chatting in his office. She had to hand it to him; he knew how to steal a good line.

A woman reporter from KPOR raised her hand and was acknowledged by Bud. "Yes, Kate?" he said.

Kate stood up and said, "I have a question for Casey."

Bud stepped aside as Casey stepped up to the podium. "Yes, ma'am?" she said, a little weakly.

"How does it feel to be the first woman player to play for the Power?" Kate asked.

Casey cleared her throat. "Well, I'm a little nervous, to be honest with you. But I'm grateful to Mr. Harley for giving me this opportunity and I'm going to play my hardest and do the best job I can to help the team win."

"What makes you think you can play with the men at this level? I mean, they're so much bigger and stronger than you, aren't they?" Kate followed.

Casey responded. "Well, yes, they are bigger and stronger than me, but this isn't a wrestling match or a football game. It's different. There's more strategy and skill involved. The pitcher still has to throw the ball over the plate, and I haven't found any guy yet who can beat me down to first base. But, like I said, I'm just going to do my best to help the team any way I can."

An older reporter from KSPT raised a hand and said, "Casey?"

"Yes, sir?" she replied.

"Can you tell a little bit about what it's like being on a team full of men? What's the interaction like? Do they treat you differently? How does it work in the locker room?"

"Well, those are some good questions. First, I usually have my own little locker room, which oftentimes isn't much more than a small converted office or something. A lot of times when I'm on the road, I'll dress in my uniform in the hotel room before I get on the bus, and then maybe I'll shower later back at the room. I'm not usually in the guys' locker room, unless there's a meeting or something, and then it's after everyone's dressed.

"As for the interaction with my teammates, I've been playing with guys all my life. It's usually a little awkward at first, for both of us. They all think they have to treat me specially at first, but as time goes on, I just become another ballplayer, which is really the way it should be."

Another reporter directed a question to Butch Morris. "Coach, when are we going to see Casey in the line-up? Is she going to start right away?"

"The team is off today, but she'll start the game tomorrow night against Omaha."

Casey snuck a look at Morris from the side of her eye. He hadn't mentioned this to her.

"A follow-up question for the coach. Do *you* believe she can play at this level?" Bud Harley shot Morris a "Don't you dare blow this" look out of the corner of his eye.

Morris was trying to hide his discomfort, and shifted a little uneasily in his chair. He tried to sound supportive, but stopped short of an outright endorsement. "Time will tell. We have a lot of positive reports on her from Richmond. She has great speed on the bases and in the outfield, and that's something our team really needs right now. She'll get her shot tomorrow night and from then on, it's all up to her."

Bud stepped in and took over the conference again. "Okay," he said, "we're going to have to wrap this up. Any last questions?"

A reporter from the second row made a wisecrack. "Yeah, Casey, you're not going to wear those high heels while you're playing, are you?" The audience let out a small laugh.

"Only when I'm batting," she countered. "It helps me reach the higher pitches." This brought a bigger laugh from the crowd, as well as a few claps.

Bud decided it was time to bring the conference to a close. "Okay," he said, still laughing lightly from Casey's response. "I think we've had enough for today. Thanks again to everyone for coming, and we invite you out to the ballpark this weekend to see Casey in action."

Fourteen

The next morning, when Casey retrieved the newspaper, she saw her first headline in the *Portland Times*. On the very front page, above the news headlines, were small boxes with headlines and teasers about various subjects. In the box titled "Sports", was the headline, "Woman Professional Baseball Player Comes to Portland." Details on C3.

Casey flipped to the Sports section to read the article:

Woman Professional Baseball Player Comes to Portland
By Ken Riley

Portland Power owner Bud Harley announced at a team press conference yesterday that they were bringing the minor league's only woman baseball player, Casey Collins, to play for the Portland Power.

Ms. Collins, a right fielder, had been playing for the Single A Richmond (WA) Tigers, where she was batting 337, with 19 stolen bases and 35 RBI's.

When asked if bringing the league's only female baseball player to Portland was a publicity stunt designed to sell more tickets, Mr. Harley denied the notion. "Absolutely not," he said. "Casey Collins is a good ballplayer. She has demonstrated that she can play and we need a right fielder. We decided it was time to move her up."

Power manager Butch Morris added, "We have positive reports on Casey from Richmond. She has good speed on the bases and in the outfield, and that's something our team really needs right now."

When asked how she felt about jumping up two divisions to Triple A, Ms. Collins responded. "Well, I'm a little nervous, to be honest with you. But I'm grateful to Mr. Harley for giving me this opportunity and I'm going to play my hardest and do the best job I can to help the team win."

Publicity stunt or not, the addition of Ms. Collins to the team is sure to generate renewed interest in the Power, who are currently in third place in the PCL, and have not been selling out their home games.

Ms. Collins will be in uniform tomorrow night when the Power hosts the Omaha Chiefs at the Powerhouse. For tickets call 1-800 GO POWER.

Casey finished reading the article, with many thoughts running through her mind. She hadn't even suited up yet and already she had an article in the paper. How had she done at the press conference yesterday? How would her new team accept her? She was still a little shaken by the reaction of some of the Richmond Tiger teammates. She had experienced some of that before, but never from people she had played with for so long. And, of course, the biggest question of all, could she play at this level?

The thoughts stayed with her throughout the day as she anticipated that nights' game. Finally, she couldn't wait any longer, and after two Diet Cokes, she made the drive to the ballpark. As she entered the player's parking lot and found a space, she noticed a crowd of about 75 people gathered around the entrance to the player's locker room. She checked her watch. 5:00 P.M. It seemed a little early for people to be looking for autographs. At her home park in Richmond, there would sometimes be 10 or 15 kids hanging around an hour before game time, but nothing like this.

Maybe at Triple A this was normal. After all, players at this level were one step away from the majors. *Yeah, that must be it*, she thought to herself, as she got out of her car. She was carrying her athletic bag as she approached the crowd.

As she got nearer, a young boy who was holding his mother's hand, pointed at her and ask loudly, "Mom, is that her?" This caused the entire crowd to turn and look at Casey, and several of the kids ran over to where she had stopped when she saw the boy pointing at her.

One of the boys, who was wearing a *Portland Power* baseball cap and looked to be about 12 years old, was the first to reach her. He stopped a few feet away and asked, "Are you Casey Collins?"

Casey was a little taken aback, but answered, "Yes."

Suddenly it seemed like a thousand kids all yelled at the same time, "Can I have your autograph?" as they swarmed around her like bees.

It wasn't like it was the first time that Casey had been asked for her autograph. Almost every ballpark she visited in Single A when traveling with the Tigers had a few autograph-seekers who wanted to see the woman who played men's baseball.

She just wasn't used to this many people. And she hadn't even played her first game yet. Still a little surprised, she placed her bag on the ground and straddled it with both legs. She took a notebook and pen from the twelve-year-old boy who had asked her the question, and as she started to sign, asked, "How did you guys even know about me?"

"It was the press conference yesterday." The answer came from one of the fathers, who, like the other parents, had come over and joined their sons and daughters.

"Yeah, and it was in the newspaper," said a mother who was holding her daughter's hand. "You're already famous here. We came tonight just to see you play." Then, nudging her daughter forward a little, she said, "Go ahead, sweetheart, ask her for her autograph, and don't forget to say 'Please'."

The seven-year-old girl stepped forward and said shyly, "Hello, Miss Collins, may I have your autograph, please?"

"Of course you can, sweetheart. What's your name?"

"Angela." Casey took the girl's notebook and pen, scrawled "Good luck Angela, Casey Collins", and gave them back to her.

"Thank you." The girl said as she scurried back over to where her mother was standing.

As she spent the next twenty minutes signing autographs, Casey noticed some of the players walking by with their athletic bags on their way into the locker room. As they saw her surrounded by the crowd, she could see some of them shaking their heads. Again, Casey felt like she could read their minds. *Look at her, she hasn't even played a game yet and already she's a celebrity.*

Finally, Casey looked at her watch and said. "Well, I have to go get ready. Thank you, everyone." They all wished her well as she made her way through, past the crowd and into the player's main entrance.

Butch Morris had asked all the players to arrive early for a brief team meeting. It was so they could be introduced to Casey. As she entered the facility, he saw her from across the room and called out. "Collins. Over here." He motioned with one arm for her to come over and join him where he was standing talking to an older African-American man with whitish hair.

Casey strolled over and said. "Hi, Mr. Morris."

Morris turned and put one hand on the black man's arm, and said, "Casey, I'd like you to meet Luscious Brown. He's our assistant manager, and he'll help you to get set up here."

Luscious reached out his hand to Casey. "Hi, Miss Casey. It's a real pleasure to make your acquaintance," he said with a genuine smile and a twinkle in his eye. "By the way, most folks around here just call me *Pop*."

Casey reached out and shook his hand firmly. "Hi, Pop," she said, pleased at his warm greeting, "It's nice to meet you."

Pop took his hand back and looked at it in mock pain. "Hey, that's some grip you got there. Remind me not to get on your bad side."

Casey smiled at him and said, "I don't think there's any danger of that, Pop," as they both chuckled.

"All right," Morris said as he put a hand on Casey's shoulder. "I'll leave you in Pop's hands." Then, as he was walking away, he pointed at his watch and said over his shoulder, "We've got the team meeting in twenty minutes, so you'd better get to it."

"Sure thing," Pop said. "We'll be there."

Sixty-seven-year-old Luscious Brown had been the assistant manager for the Portland Power for seven years. An African American with white hair and a white mustache to match, Luscious looked like he had been through some interesting times, and, in fact, he had. He had been a bat boy for the Brooklyn Dodgers, and his main claim to fame was that he knew Jackie Robinson. Luscious actually played in the minors for seven years himself, but never made it to the majors.

Even at sixty-seven years of age, Pop stood tall and firm, and walked with the kind of pride that came from overcoming a lifetime of adversity. He had a kindly face which was emphasized by wrinkles that appeared around his eyes when he smiled, which was often. He had a million and one stories, which he was always ready to tell when asked, and oftentimes even when not.

If Luscious Brown had been born in a later era, he would most likely be a head manager at a professional baseball level, if not in the majors, then certainly in the minor leagues. But by the time African Americans finally broke the color barrier in the major league manager ranks, it was a little late for Luscious.

This did not change the fact that he knew a lot about baseball, and it was people's respect for his baseball knowledge, and for the way that he carried himself, that made him a respected coach. Players would often seek his advice on their swing or some other aspect of their game that they were having trouble with at that time. It was Luscious Brown's patience and gentle manner in which he delivered his advice that caused people to call him Pop.

Pop was the kind of guy that you could tell just loved to be around the game, and would probably die on or around a baseball field.

He motioned for Casey to follow him down the hall, to an office door with a glass pane at the top. He had a key chain hanging from a small clip on his belt, and he unhooked one of the keys and opened the door. He went inside first and flipped on the light, as Casey followed him in.

The office was small, 12 by 12 feet, and smelled a little dank. It still had a metal desk up against one wall, and there was a 36-inch-square mirror with a wooden frame sitting on top of the desk and leaning against the wall. There was a single bench along the opposite wall and a wooden coat rack in one corner. On the bench were a folded uniform and a cap.

"We only found out on Monday that you were coming, so there wasn't a lot of time to get you set up properly." He motioned with his head to the uniform on the bench. "I was able to call down to Richmond and get your measurements, so it should fit you."

Casey walked over to the bench and put the baseball hat on. If felt like it fit okay. Then she unfolded the shirt and held it up against her chest. It was a black button down jersey with *The Power* written across the chest in gold lettering. Piercing *The Power* diagonally was a jagged gold lightning bolt, separated in the middle to allow the words to spread across the chest. It also looked like it would fit.

She refolded the jersey and put it back on the bench, then picked up the baseball pants and held them up against her. The pants were all white, with very thin black stripes running vertically from top to bottom, and they included a black expandable belt running through the loops. They also appeared to be the right size.

"They look like they'll fit all right," she said to Pop as she refolded them and placed them back on the bench. "Thanks."

"No problem," he said. "I've got another set for you in my office. I'll give them to you later."

"So where do I shower?" she asked.

Pop had both hands on his hips, and he frowned. "Well, that's a bit of a problem right now. Like I said, we didn't have a lot of time to prepare for you. Mr. Morris and I share a shower between our two offices and you'll have to use that one. But only for a couple of days. We go on the road next week and we've got plumbers and carpenters coming in. They're going to knock out the adjoining office and put a bathroom and shower in there for you. Nothing fancy but it should suffice."

"It's okay," she said, "I deal with this stuff all the time".

"I bet you do," he smiled, and starting walking toward the door. "Well, I'll let you get changed and then we'll head on into the other locker room and you'll meet the team. All right?"

"All right," she replied, then watched as Pop left the office and closed the door. She placed her athletic bag on the bench, and changed into her new uniform. She walked over and stood in front of the mirror to see how she looked. The uniform actually looked a little big on her, but it wasn't too bad. She did feel a little strange dressed in the white pants and black jersey, after wearing the red Richmond Tigers jersey for the last five years.

Well, this is my new uniform. I guess I better get used to it, Casey thought to herself. She hung her street clothes on the coat rack and grabbed her glove from her bag. She walked out the door, closing it behind her, and headed back up the hallway to Pop's office. The door was open, and she gave it a light rap with her knuckles.

Pop's office was a bit bigger, and was littered with baseball equipment. A cloth bag full of baseballs rested in one corner, and an orange plastic water container sat in the other. A few bats, spikes and assorted other baseball equipment was scattered around.

Pop heard the rap on the door and looked up from a scouting report he was reading. He was wearing half-moon reading glasses, and he peered over the top to see who was at the door. He sprang up when he saw it was Casey.

"Hey, Casey, come on in!" he said as walked around the desk. He gave a quick look up and down at her in her uniform. "You look great. Everything fit okay?"

With her thumb and forefinger, Casey pinched a piece of her jersey where it hung over her pants slightly, and said, "Actually, it's a little big, but not too bad."

"Oh, we'll take some real measurements later and get you a better fit. But it looks okay for now." He glanced briefly at his wristwatch and asked, "So, are you ready to meet your new team?"

"Sure," she replied, a little apprehensively.

Pop sensed her uneasiness and gave a reassuring smile. "Hey, don't worry, it's normal to be a little nervous, joining a new team and all."

"I think I'm more than a little nervous," she frowned.

Pop dismissed her comment with a wave of his hand. "Nonsense. It'll be all right. If anybody gives you any flak, you just let me know, and I'll deal with them. Now, come on and follow me."

He shuffled her out the door and they headed towards the main locker room. As they approached the door, he halted and said, "Why don't you wait out here? I'll grab Mr. Morris so he can introduce you to the team."

Casey waited outside for what seemed like a half an hour, but, in reality, was only a few minutes. Her palms were sweating slightly and she was wiping them on her pants when the door opened and Butch Morris came out.

He looked at her up and down as she stood there in her uniform, and gave a slight grunt. "You ready?" he asked.

"Sure," she said, trying to sound convincing.

Morris opened the locker room door and went inside, reaching back with a hand to keep the door from closing shut, as Casey and Pop followed him in. The locker room was a large cement floored room with a long row of metal lockers up against the right and left walls. In front of each row of lockers was a long wooden bench running the length of the lockers. The back wall had a 10-foot-wide opening in the wall, which was the entry to the bathrooms and the team showers.

There were about twenty men scattered around the locker room in small groups, some sitting on the benches, some leaning against the lockers talking. Morris was carrying a clipboard as he walked into the room and commanded loudly, "All right, everybody, listen up!"

As the conversations slowly died down and the players turned to face the front of the room, Casey saw twenty sets of eyes all staring at her. She suddenly felt like she was the eight-year-old girl back at the neighborhood ball field, facing a bunch of boys all looking at her. *Another group appraisal.*

Morris addressed the team in a loud voice. "Okay, you guys all know what's going on by now, so I want you to meet our new right fielder, Casey Collins. Why don't you guys come up and introduce yourselves?"

The players looked to the front of the room, and saw a lean woman dressed in full uniform, complete with the black *Power* baseball hat. She was attractive, and it looked like she was in pretty good shape. Her bare arms were well defined without being overmuscled, and her legs appeared to be the same.

Her baseball socks were pulled up a little high, a touch of cockiness, and she had a serious look on her face — this was not someone who was just playing at this. *She looked like a ballplayer.*

Casey gave an awkward nod of her head and a small wave of her hand as she was introduced, and managed to get out a weak, "Hey". She stood there with her hands by her side and waited for the players to come and introduce themselves.

Four players that had been standing by the lockers closest to the front of the room broke out of their small group and came up to Casey one by one. The first one to approach her was the big first baseman with the round baby face. He reached out his hand and said, "Hi, I'm Eric Davis, first base. Welcome to the team."

Wow, he's huge, she thought to herself as she looked up at the 6'4" man. "Hi, Casey Collins," she smiled in return, thankful to have the first one over with.

Next up was the second baseman. "Hi, Bobby Turner, second base. Nice to meet you."

"Hi, Bobby. Casey Collins. Nice to meet you."

After Bobby came Scott "Stud" Wilson, who gave Casey a warm handshake and a charming smile. *Wow, Anne was right, he is gorgeous,* Casey thought to herself, trying not to stare too hard.

One by one, they all came up to introduce themselves. As Casey greeted each of them, she noticed a wide variety of ways in which they reacted to her. Some, such as the gentle Eric Davis, were generally warm and sincere as they welcomed her to the team. A few seemed indifferent, and Dale Roberts, whom Anne had called the Turk, was just as Anne had described him.

He wasn't wearing his baseball hat, and his short blonde crew cut stood straight up. Turk did not look like a happy person, with his little pug nose, beady eyes, and a perpetual scowl on his face. He walked up with his head tilted back, and had tried to squeeze Casey's hand extra hard in an effort to hurt her, but was shocked to feel how strong her grip was in return. He grunted a greeting. "Dale Roberts, starting pitcher. I hope you can play. I'm starting tonight."

A little taken aback by his curt greeting, all Casey could say was, "I'll do my best," while thinking to herself, *Asshole.*

Roberts grunted and walked away. Pop, standing there with his arms crossed, just shook his head as he witnessed the exchange.

Casey supposed the variety of reactions she encountered was just like any social group meeting a new member, but she also knew it was a little more than that. Since she was the only woman baseball player currently in the minor leagues, this was as new to them as it was to her.

After the players had taken their turns in greeting Casey, Butch Morris spoke up again. "All right. Now that the pleasantries are all done, let's talk about some baseball. Everyone take a seat." The players each took a seat along one of the benches, and Casey joined them, sitting up front.

Morris had his clipboard in hand and was about to continue when he surveyed the group. He ran a hand over his day-old stubble as he looked them over, and asked, "Hey, has anybody seen Moran?"

Just then, as if on queue, the loud sound of a toilet flushing came from one of the stalls at the back of the locker room. The stall door opened and Mike Moran came out, pulling up his pants and tightening his belt. He was tall and wiry at 6'3 and 180 pounds, with curly brown hair that stuck out from his baseball hat. His hat was tilted slightly to the left as he walked over to one of the sinks and washed his hands. He then grabbed a paper towel, and as he was drying his hands, turned and looked at the rest of the team, who were all staring and laughing at him.

Casey laughed along with the rest of the team, as Moran casually walked over to one of the benches and took a seat. "Sorry, Skip," he said to Morris.

This caused everyone, except for Morris, to laugh even more. Shaking his head at Mooch's antics, Morris got back to business. "First, tonight's line-up, for those of you who haven't seen the list on my door. Johnson, you're leading off as usual,

Turner, you're second..." He read through the list until he got to the last position. He looked up from his clipboard. "Collins, you're in right field, batting ninth."

Casey replied with a nod, as Morris continued. He moved the line-up page to the back of his clipboard, and looked up at the group. "All right, before we head out, I've got a memo here from President Jacobs."

A collective groan went up from the team, but Morris silenced them with a single look. "Now, listen, this is serious stuff. This is in reference to all the fighting that's been going on in the league. Bud Harley was summoned to an owner's meeting last week, and Jacobs issued this memo."

Morris read the memo from the league president, including the punitive measures that would be taken against any player that was involved in a fight. Finishing up the memo, he looked at the team. "Now, I don't think any of you want to fork over a grand to the league, and you can be damn sure you don't want to be the cause of me having to fork over any money. Understand?"

The group muttered their agreement as Morris looked at Jason Taylor, who they called Grunt. "This means you especially, Taylor. If I see you make any more moves toward the pitcher, I'll tackle you myself. You got it?

A few players chuckled as Grunt grinned sheepishly. "I got you, Chief."

Morris looked at his watch. "All right, enough of that. Now let's go get some solid batting practice in and have a good game tonight. We're facing Gardner, their lefty, so let's get to it." The players all rose and began filing out of the locker room, heading towards the tunnel that lead up to the playing field.

As Casey started to file out, Michael Moran came over to her and reached out his hand. "Hey, how are you doing? I'm Mike Moran. Everybody calls me Mooch."

Casey shook his hand and looked up at him, "Hi, Mooch, Casey Collins. Nice to meet you."

Mooch then reached into his back pocket, pulled out a pouch of chewing tobacco, and held it out in front of him. "Want some chew?" he offered.

Casey's face suddenly contorted in revulsion, and she lashed out at him. "Ugh, how can you chew that disgusting stuff?"

"What?" he asked, a little surprised at the intensity of her reaction. He could not have known that his next line was even worse. "It's not so bad, it's not like it's going to kill me or anything."

She just shook her head and walked away in disgust, leaving him standing there with a bewildered look on his face, still holding out the tobacco pouch, "Geez, I didn't know it was such a big deal," he said, more to himself than anyone else.

Pop was standing nearby and had noticed the exchange. He walked up to Mooch and said, "What was that all about?"

"I don't know," he replied. "All I did was offer her some chew and she went off on me. I thought she'd been around baseball and guys long enough that she wouldn't be offended by it. I was just trying to be cordial."

Pop gave a knowing smile and put his hand on Mooch's shoulder and said, "Well, let me tell you something."

When Pop had called down to Richmond to get Casey's measurements for her uniform, he also took the time to ask about her background, which is when he heard about Casey's father. He filled Mooch in on the story. When he was done talking, Mooch had a concerned look on his face as he looked at Pop. "Wow, geez, I didn't know. I mean, how was I supposed to know? Should I go apologize now?"

"Relax," Pop said. "Maybe you should just let her cool down a little and you can apologize later. I'm sure she'll understand."

Luscious Brown had showed one reason why they called him Pop. Part coach, part counselor—always there to offer advice.

Fifteen

Following the other players, Casey made her way out of the tunnel and up into the dugout. It was her first opportunity to get a look at the new field, and she went right to the top of the stairs and looked around.

The first thing she noticed was that the Power stadium was easily three times bigger than any stadium she had played in in Class A. Portland Stadium, or The Powerhouse, as it was often called, held 35,000 seats, while Richmond Stadium only sat 7,500.

The Powerhouse was also much more elaborate than Tiger Stadium, and resembled a major league park. The press box behind the plate consisted of two levels, and wrapped around home plate so that it stretched about 20 feet along each base line. There was room for about 40 journalists, with Plexiglas walls extended from the floor to the ceiling.

The outfield wall was 8 feet high and painted dark green. Bleacher seats wrapped around the entire outfield, with the exception of center field. There was a 40-foot break in the first 20 rows of the center field bleachers, where there was a 15-foot high water fountain. On either side of the fountain was a screen-enclosed bullpen, one for each team.

Behind the fountain, at the top of the stadium, was a 20' by 30' electronic scoreboard, equipped with the latest in computer generated graphics, including a radar gun readout which showed the speed of every pitch.

Just like in the majors, Casey thought to herself.

The other major difference she noticed was that the field was made of artificial turf. Portland got enough rain that they chose not to use natural grass. She went out onto the field and walked around to get the feel of the turf. None of the minor league parks she had played in used artificial turf. They all used natural grass, which was less expensive to maintain, but also caused widely varying qualities in the playing surfaces from ballpark to ballpark. This was not the old Astroturf of the late 'seventies, this was the new cushion turf, and felt much closer to natural grass. *This stuff is amazing*, she thought to herself as she felt around with her feet.

She jogged out to right field and walked around, making exaggerated steps and pressing down to feel the spring of the turf. As she was getting the feel of the field, other players were running out to various spots of the field and starting their warm-up routines. Some were doing calisthenics, some were jogging to get loose, and some were tossing balls to each other. Casey walked out to the "Warning Track", which was a 15-foot-wide patch of dirt stretching the entire length of the outfield fence. It extended from the fence into the outfield, and provided a noticeable break from the turf. The purpose of this was to warn an outfielder chasing a fly ball and running back towards the fence that they were getting close, so they could make adjustments and avoid a collision.

As she was looking around, the centerfield wall opened up and the equipment manager came through, riding a small green tractor. He was towing a batting cage behind him, and heading towards home plate. This was definitely different than Class A, Casey thought to herself.

In Richmond, the manager would usually enlist a few "volunteers" to manually pull the batting cage behind the plate. In fact, some of the parks didn't even have a batting cage.

As the equipment manager towed the cage to home plate, a few of the players standing near the dugout grabbed some bats and started to take some practice swings. Once the cage was set up, he hauled out a couple of cloth bags full of baseballs, and placed them out behind another small cage by the pitcher's mound. The pitching cage was just a small wire mesh fence that was about waist high. When someone was throwing baseballs for batting practice, he would stand behind the cage, which would protect him in case the batter hit one back to the mound.

Typically, it was the pitching coach or assistant manager who would throw batting practice. In this case, the pitching coach, Manny Rodriguez, took his position behind the pitching cage and motioned for the first batter to step in.

Casey took a ready position in right field as "Grunt" Taylor stepped into the batting cage. Although most of the players in the field were standing around in small groups, Casey was by herself. Manny began throwing a series of medium fastballs to Grunt, who took his swings and began scattering the balls around the infield and outfield, until his time was up.

One by one, the players stepped into the cage and took their turns. Casey fielded a few grounders and fly balls, which helped to loosen her up a little. She did notice out of the side of her eye that a few of the players were watching to see how she handled the balls that were hit to her. Since all of the players that had batted so far were right-handers, she only fielded a few, and did so easily, following up by throwing the balls back in towards the infield.

After a few players had taken their swings, the pitching coach motioned, with a wave of his hand, for Casey to head in and take her turn. She trotted in towards the dugout where the center fielder was just finishing up, and one of the back-up infielders was taking his swings.

She grabbed her bat from her bag and put the metal doughnut over the end, stepped into the on deck circle and started taking a few practice swings. As she took her swings, she watched the pitches being thrown into the batter, so that she could gauge the speed.

The infielder finished his swings, and then it was Casey's turn. As she stepped into the batter's box, every player stopped what they were doing in order to watch her, and the managers did as well. Although she expected to attract some extra attention, having everyone just stop and watch her was a bit unnerving.

Relax, it's just batting practice, she told herself.

The pitching coach held a single ball high in the air over his head, which was a way of asking Casey if she was ready. She assumed her batting stance and nodded that she was ready. She watched the first two pitches go by, way outside, and noticed that they were a little slower than they were for the last couple of batters.

Like all men who pitched to her the first time, the pitching coach was a little thrown off pitching to a woman. She grinned, took a step out of the box and called out to him. "It's okay, Coach, just throw at your normal speed."

Realizing what he had been doing and feeling slightly embarrassed by it, Manny gave a little chuckle and said, "All right. I get it. Sorry."

Casey stepped back into the box as he wound up and threw a medium-speed pitch right down the middle. Casey watched his windup closely, looking for the release point of the pitch. She followed the ball as it came to the plate, shifted her weight forward and stepped into the pitch, giving a solid, level swing.

She connected with the ball and it zinged straight at the coach's head. "Whoa," he exclaimed, as he ducked behind the cage just in time for the ball to sail over his head and bounce right behind second base. "Good wood."

"Thanks, and sorry about that," she replied.

It felt good to hit the ball, and Casey began to feel more at ease with each passing pitch. She took about 20 swings, connecting well on most of the pitches. As she scattered the balls around the outfield, the players resumed their various activities.

Casey finished up, nodded thanks to the pitching coach and stepped out of the cage. The next batter up was Bobby Turner, and he said, "Looking good," as she walked by.

"Thanks," she replied. She placed her bat back in the bat rack, grabbed her glove and jogged back out to right field.

Crush Davis was standing by first base, and he nodded to her and said, "Good hitting," as she jogged by.

"Thanks," she said. "You were really crushing the ball yourself. I guess that's how you got your nickname." Crush grinned in return.

Casey noticed that the stands had been filling up, and there were already twice as many people as she was used to seeing at her games. After batting practice was finished, she jogged in to the dugout, where Pop was moving a few things around. He was standing at the top of the steps at the outfield end of the dugout, and he greeted her as she jogged in.

"How are you feeling, kid?" he asked.

"A little nervous," she responded. She descended the stairs and dropped her glove on the end of the bench, as the players from the visiting team ran out and took their turn on the field.

"Don't worry," Pop said with a reassuring nod. "You'll be all right."

A few minutes after the visiting team had taken their turn on the field, the public address announcer's voice came over the microphone. "Ladies and gentlemen, please rise and join us for the playing of the national anthem."

The players from both teams stood in front of their dugouts, holding their hats against their hearts. When the recorded song finished playing over the PA system, Butch Morris clapped his hand together a couple of times as he turned to his players and said, "Okay, guys, let's take the field. Lots of hustle out there tonight. Let's go!"

The hometown crowd cheered as the players for the Portland Power jogged out to their positions, with Casey taking hers in right field. She looked around the stadium and was amazed at how many people there were. Unlike back at Richmond, where most of the fans sat behind the dugouts along either baseline, here there were actually people sitting in the outfield seats.

The pitcher finished his last warm-up toss to the catcher, who jumped up and threw the ball down to the second baseman, who caught it and flipped it the shortstop, who tossed it to the first baseman, who then threw it to the third baseman, who finally tossed it to the pitcher. It was a process know as "*Throwing it around the horn*", and was a ritual that teams followed in between innings and after every out was made. It was a way of keeping the infielders loose and into the game.

Finally, the umpire called "Play Ball", and the lead off batter for the Omaha Chiefs stepped into the box. His name was Maurice "Scooter" Jones and he led the league in stolen bases. He batted left-handed, and was known for trying to bunt his way on base. Once he got on, he was trouble.

Casey's stomach was turning summersaults, and for the first time she could ever remember, she secretly wished that they didn't hit the ball to her, at least not right away. *Gotta have a good game. Gotta have a good game*, she willed to herself.

Dale "Turk" Roberts was on the mound for the Power. He had a record of 3 wins and 3 losses so far this year, and was looking to move into the plus column with a win tonight. He wound up and started Jones off with a fastball down the middle for a called strike one. The first and third basemen, expecting a possible bunt, had inched in towards home plate a few steps, and they retreated to their normal positions after the called strike.

Roberts wound up again, and again the first and third baseman moved in closer to the plate. But the batter turned his body and bunted the ball straight out in front of home plate. Grunt tore off his catcher's mask and went running out after the ball, but it was too far out towards the pitcher for him to retrieve. Roberts was a little slow in his follow-through, and by the time he came off the mound and retrieved the ball, Jones was well on his way to first base. Roberts made the throw to first, but it wasn't even close. "Scooter" was safe by two feet.

One man on and nobody out. The number two batter came up and also bunted, but he made no attempt to get a base hit out of it. Instead, he executed a "sacrifice bunt", bunting the ball firmly to the pitcher so that he had to field the ball, but not so firmly that he had time to turn and throw the base runner out at second. Roberts' only choice was to throw the batter out at first, which he did.

The second baseman, who was covering first base because the first baseman had taken a few steps in to help cover the bunt, caught the ball from the pitcher. Casey had run in about 20 feet behind first base, to "back up" the play in case there was a wild throw. Once the out was made, she jogged back to her position in right field. It wasn't much, but at least it got her into the game and got her heart pumping a little.

One out and a man on second. The number three batter for the Omaha Chiefs, David Riggs, came up to bat. A right-hander, he had decent power, with 4 home runs this year, but he hit mainly line drives for singles and doubles.

Casey assumed her ready position as Roberts prepared to deliver the pitch. It was a fastball over the outside corner. Riggs swung hard at the pitch and connected with a loud crack. The ball took off on a searing line drive directly towards Casey.

It was the hardest catch for an outfielder to make. When a ball is hit high in the air, or to either side of an outfielder, they can get a sense of how high and how hard it is hit, and it's much easier to "judge" where to position themselves in order to make the catch. But when a ball is hit on a line drive directly at them, it's much more difficult to get a perception of how hard and how far the ball has been hit.

The ball that Riggs hit was screaming right at Casey. At first, the ball looked like it was going to fall short of her, and she immediately took a few steps in towards the ball. That's when she realized she had made a big mistake. The ball had actually been hit a lot harder than she initially thought, and it was going to go over her head.

Oh no! she thought to herself, in panic.

She quickly tried to back peddle as fast as she could, in order to compensate, but it was not fast enough. As the ball went speeding over her head, she waved at it feebly with her glove, but missed it by a good three feet. The crowd groaned as Casey turned around and raced after the ball at full speed. The ball rolled all the way to the outfield fence, and by the time she caught up with it, Scooter Jones had already scored and Riggs was rounding second base.

Casey picked up the ball and threw it with all her might to the second baseman, who had come running out into the outfield when he saw that Casey had misplayed the ball. He caught her relay throw, then turned around and threw it into the infield, where the first baseman caught the ball about twenty feet in front of the catcher.

Riggs stopped at third base for a stand-up triple. Top of the first inning, only one out, and already the Power was down by one run. And it was Casey's fault. If she had made the catch, there would have been two outs and a runner on second. A strikeout, a fly ball or a ground out would have gotten them out of the inning.

It was the first error Casey had made all year, and it came on her very first play in front of her new coach and her new team. Every ballplayer feels bad when they make an error, but when that ballplayer is brand new and trying to prove themselves to their teammates and their coach, it's even worse. And when that player is a woman trying to show that she can play with the men, it was downright awful.

Casey knew her teammates were all looking at her, but she didn't dare look at any of them. She had caught a glimpse of Butch Morris shaking his head right after the play was over, and she saw the pitcher, Roberts, glaring at her from the mound. The fans were buzzing all around her, wondering if this was a hint of things to come. Was *this* their new right fielder?

Casey stood there in right field with her hands on her hips, her glove dangling from her right hand. She was shaking her head in disgust as she watched the number four hitter for Omaha step up to the plate.

She heard Pop yell from the dugout, "It's okay, Casey, shake it off now. Let's get the next one."

It didn't help. She wanted to crawl into a hole. Her confidence was shaken, and she was extremely nervous that she might make another mistake. She still felt Turk's glare as he prepared to take his position back on the mound.

Roberts, feeling like he had to make up for something, bore down and struck out the next batter. Two outs and a man on third.

The number five batter was left-handed, and on the second pitch, he hit a high fly ball into right field. Casey could feel her team and the entire home crowd hold their breaths as she positioned herself under the ball. As the ball descended to where she was standing, it looked a little blurry, and although she caught the ball, it bounced around in her glove a little and she had to make a second grab at it to haul it in. She could hear the crowd react with a collective "Oh", as the white of the ball was showing at the top of her glove. She made the catch, but it was shaky.

Three outs, finally, in the longest half inning of Casey's life. She tossed the ball back in to the infield and started to jog back towards her dugout. She was in no particular hurry to get there, and when she did, she wanted to just keep on going into the tunnel and right out the back door of the stadium.

But she was a professional, literally, and professionals act like it. She had to face it.

Pop was waiting at the top of the dugout when she arrived. He took a few steps out towards her and clapped his hands a couple of times in encouragement. He knew she would be feeling low and he tried to cheer her up. "Hey, it's okay," he said as she approached. "It's still early and we've got plenty of time."

Casey shook her head in response. "I can't believe I did that," she said. "I looked like a little leaguer out there."

Pop continued to be positive. "Don't be ridiculous. It happens to everybody, and it's your first game. Just put it behind you and concentrate on the rest of the game. All right?"

He tilted his head slightly, looking for acknowledgement from Casey that she got the message. "Yeah, all right," she said, clenching her lips together, still disgusted at her play.

She went into the dugout and plopped down on the end of the bench, as far away from everyone as she could get. "Sorry, guys," she muttered weakly, to no one in particular. She sat there holding her glove on her lap with her arms wrapped around it, looking down at her feet.

The other players were milling around, storing their gloves beneath their seats on the bench, or for the first few batters due up, grabbing their bats and putting their batting gloves on Usually when one player makes an error, their teammates rally around that player and offer their support. Everybody makes errors at some point, and sometimes it's just your turn. A few of the players around Casey muttered the standard responses, "Hey, don't worry about it", "Shake it off", and "Get 'em next time."

A few of them didn't say anything, and one player in particular, Turk Roberts, who waited to catch her eye, gave her another look of disgust from the other end of the dugout.

The Omaha Chiefs had taken the field and completed their warm-ups. When the umpire yelled "Play Ball," the focus in the

Power dugout changed to the offense. The first and third base coaches ran to take their respective positions, and Butch Morris took his place at the head of the dugout. He was clapping his hands in encouragement and calling to everyone, "Okay, let's get some runs now."

The leadoff hitter stepped into the batter's box, while the number two man made his way to the on-deck circle. Some of the players remained seated on the bench, and some of them stood with their arms hanging over the short fence separating the dugout and the field. Casey remained seated on the bench, still fuming over her bad play.

She watched as the first batter for the Power got on base, but the next three were retired in order. The pitcher for Omaha was a left-hander, and after giving up a leadoff walk, he struck out the next two batters and got the third out on a ground ball to the shortstop. It looked like he had good stuff, throwing a mixture of fastballs, curve balls and sliders.

Their half inning went quickly and, suddenly, it was time for the Power to take the field again. Casey grabbed her glove and jogged out to take her position in right field. She vowed to herself that there would be no mistakes this time, and there weren't. All three batters for Omaha grounded out to the infield, and it was back into the dugout for the Power as they prepared to take their turn at bat in the second inning.

Leading off the second inning was the Power's number five hitter, first baseman Eric "Crush" Davis. On the first pitch, Crush lived up to his name. He launched a high fastball into the gap in left center field for a double. Unfortunately for the Power however, the next three batters couldn't get him in, and he was left stranded at second base. Casey was in the on-deck circle when the Power made their final out of the inning, which meant she would lead off the next inning.

After their defensive half of the inning, Casey jogged back into the dugout and stored her glove. She grabbed her bat and climbed the few steps leading up to the field. As she walked out to the on-deck circle, she could see all the fans watching her. She tried to ignore them and concentrate instead on the pitcher as he took his warm-up tosses. She bent over and picked up the doughnut, put it on her bat and started taking her practice swings. Since the last inning had ended with her in the on-deck circle, she had gotten a chance to get a feel for the pitcher's delivery, and to see some of his pitches up close.

Stan Marx, the play-by-play announcer for the Power, was in the press box behind home plate, and he introduced Casey to the radio audience. Tim "Gunner" Thomas, an ex-pitcher for the Los Angeles Dodgers, was sitting next to him doing the color analysis. Both men traveled everywhere with the team, and were local celebrities around the Portland area.

The PA announcer spoke into the microphone, "The right fielder, number nine, Casey Collins." There was a smattering of applause as Casey stepped into the batter's box, wearing a single batting glove on her right hand, ready for her first at bat with the Portland Power. She clicked her bat against her spikes a couple of times, and took her stance at the plate as the pitcher stood on the mound to receive the signal from the catcher.

The left-handed pitcher went into his windup as Casey stood at the plate with her bat held high behind her head. He delivered a fastball right down the middle of the plate, which Casey watched go by for a called strike one. She glanced over at the radar gun readout on the mini scoreboard over the third base dugout. *93 mph.*

The catcher returned the ball to the pitcher as he shouted encouragement out to the mound. "Attaboy, Tommy. Good start. Keep it coming, babe."

The pitcher caught the ball from the catcher, took his position on the mound, and looked backed in at the catcher for the sign. He wound up and threw the next pitch, letting out a loud grunt as he released the ball. Another fastball, this time on the outside corner. Casey thought it was too far outside, but the umpire didn't. "STRIKE TWO," he called as he held out his right hand, signaling that the pitch was a strike.

Now, it was zero balls and two strikes, or "Oh and Two", as they say, and Casey was behind in the count. The scoreboard had registered 94 mph on the last pitch. She took a step out of the batter's box, and choked up on her bat a little. This pitcher had good speed and she needed the bat to feel a little lighter.

When a pitcher has the pitch count in his favor over the batter, such as when there is one ball and two strikes, or, as in this case, no balls and two strikes, they usually applied one of two strategies.

If they felt like they were really "on" that day, they would go right after the batter, throwing a strike and trying to get them out immediately. Alternatively, since the pitcher was ahead in the count, they might "waste" a pitch or two, throwing a ball that was close to being a strike but was really not in the strike zone, hoping to get the batter to "go fishing" and swing at a bad pitch.

Casey stepped back in to the box, and watched the pitcher closely as he went into his windup. Again, he let out a grunt as the ball came zinging out of his hand, right at Casey's shoulder. She took a step back away from the plate, but at the last minute, the ball curved away from her and went right down the middle of the plate. It was a slider, which was a pitch that was thrown hard and meant to look like a fastball, but it had spin on it so it curved at the last moment. Basically, it was a fast curve ball.

"STEE-RRIKE THREE!" the umpire called. He rose up from his crouch and made an emphatic motion with his hands, essentially letting everyone in the stadium know that the batter had struck out.

Casey felt foolish. She had "bailed out" of the batter's box like a little leaguer who was afraid of the ball. Focusing too much on the speed and the placement of the ball, she had not picked up on the fact that it was spinning horizontally, the signal that it was not a straight fastball.

She turned around and headed back to the dugout, shaking her head in disgust. She heard a man yell from the stands. "It's okay, Casey, get 'em next time." A woman also shouted encouragement. "Yeah, Casey, let's go!"

It was one of the advantages of playing in front of the home crowd. You usually got the benefit of the doubt. Most fans were loyal and wanted to see their home team players do well.

But Casey knew that it didn't take too long before they turned on you. At some point, you have to deliver.

As she passed James Johnson, who had been in the on-deck circle and was now making his way to the plate, all he said was, "Slider, huh?"

"Yeah," she replied. "A good one."

As she got back to the dugout and returned her bat and helmet to the rack, no one said a word to her. She made her way back to the end of the bench and plopped back down, not paying attention to the action on the field.

What a great start, Casey thought to herself in disgust. *I didn't even take the bat off my shoulder. Pathetic.* She sat there brooding by herself, and didn't really notice that the next two teammates had also made outs, and it was time again for the Power to take the field.

When the rest of the players started grabbing their gloves to head out to the field, it snapped her out of her self-reflection, and she grabbed her glove and went back out to her position in right field.

Casey batted three more times that day, also striking out her second time at bat, this time going down swinging. Her third time up, she walked, and was on first base with one out. But on the very next pitch, the batter hit a hard grounder to the shortstop, and he easily turned it into a double play.

She had slid in hard to second base, trying to "break up" the double play by interfering with the shortstop's concentration, but he easily moved out of the way. "Nice try, honey," he said with a smirk, as he turned around and trotted back to his dugout.

On her last at bat, Casey fouled off the first pitch, swinging very late, causing the ball to careen into the opposing players' dugout. There was a player on second base, and a hit would have tied up the game. But she hit a feeble line drive to the third baseman, which he caught easily to end the game. The Power lost one to nothing, and officially, she was 0 for 3 at the plate.

Prior to her last at bat, she overheard Turk Roberts say, "How about a pinch hitter?" He was living up to his nickname of

Turk the Jerk. After the game, he was fuming. Instead of being 4 and 3, he was 3 and 4. It would now take him two wins to get into the plus column.

The northern division leader, Calgary, had won, so the Power slipped another full game in the standings. After the game, Casey didn't say a word to the other players, and no one said much to her either. She purposely walked slowly back to the dugout, and milled around long after the game so that she didn't have to walk back through the tunnel with the rest of the team.

She did run across Butch Morris, and she felt like he was her father and she had spilled ice cream on his favorite shirt. "Sorry, Skip," she said in apology.

He grunted, "Don't worry about it. Get 'em next time."

Of course she had had bad games before, but it was usually more a matter of poor performance at the plate. Even the best hitters fail two-thirds of the time, and she was no different. But this was more. She had looked and felt like a little leaguer in the field, and she was embarrassed by it. She *was* better than that, although no one in attendance at tonight's game saw any evidence of it.

This was one time when she was thankful that she had her own room in which to change, even if it was just a converted old office. She slumped down on the bench and looked over at the wooden framed mirror on top of the desk.

What a sight, she thought, as she saw the image of herself sitting there on the bench in her dumpy little office, in a uniform that was a little too big, with her shoulders hunched over. She reflected on her performance in her first game with the Power.

She hadn't contributed. In fact, she had detracted from the team's effort. The loss was mostly her fault. Not only the error, but the chance to tie the game up at the end, and she had choked. She felt the self-doubts starting to surface—for the first time in her career.

Professional baseball players, like professional athletes in general, have a great deal of pride. They wouldn't have gotten to this level if they hadn't experienced a lot of success in their careers. So, when they played poorly, they sometimes got down on themselves. Casey was no different. She really hadn't experienced a lot of failure in her career. She, like every other player, had occasionally gone into slumps before, and had always pulled out of them. But she had really wanted to prove herself in her first game, and instead she had done just the opposite.

She had been sitting there brooding for about twenty minutes when there was a knock on the door. "Come in," she said.

The door swung open and Pop walked in. "How are you doing, kid?" he asked with a sympathetic smile.

"Not all that great," Casey replied with a shrug. She was sitting on the bench with her legs on the floor and each hand on either side of her, grabbing the front of the bench. "I stunk tonight."

Pop closed the door behind him, walked over to the desk opposite the bench and leaned up against it with his rear end, half sitting but with his feet on the floor. He crossed his arms. "Hey, it wasn't that bad," he said, trying to cheer her up. "It was your first game with a new team in a new stadium. You were a little nervous, that's all. It's to be expected."

Casey looked up at him from the bench. She raised her eyes. "I cost us the game, and I struck out twice. I haven't done that all year. You know, I'm better than that. I really am."

"I know you are," he said.

"Skip probably hates me," she continued chastising herself.

The wrinkles around Pop's eyes showed again as he smiled. "Nonsense. Skip's been around for a long time, and I've worked with him for a while. He understands what's going on. All you need to do for him is to go out and do your best tomorrow."

"Yeah, I guess," Casey said, as she shifted a little on the bench.

Pop stood upright and starting walking towards the door. "Well, why don't you get your stuff and go grab a shower? Skip's already showered, and I'll be here late. Come on, I'll show you where it is."

Casey grabbed her bag and followed Pop down the hall to where his and Skip's offices were adjoined. He walked to a door near the back of the room and opened it up. "The shower's in there," he said. "There are some towels in the cabinet, and soap and shampoo and stuff are in there. The doors both lock, so take your time. Okay?"

"Okay. Thanks, Pop."

After showering, Casey went back to her office, tidied up a little bit, and left, locking the door behind her. By the time she had finished, the other players had all gone home, a fact for which she was very thankful.

When Casey got back to the hotel room, it was almost midnight. She immediately got changed into her oversized Cincinnati Reds T-shirt and got into bed. She curled up in a fetal position and pulled the covers up to her neck, trying not to think about the night's game. Feeling very tired, she fell asleep in a few minutes.

Sixteen

The next morning, Casey woke up around 9:00, and ordered room service—some scrambled eggs, toast and coffee. She put on some sweats and flipped on ASN and was watching the highlights from last night's major league games, when the room service waiter came to the door.

He brought the tray in as Casey instructed, and set it on a small table in front of a chair by the window. He poured her a cup of coffee out of the small pot, and started to walk out the door. Casey tipped him a couple of dollars, said thanks, and escorted him to the door. As he stepped through the door, he bent over and picked up a newspaper that was sitting on the floor right outside the doorway.

"Oh, Miss Collins, here's your newspaper," he said as he handed her the paper.

"Thanks," Casey said, taking the paper from him and skimming the front page as she made her way over to the easy chair by the window. She plopped back into the chair and crossed one leg over the other, spreading the paper out on her lap.

She opened the paper to the sports section and looked at the scores for, first, the American league on the left page, and then the National League on the right. She read the headlines and a few details on some of the games, while pausing now and then to eat her eggs and munch on some toast. She had just finished taking a sip of coffee when she turned to the next page, which was titled "Local Sports Scene". That was when she saw the headline.

CASEY'S DEBUT NOT SO MIGHTY

She sat forward in the chair and put both legs on the floor, holding the paper a little closer as she read the body of the article:

Much has been made the last couple of days over Casey Collins, the young woman baseball player from Richmond, Washington, who joined the Portland Power on Thursday. Ever since the special press conference on Thursday afternoon, the city has been buzzing over the arrival of Miss Collins in our fair city.

Last night, she suited up for the Power for the first time. Seventeen thousand eight hundred sixty-three fans, the most so far this year, showed up at Portland Stadium to see her debut. Unfortunately for Collins, and for the Power, her first game was anything but stalwart. In the first inning, she committed an error that lead to visiting Omaha's first and only run, which turned out to be the game winner.

Her performance at the plate wasn't much better, as she went 0 for 3 with two strikeouts. Collins had an opportunity at her last bat in the ninth inning to tie the game with a base hit, but instead, ended the game with a fly out to the third baseman.

When asked about Collin's performance after the game, Portland manager Butch Morris commented. "Yeah, she had a rough outing, but it was her first game, in a new stadium, facing some great pitching. I'm more concerned about the fact that the rest of the team didn't hit last night either. You can't win if you can't score."

Fans interested in seeing Collins play will have another chance tonight, as the Power take on the Omaha Chiefs in the second game of a three-game series, at 7:05. For tickets. Call 1-800-GO-POWER.

Casey slumped back in her chair. *Great,* she thought to herself. *One game—one bad game—and they make it the headline.*

She had read her name in the paper before, of course, many times. Even when she had bad games, which admittedly wasn't that often, she had gotten used to it, or thought she had.

But this one hit hard. Making the headline in a city of 100,000 was one thing, but making it in a city of a couple of million was another. Especially when she made the headline for costing her team the game.

Shake it off, she told herself. *It comes with the territory. If I want to play at this level, then I have to PLAY at this level.* She gave herself some new resolve, and decided right then that she would get to the ballpark early that night so she could take some extra batting practice. *It was*, she decided, *time to step it up.*

Casey did arrive early, and took about 20 extra swings at batting practice. Unfortunately, it didn't help much. She went 0 for 3 again, with one strikeout and two ground outs to the third baseman. She did execute a perfect sacrifice bunt in the fifth inning, but on the very next play, the runner was thrown out trying to steal third, and the impact turned out to be minimal.

She made a few routine plays in the outfield, and did not commit any errors. But the *Power* lost 3 to 1. Fortunately for them, the Calgary Cowboys also lost, so they didn't lose any ground in the standings, but they were still seven games out of first place.

The third game, on Sunday afternoon, went pretty much the same, with the Power losing again. This time, she had three official at bats, getting walked once, but again went 0 for 3, with a strikeout, a groundout and a fielder's choice. The *Power* now was 0 and 3 with Casey Collins in right field, and she was 0 for 9 at the plate.

She waited until the other players had returned to the locker room, before slowly making her way to hers. She had heard some of the players talking about going out for a beer after the game, but no one invited her. Not that she would have gone anyway, feeling the way she did. Still, it would have been nice to have been asked.

By the time Casey got changed and made it back to her hotel room, it was early Sunday evening. She walked in the room, threw her keys on the bed, and looked in the mirror. *I look like crap*, she thought to herself as she sat on the edge of the bed. Her shoulders were sunken and she had a desolate look on her face. *What am I doing here*? She asked herself.

She stared at the phone for a long moment, then picked up the receiver and slowly dialed her home number. Her mom answered on the second ring. "Hello?"

"Hi, Mom, it's me," Casey said with a sigh.

"Hi, sweetheart," Sue answered, excited to hear from her daughter. "How are you?" she asked cheerfully, although her mother's sense told her that something was wrong.

"Oh, not so good, Mom," Casey said dejectedly. "I really stunk it up bad. My big debut and I totally choked. Zero for nine in three games, with an error. The fans were taunting me the whole time and I'm sure some of the players hate me already."

"Oh, I'm sure you're exaggerating, Casey, but what did you expect?" Sue asked. "You jumped up two levels to a whole new league and you're playing with a completely different team. Did you expect to walk in and hit three hundred right away?"

"No, I guess not," Casey replied. "It's just hard. These guys are really good. They're big and they're strong and they're fast. It's amazing. The pitchers are throwing four or five miles an hour faster, and they're control is so much better."

Sue continued the motherly support. "Well, those players were all where you were a few years ago, right? If they were that much better, then they would be in the majors by now, wouldn't they?"

"Well, yeah, I guess, but..."

"And what would your father tell you – choke up on the bat, or start your swing earlier, or...well, you know. He would tell you to find an angle, wouldn't he? And you've always been able to do that, haven't you? You know you have the talent. I think you just need some time to figure it out, that's all. And your father would be so proud of you. Just like I am. We're all so proud of you here, sweetheart. The whole town is talking about you."

Then, trying to change the subject, Sue continued, "So, how is Portland?"

Casey knew what her mother was doing, and she appreciated it. "Oh, I barely even know," she replied. "It looks like a great city, but I've been so busy ever since I got here I haven't really seen too much of it. Everyone else seems to love it here."

"Well, you take care of yourself, sweetheart, and don't worry about things so much. Just be yourself and everything will work out for the best. I have faith in you."

"Thanks, Mom," Casey said. "I guess I should go now. Say hi to everybody at the restaurant for me, will you?"

"I sure will, sweetheart. Take care. I love you."

"Bye, Mom, I love you, too."

Casey felt a little better after she hung up the phone. Sometimes, you just need to talk to your mother. She got changed into her oversized Reds jersey and got in bed, curling up into a ball and pulling the covers up to her neck. As she started to nod off to sleep, she wondered to herself, *Can I really do this?*

Seventeen

The following morning, it was time for Casey's first road trip with the Power.   They had a three-game series against Vancouver, which was a six-hour bus ride from Portland.

The players all met at the Power Stadium parking lot at 9:00 Monday morning.   Although Casey had taken a lot of bus trips with the Richmond Tigers, she was feeling a little apprehensive about her first trip with the Power.   Her poor performance in her first three games over the weekend had left her feeling defensive. She was not looking forward to spending so much time in an enclosed environment with a bunch of players whom she was sure felt the same way as she did—that she had let them down.

When she arrived at the player's lot, the Greyhound bus was already there, and there were several players milling around outside.   No one was in any particular hurry to get seated when they knew they would be that way for the next several hours.   The team managers were standing a few feet away in their own little group, with Pop holding a clipboard and Butch Morris drinking coffee out of a Styrofoam cup.

After parking her car, Casey sauntered uneasily over to the group of players.   A few of them nodded; a few ignored her and continued their conversations.   Not feeling comfortable just going up and starting a conversation with them, and not knowing what else to do, she just continued over to the front of the bus and went inside.

The bus driver nodded as she came up the few stairs, and then gave a second look as he noticed it was a woman entering the men's team bus.   *He probably thinks I'm the equipment manager*, she thought to herself, as she turned and continued down the rows of seats.   She went about a third of the way down the aisle, threw her bag in the overhead bin and plopped into a seat next to the window.   She gave a brief glance out the side of her eye to the group of players still standing around, and wondered if they were talking about her.

More players had arrived, and after a few minutes Pop spoke up. "All right, guys, time to hit the road." He positioned himself outside the front door of the bus, checking off the names of the players on his clipboard as they broke from their groups and filed on to the bus.

One by one the players found a seat, some doubling up and some sitting alone. The coaches and the trainer sat up front in the first couple of rows, leaving a seat for Pop next to Butch Morris.

When it looked like the bus was almost full, Pop walked up the stairs with his clipboard and looked down the rows of seats. He had a frown on his face. "Has anyone seen Moran?" he asked loudly.

This immediately caused a smattering of chuckles and comments from the other players. "He's probably still asleep," someone called from the back of the bus.

Just then, a red 1975 Corvette came speeding into the parking lot, causing everyone's head to turn. The car spun around, with its brakes squealing as the driver raced towards an empty spot, pulling the car into the space and screeching to a stop.

The door flew open as Mooch Moran jumped out of the car, dragging his athletic bag behind him. The players all stood up to look out the window at the humorous scene taking place in the parking lot, and broke into laughter as Mooch tried to slam his car door shut while he started running. But his bag got caught in the door, yanking him backwards and causing the door to bounce back open, hitting him in the knee.

The players howled as Mooch threw his bag over his shoulder, closed the car door again, and sprinted around the back of his car towards the bus. The bus driver had already closed the doors and had to reopen them for Mooch. The *whooshing* sound made by the reopening of the rubber seal on the doors added a comical punctuation mark to the whole scene.

The players had all retaken their seats, and were facing the front of the bus as Mooch came up the stairs. He turned sideways and tried to slide by Pop, offering a weak, "Sorry."

"Moooch," several players chided in a low voice, as he made his way down the aisle.

Pop turned around and called after him. "Moran, that's a hundred bucks for being late. You know the rules."

"C'mon Pop, I'm not late," Mooch said, looking at his wrist, which did not contain a watch. "It's only nine fourteen and a half. I've got thirty seconds yet." This, again, caused everyone to laugh.

"Thirty seconds, my ass," Pop retorted, only half angrily. "Just sit yourself down so we can get moving." Then, taking a seat next to Morris, he muttered, "That boy's going be the death of me yet."

Morris grunted in acknowledgement, as Mooch fumbled around with the overhead bin for a few seconds. He slammed it shut and plopped down in the seat across the aisle from Casey, giving a nod in her direction. "Hey," he said.

"Hey," she responded, shaking her head and still chuckling at his recent antics.

The bus driver had closed the doors again and the bus started to pull out of the parking lot. After a few minutes, they were leaving Portland and heading onto I-5 on their journey north to Vancouver.

A few hours later, some of the players were listening to music on their Walkmans, some were talking and a few were sleeping. Casey hadn't thought to bring anything to read or to listen to, and so she just sat there staring out at the scenery going by.

She had been sitting there looking out the window for a couple of hours, when a voice from the aisle got her attention. It was Mooch. "Care for a chew?" he asked as he held out a pouch to her.

Starting to get upset, she spun around to look at him, and noticed that he was grinning. She followed his look down the length of his arm, and saw that what he was offering her was a pink pouch full of shredded bubble gum. Her initial look of hostility subsided, and all she could do was laugh.

"Mind if I sit down?" Mooch asked.

"No, go ahead," Casey answered with a wave of her hand.

Mooch plunked down next to Casey, his long legs reaching under the seat in front of him. Still holding the pouch of "chew" open, he held it out to her. "So, you want some?"

"No, thanks," she said. "I'm good."

Mooch closed the pouch and stuffed it into his back pocket. Then he got a serious look on his face as he turned to face Casey. "Hey, look," he said. "I want to apologize for the other day. I didn't know about your father."

Casey waved her hand in dismissal. "No, it's okay," she said. "I'm the one who should apologize. I overreacted a little." She paused, then asked, "So how do you know about my father?"

"Pop told me. He overheard our little exchange."

"Oh, good old Pop. Boy, he doesn't miss a thing, does he?"

"No, he really doesn't. He's great. He knows everything about baseball. But that's because he's like a hundred and thirty-seven years old and he's been around forever. He's been a real mentor to me, and he's helped me a lot with my pitching. Not that it shows."

Casey laughed, as Mooch changed the subject. "So, rough series over the weekend, huh?" he said, looking at her out of the side of his eye.

She crossed her arms, looked down at the floor, and snorted, "Yeah, thanks for noticing."

He turned a little to face her more squarely. "No, that's not what I meant. I was talking about the team dropping three to Omaha."

"Oh, sorry," she apologized. "I'm feeling a little defensive at the moment. I mean, most of it was my fault. I really stunk."

Mooch tossed his head back as he laughed. "Don't be ridiculous. I wouldn't call the team batting .190 for the series your fault. Besides, I stunk a lot worse when I first came up. I couldn't even find the strike zone. Still can't, sometimes."

Casey laughed lightly. That made her feel a little better, and she was happy to have someone to talk to, but wanting to get off the subject of her performance, she changed the subject again. "So, how long have you been in the minors?"

"Four years," he answered. "I started in Tempe. Played there for a year and a half and I've been here for about two and a half."

"Are you from Tempe?"

"No, Oklahoma actually—a small town called Rangeville. How about you, you're actually from Richmond, right? I remember reading about you when you signed your contract with the Tigers."

Casey chuckled. "Yeah, I was a blurb in the newspapers. My fifteen minutes of fame."

"Hey, it's more than I ever got," Mooch said with a grin.

Casey snorted. "Yeah, well, I've gotten a lot more than that since I arrived in Portland, and it hasn't been all that great. Of course, it's my own fault; I should have played better." She paused, then asked, "So how come you haven't been called up yet? I saw you clocked at 96 miles per hour last Saturday."

"Did you also notice that I walked two guys?"

"Oh, control problems, eh?"

"That's an understatement," Mooch replied with a frown. "I've been all over the place all year. When I'm on, I'm on, but when I'm off, I'm way off."

"What do you think you're problem is?

"Well, Manny says it's my follow-through, but Pop tells me it's just my concentration. Probably a little of both."

Casey felt exhilarated to be talking to someone who *really was* one step away from the majors, probably with the expectation that he would actually get there. "But you're expecting to make it to the majors, right?"

Mooch nodded. "Yeah, I think so. I mean, I have the arm; I just need to get my mechanics worked out and get a little more under control. How about you, you think about it?"

Casey snorted. "Making the majors? Of course, I think about it. More like fantasize about it. But for me, I just came from Single A, and an independent team at that. I'm not even sure I can make it here yet. I'm more concerned about that than anything else right now."

"Well, don't worry about it. I'm sure you'll do fine. But hey, can I ask you a question?" Mooch asked tentatively.

138

"Sure," Casey answered with a shrug. She prepared for the question she was sure was coming – *Are you seeing anyone?* – and was ready to respond that she was. But that wasn't the question that came.

"Well, how do you do it? How can you play with guys at this level? I mean, not to sound sexist or anything, but there are thousands of male baseball players that can't even make it to this level, but here you are. It seems kind of amazing to me."

Mooch turned slightly in his seat, staring intently at her, and Casey could see that he genuinely wanted to know how she did it. She looked at him. He wasn't a great-looking guy. Not ugly or anything; he just didn't look like the kind of guy who was a professional athlete, someone who could throw a baseball 96 miles an hour. But he seemed honest, and she felt very at ease talking with him.

"Well, I think it started with my parents. My dad was a great baseball player who only made it to the majors briefly, but even to make it to that level at all, you have to be great, right? And my mother was a track star in high school, so I got a lot of speed from her."

She continued, with Mooch's full attention, "So, part of it is good genes. Then, my dad, who, I'm sure, really wanted a boy, pushed me since I was a kid to be a baseball player. It seems like that's all we did when I was younger, every weekend when he was in town, out in the backyard playing baseball. So I got my mechanics and my knowledge of baseball down early. Plus, my dad was always showing me how to find some kind of angle. Trying to figure what the pitcher was going to throw next, going to the opposite field, things to key off of when stealing bases, etc.

"Once I started having success early, it just seemed to build on itself, but I really thought I had gone as far as I was going to go in Richmond, until Mr. Harley gave me this shot."

Outside, the Washington scenery was flying by, as they passed through Seattle on their way north to Vancouver. Casey glanced at her watch and yawned, trying to cover it by putting a hand over her mouth. "Sorry," she apologized.

Mooch didn't know whether to take this as a sign of boredom with the conversation, or if Casey was just tired. He decided to play it safe. "Well, I wish you the best of luck." Then he placed a hand on the seat in front of him as he stood, and said, "Hey, I've got to hit the head...I mean, go to the bathroom. Uh, anyway, it was good talking to you."

Casey smiled. Men were always a little uncomfortable around her at first, and it took time for them to treat her as one of the guys. "Yeah, it was good talking to you, too. I'll see you later."

Mooch walked to the bathroom, and on the way, paused to chat with a couple of players who were talking near the back of the bus. After a few minutes, he returned to his seat, put it in recline mode, and made himself comfortable. He glanced across the aisle to look at Casey, who was sound asleep with her head resting on a pillow propped against the window. Mooch closed his eyes, and also fell asleep in a few minutes.

The first two nights in Vancouver went well for the Power as they won both games, but not so well for Casey. In the first game, on Monday night, she had gone 0 for 2, reaching base on a throwing error by the pitcher. On the very next pitch, the batter hit her into a double play, so she didn't even get a chance to run the bases. On her last time up, she did execute a perfect sacrifice bunt, and this time the runner went on to score, but it was a very minor victory for Casey.

Earlier in the game, after Casey had struck out at the plate, Pop noticed that she was heckled by a fan, who called her a derogatory name. She seemed to be a little shaken as she got to the top of the dugout on her way out to the field, and Pop met her there. He had a concerned look on his face as he put his hand on her arm.

"What's the matter, Casey, did something happen back there?" he asked.

Casey looked disgusted. "Oh, some guy just called me a filthy name. It was disgusting, really. But no big deal; I've heard most of it before."

Pop grunted knowingly. "Honey, I know the feeling. I used to get called some pretty nasty names back when I played. Mostly racist stuff. But you can't let it bother you. It all comes from ignorant people who don't even deserve the energy it takes to show your indignation. You know what I did when people called me a name like that?"

Casey had her arms crossed and was listening intently. When Pop used the term "honey" or "sweetheart" with Casey, she knew it was from genuine affection and not meant to be derogatory. She leaned into him a little, and for the first time, noticed that his eyebrows also had a little tint of white around the edges. "What?" she asked anxiously.

"I used to smile at them and say, thank you very much," he said with a smug look, the wrinkles around his eyes contracting as he smiled.

"You said thank you?" she said, raising her eyebrows in astonishment.

"Oh, yeah," Pop said with a laugh and a wave of his hand. "It's great. They don't know how to handle it. They're expecting you to be all upset and everything, and when you just turn around and give them this big warm smile, it really throws them off. You should try it sometime."

Casey laughed. "I just might do that," she said, as she grabbed her glove and jogged out into the field.

Tuesday night did not go much better for Casey. After fouling out to the catcher in the third inning, in the fifth, she hit into what should have been a double play. Her speed in getting down to first base kept the Power out of the double play, but again it was a very small positive, as the next batter lined out on the first pitch to end the inning.

In the eighth inning, with Vancouver leading by a score of 3 to 1, they brought in a left-handed relief pitcher. Casey, who had been standing in the on-deck circle getting ready to bat, was called back to the dugout by Coach Morris.

"We're going to go with a right-handed bat," he explained gruffly to Casey as she walked back to the dugout. He was indicating that he wanted a right-handed batter to face the left-handed pitcher, as that typically gave the batter an advantage.

"Sure, no problem," Casey answered dejectedly, wondering if that was really the reason. She walked past everyone in the dugout to the far end of the bench, and plopped down in disgust. She did not say a word to anyone; nor did anyone say anything to her. Things were not getting any better; in fact, they were getting worse.

It added to her feeling of isolation. Earlier, before the game, since the Vancouver stadium only had one visiting locker room, she had to change in a women's rest room stall, suffering the stares of the other women as she walked out in her uniform.

After the game, she had to wait until all the players had taken their showers and vacated the facilities before she could shower. By the time she was finished, all the other players were waiting in the bus, and she had to enter last, knowing they were holding the bus for her. It was a miserable feeling, made even worse when she overheard Turk say, "Why don't we just get her her own limo?"

But the comment from Turk was just a small example of her negative interactions with him, and the next night was to bring an even bigger one. As she was heading through the tunnel towards the dugout, she came upon Turk talking with two of the backup players, one an outfielder who was called up from Double A Salem, and felt like he should be playing instead of Casey, and the other, a backup infielder playing behind Bobby Turner at second base.

As Casey walked by the group, she heard Turk say, loud enough for her to hear, "Why does she need her own locker room? She probably pees standing up, anyway." This was followed by chuckles from the other two players.

Casey heard it loud and clear, and she had had enough of Turk's antics. She wheeled around to face him, spread out her arms and said, "Hey, pal, what the hell is your problem, anyway? What did I ever do to you?"

This only incensed Turk, who pointed a finger at her, as his already sour face twisted in anger, his lip curling up at one end. "You're my problem, bitch, walking around here like a queen bee, thinking you're something special. Why don't you just go back to Single A where you belong?"

Casey was now face to face with Turk, as she lashed back at him, "Yeah, well, why don't you go back to your cave where you belong?"

This caused the other two players to laugh, and the reserve outfielder made a sound like "ooohhh," egging Turk on, though he really didn't need it.

He suddenly grabbed Casey by the collar with both hands, spinning her around and slamming her hard against the wall, his speed and strength surprising her. He held her against the wall by her collar with one hand, while he raised his other hand in a clenched fist in front of her face. "You think I won't hit you, bitch? You women want to be considered equal, how about I smash my fist into your face?"

Casey tried to push back, but Turk's weight was too superior, and he kept her pinned against the wall. She sputtered, "Go ahead, if that'll make you feel like a man."

Casey could see Turk considering the ramifications if he actually did hit her, when the backup infielder put his hand on Turk's arm and said, "Hey, come on man, it's not worth it. Let her go."

Just then, Pop came around the corner, carrying a clipboard, and saw the commotion. "Roberts! What the hell are you doing?" he shouted as he rushed over to where they were standing. Turk released Casey and took a step back, as she smoothed out her uniform, trying to gain her composure while still glaring at Turk.

"Casey," Pop said as he looked alternately at the two of them. "What's going on here?"

"Nothing, Pop, we're okay."

"Nothing! It sure as hell doesn't look like nothing to me!"

"Honest, Pop," Casey insisted, "We were just having a discussion, that's all."

Pop knew better, but he also knew the code as well as Casey did. You don't rat on your teammates, regardless of what you think of them. You dealt with them on your own. Although he respected Casey for it, he was not going to let anything interfere with the dynamics of his team. "Well, I don't want to see any more of this *discussing*," he said, looking at the two of them. "Am I clear?"

"Yes, sir," Casey replied.

"Yeah, sure," Turk said, still glaring at Casey.

"Now, get out on the field, we've got a game to play," Pop said as he shook his head in disgust and headed out towards the dugout.

The two reserve players left immediately, while Turk turned and sauntered along behind them, a smirk still on his face. Casey waited a few seconds, and then followed them out to the field. She was shaken, but vowed not to let it show.

That same night, after the game, Pop made all the players wait outside the locker room until Casey took her shower first. Pop's heart was in the right place, but the timing could have been better. She heard some of the players grumbling about it, and later she respectfully asked Pop not to show her that kind of special treatment again.

Now it was the last game of the series. Casey was now 0 for 15 since she had joined the Power, and she was desperate to do something positive. Batting ninth, she came up to bat in the fifth inning.

On the mound for Vancouver was Jules Dawson, the number three pitcher in their rotation. Dawson was a right-hander, 6' 1" and 190 pounds, with a medium-speed fastball, but a good curve and a great change-up. The Power only had two hits against him in the game by the time Casey came to the plate. She had grounded out to the shortstop her first time up, and this time, she noticed the first baseman playing at his normal depth, about two feet behind first base.

She was up in the count at one ball and no strikes, when the pitcher threw an off-speed pitch that curved down the middle of the plate. As the ball approached the plate, Casey first squared around in the normal bunting position, then continued pivoting her body towards first base as she slid her left hand up the bat a few inches.

As the ball reached the plate, Casey gently "dragged" the ball down the first base line as she took off running with her head down and her arms and legs pumping hard.

By the time the first baseman realized it was a bunt and ran in to pick up the ball, it was too late. Casey had already reached base with her very first hit for the Portland Power.

Casey had run full speed down to first and had gone about fifteen feet past the bag. As she was returning to take her position on the bag, Pop, who was coaching first base, gave Casey a high five. "Great bunt," he congratulated her. "Feels good to get that first one, huh?"

"Thanks. It sure does," Casey replied with a grin.

Up in the press box, Stan "The Man" Marx was calling the play-by-play. "And there it is, folks. Casey Collins gets her first hit for the Power on a perfectly executed drag bunt down the first base line. How about that, Gunner?"

Gunner Thomas, the color announcer, replied, "I'll tell you, Stan, that was a textbook drag bunt. She did everything right on that play. And I'm amazed at how fast she got down the first base line. She has definitely got some speed. Now, let's see what she does on the base paths."

Back on the field, Casey had taken her position on the bag at first base, while the leadoff batter for the Power, James Johnson, stepped to the plate. The ball had been returned to the pitcher, and he looked in to the catcher to get the signal for the next pitch. Casey took a few steps off of first base as the pitcher went into his stretch.

The stretch was a means for a pitcher to hold a base runner close to the base in order to prevent them from stealing. If a pitcher went into a full windup, the base runner was able to take off towards the next base anytime they wanted, and the pitcher was prohibited from interrupting his windup to try to throw them out.

However, if a pitcher went into a stretch, which was a sideways stance on the mound, with sort of a half windup motion that brought his legs together in front of the pitching rubber, he could throw over to the base at anytime, as long as he did not turn towards home plate and start to pitch to the batter.

Casey watched the pitcher closely as he went into his stretch. She took a few more steps towards second, and hunched over facing the pitcher, dangling both hands in front of her. The pitcher completed his stretch, looked over at Casey, "checking the runner", and threw a slider over the plate for a called strike one.

Casey walked back to the bag and tagged it with her foot as the catcher returned the ball back to the pitcher. She again took her lead as the pitcher went into his stretch. In the ready position again, Casey watched closely for any sign that the pitcher was going to throw home, instead of throwing over to first base to try and pick her off.

As the pitcher stood sideways on the mound, looking over his shoulder at her, Casey saw the sign she was looking for. Once the pitcher committed to throw towards home plate, he could not throw anywhere else. The moment Casey saw this, she broke towards second base, first pivoting on her right ankle, then crossing over with her left leg and digging hard into the dirt. She pumped her arms hard and ran several steps towards second base.

She looked in at the plate and saw that the batter had swung at the pitch and missed. The catcher had caught the ball and was in the process of standing and throwing the ball when Casey glanced in at him. She was now at full speed as she turned her head back toward second base, and saw the shortstop coming over to cover the bag. About five feet from the bag, Casey threw her feet out in front of her, hooking one leg under the other. She went straight into the bag, and as soon as she made contact with the bag, she popped straight up onto her feet.

The ball was late in arriving and the umpire had spread his hands out wide with his palms flat down, the signal that the runner was safe at second. Less than five minutes after Casey got her first hit in Triple A ball, she also had her first stolen base.

"And Collins slides safely into second with her first stolen base," Stan Marx called to the radio audience. He looked over at Gunner. "Wow, she really got a great jump on that one."

"She sure did, Stan," answered Gunner. "She stole that one on the pitcher. The catcher didn't have a chance."

Stan continued, "She has really got some speed, hasn't she?"

"I'll say," replied Gunner Thomas. "I'd love to put a stop watch on her. But her mother was a high school track star, so I guess we shouldn't be too surprised."

Casey couldn't hear their comments, of course, but was feeling pretty good about herself as she stood on second base. Her first hit and her first stolen base. Maybe this would turn it around for her.

She was now on second base with two outs, and a base hit would allow her to score. "C'mon, James," she called in to the center fielder, who had a two-and-two count on him at the plate.

She looked back in to the pitcher, who again glared at her as he went into his stretch, while she took her lead off of second. He delivered a nasty curve ball which Johnson swung at and missed. Strike three and the end of the inning. Casey was stranded at second base.

It was too bad for the team, and she really wanted to score, but Casey did feel a little better as she jogged in towards the dugout. *At least I finally did something positive*, she was thinking to herself. But her good mood was shattered when she reached the dugout.

Butch Morris was standing at the top of the dugout. Casey had a grin on her face and she was expecting to be congratulated. But it was anything but congratulations.

As she approached the dugout, Morris took a step toward her and spread his arms open wide. He had a look of consternation on his face, which confused Casey. "Collins, what the hell was that?" he said, loud enough for everyone within twenty feet to hear.

Upon hearing the tone in Skip's voice, the grin immediately disappeared from Casey's face. "What do you mean?" she asked, a look of bewilderment on her face.

"Did I tell you to steal?" he asked in an interrogating manner, about three inches from her face. "I don't remember telling you to steal.   Did I give the steal sign?" He was relentless.   "Did you see a steal sign from somebody? Because I sure as hell didn't give one."

Casey's eyes were wide open, and every player on the bench was watching the scene taking place at the top of the dugout.

"I'm sorry, Skip," Casey said meekly. "In Richmond, I always had the green light. I saw an opening and I took the base."

Morris had both hands on his hips. He took one hand off to point at Casey with one finger.   "Well, this isn't Richmond, missy," he said. "And you better realize that pretty damn quick. You do *what* I tell you, *when* I tell you. Is that clear?" he asked, glaring at her.

"Yes, sir," she replied sheepishly as she looked down at the ground.

"Good!" Morris exclaimed as he wheeled around and headed back to the dugout, leaving Casey standing there feeling like she had just been yelled at by the teacher in front of the entire class. Stunned, she turned and walked with her head down to the far end of the dugout, where she retrieved her glove and prepared to take the field.

She was crushed.   Her brief feeling of euphoria had evaporated into a cloud of bewilderment. She had never felt so down in her life. Never before had she been yelled at like that. Not by her father, not by a teacher, and not by any of the nine different coaches she had had in her career. Never.

Bobby Turner was sitting nearby, and he turned to her. "Hey, shake it off, Casey," he said in encouragement. "It happens to all of us."

"Shake it off? I was safe!" she said in objection.

"That's not the point," Turner said. "Skip's in charge and he wants to make sure that everybody knows that."

"Well, I guess I get it now," she said with a shrug.

"Don't let it bother you," he said as he slapped her on the knee, "we all get yelled at, at some point or another. It don't mean nothing." He smiled as he started to get up off the bench and headed out towards the field.

"Thanks, Bobby," Casey said as she followed him up the dugout steps.

"Don't mention it," he called back over his shoulder as he took his position at second base.

Up in the press box, Stan Marx and Gunner Thomas caught the whole scene. Stan started off the commentary. "Well, there seems to be some commotion over in front of the Power dugout. Coach Morris seems to be reading the riot act to Casey Collins, who strangely enough, just got her first base hit and her first stolen base. I wonder what that's all about."

"Well, I don't know for sure," Gunner responded. "She may have missed a sign or something, and we know that Morris doesn't go in for that sort of thing. He likes to keep a tight reign on his players. Other than that, I can't think of anything. It seems like she did everything else right in that inning."

"Well, whatever it was, I'm glad I wasn't on the receiving end of that exchange," Stan commented.

"Yeah, me, either."

Casey barely managed to find her way back into right field. She was totally demoralized, and thoughts of quitting went through her mind. She told herself that she had to snap out of it and concentrate on the game, and the umpire's call of "Play Ball" helped refocus her attention back towards the infield.

She watched as the first batter of the inning for Vancouver popped out to the left fielder, Darnell Jenkins. One out and nobody on. Casey was in the ready position as the next batter came up and smacked one into the gap between her and the center fielder. Casey, with her speed, was the first to reach the ball. She fielded it backhanded with her glove, planted her feet, and transferred the ball to her bare hand, preparing to throw.

The second baseman, Bobby Turner, had come out into right center field to take the relay throw. As Casey wound up to make the throw, the frustration of last inning's scene with Morris combined with the futility she felt over the last several days. She threw the ball as hard as she could and it sailed a good three feet over Turner's head, and went bouncing towards the shortstop, who was covering second base.

A good relay throw would have held the base runner at second base, but when he saw that Casey had overthrown the relay man, he kept going on to third base. Now, there was a runner at third base with only one out, and a sacrifice fly would allow him to score. It was another mistake—another error—by Casey, and again it put her team at a disadvantage.

Every now and then, when there's a crowd of people and a lot of background noise, a situation occurs where everyone seems to suddenly stop talking at once, and it gets unnaturally quiet. This is the time that one voice comes over loud and clear. In this case, a particular fan yelled "Hey, Collins, have you ever heard of a relay man?"

Another voice chimed in. "Yeah, that's the guy that ran all the way into the outfield to catch your throw." It was followed by a round of laughter from the other people sitting in the section.

Casey heard the words loud and clear, along with the laughter, and they stung. It did not help matters any that the very next batter for Vancouver did hit a sacrifice fly to center field, and the runner on third scored, putting them ahead, 3 to 2.

When Crush Davis ended the game with a fly out to center field in the top of the ninth, Casey stood in the dugout staring out at the centerfield scoreboard. Vancouver 3, Portland 2.

The neon scoreboard blazed into her brain. The Power had lost four games since she joined, and she was directly responsible for two of the losses. She couldn't have done worse if she tried.

Again, Casey waited until every other player had left the dugout. She was standing there with her arms hanging over the chain-link fence, when the bat boy came up to her and uttered the words that no baseball player ever wants to hear. "Coach wants to see you in his office."

The words hit her like a ton of bricks. This could not be good. She was sure that Morris was not calling her in to congratulate her on her wonderful performance. A hundred thoughts were racing through her mind, and none of them were good.

Was he going to send her back down to Single A? Already? Was this as far as she could go? Had she finally reached the limit of her athletic abilities? Now what? Try to go back and play for Richmond again? Could she even do that? Would she have even been playing in Richmond if the owner hadn't known her and signed her on his own?

Casey reviewed her stats in her mind. 1 for 16 with 6 strikeouts, two errors. *No, this could not be good.*

She languished over these thoughts for a few moments, then decided that she was probably already in enough trouble and that she shouldn't make matters any worse by keeping Skip waiting. She grabbed her glove and bag and made her way through the back of the dugout and into the locker room area.

She walked toward the visiting manager's office like she was walking to the electric chair. She was in no hurry and dreaded the upcoming conversation. Eventually, she arrived at the office door and knocked on it softly, hoping that maybe Morris wasn't there.

But he was, and he answered gruffly, "Yeah?"

Casey opened the door a crack and said, "Uh, it's me, Skip. Casey. Tommy said you wanted to see me?"

Morris was sitting at his desk, looking over the official team scorebook. He still had his uniform on, although his hat was sitting on a corner of the desk, and he looked up upon Casey's entrance. "Oh, right, come on in and have a seat. And close the door behind you, if you would." He motioned to an old brown leather couch that was located opposite his desk.

Casey closed the door and took a seat on the couch. Her heart was racing and she felt short of breath. She was sitting at attention on the front part of the couch, with one hand on each leg, looking apprehensively at Morris.

He dropped the scorebook on the desk as he came out around to the front of the desk and leaned up against it, his paunch hanging out over his belt. He crossed his arms and looked at Casey, then got right to the point. "I wanted to talk to you about your performance. I..."

Casey moved forward a little more, as she interrupted with a verbal barrage. "Skip, I'm sorry about the sign. I should have known better. It won't happen again and I know I can play better." Then, realizing she had interrupted Morris, she stopped and looked at him. "Sorry," she said, wincing.

Morris was grinning slightly, as he uncrossed his arms and held them up in the air in a "hold everything" motion. "Hey, relax," he said. "This isn't about the sign."

"It isn't?"

"No, not completely. I mean, you should know better and I think you do now. But the real reason I called you in here is just to talk about the last few games."

"I know. I really stunk. I'm sorry, but I know I can do better." She stopped when she realized she had interrupted him again.

This time he just continued. "Look, I wanted to wait a few games so I could see how you play. I've watched you in batting practice and in games. You have a good instinct for the game. You have talent, you hustle and you move well. You're just pushing too hard. I know you want to prove yourself, but just relax." ·

Casey sat back a little on the couch. *Wow*, she thought to herself. *He's not sending me down.* She verbalized this to the skipper. "So you're not sending me back to Richmond?"

"No," he said. "I'm not sending you down, at least not yet. You're still going to have to prove yourself, but I promised Harley that I would give you a fair shot and I will. You'll get the same chance that any other ballplayer would get."

Oh, Harley, she thought to herself. *That was the main reason she was still there.* She wondered if Morris resented the fact that she was forced on him by the owner.

"I guess that's all I can ask for." Casey paused for a few seconds, then added, "So, can I ask you a question?"

"Shoot."

"Do you think I can play at this level?" she asked with some hesitancy, not really sure if she wanted to hear the answer.

"I don't know the answer to that yet. Like I said, you have some talent. But talent alone isn't enough. It needs to translate into performance."

"I'll do better. I promise."

"Well, let's worry about it when we get back to Portland," Morris said. He walked back around to the rear of the desk and looked down at his paperwork, indicating that the session was over.

"Okay, Skip, thanks," Casey said awkwardly, and left the office.

After she showered and got on the team bus for the trip home, again sitting alone, she stared out the window, in her mind reviewing her meeting with Butch Morris. She wasn't quite sure what to make of the whole conversation. He wasn't sending her back down, which was good, but he had also made it clear that she needed to perform. It wasn't anything she didn't already know herself, and it just gave her added resolve to try and turn things around. But one thing was very clear — the pressure was definitely on.

Eighteen

By the time the team bus arrived back in Portland, it was 7:00 the next morning. The team had an off day, which was good, since everyone was tired from the series and the long bus ride home.

When Casey arrived back in her hotel room, there was a message on her voicemail from Bud Harley's secretary telling her that her furnished apartment was ready at the Riverview apartment building. Bud Harley had arranged for special rates for the players, so most of them stayed at the Riverview, which was only about fifteen minutes from the stadium.

After catching a few hours of sleep, Casey packed up her clothes and moved over to her new apartment, which was a nice one-bedroom with a kitchen, a living room and a small laundry room with a washer and dryer. It had a small patio, with a balcony that overlooked the Willamette River. She made a quick trip to a local shopping center and purchased supplies to stock her kitchen and bathroom.

Once she was settled in, she called Anne and invited her over for a "house" warming drink. A couple of minutes after six o'clock, Casey was in the kitchen when the doorbell rang. She went to the door and opened it, and Anne was standing there with a bottle of wine with a ribbon around it. She was wearing jeans, New Balance sneakers, and a plain white T-shirt with a light blue blazer on top.

"Hi, Anne, thanks for coming. Come on in," Casey said, swinging the door open and motioning for Anne to come in.

"Hey, girl, how're ya doin'? I brought you a little house-warming present," Anne said, handing over the bottle of white wine. "I thought you might like to try some local wine. It's one of my favorites, Chateau Benoit."

"That's great, thanks. We can drink it out on the terrace." They stepped into the kitchen, and Casey opened one of the cupboards. "I don't think I have any wine glasses. Water glasses close enough?"

"Works for me."

"I'm also not set to make anything for dinner, so I just ordered some pizza. It should be here pretty soon." Then, opening and closing a few drawers, she frowned. "Oh, damn, I don't have a wine opener."

Anne smiled and reached into her side jacket pocket. "Voila!" she said, producing a wine opener. "Shall I?" she said as she grabbed the bottle and proceeded to open the wine.

Casey laughed. "Boy, you think of everything, don't you?"

"Hey, I was a Girl Scout—always prepared and all that."

Anne poured glasses of wine for them both, as they chitchatted for a few minutes, until the pizza arrived. Casey paid the delivery person, and grabbed two plates and some paper towels, then the two of them headed out toward the balcony. Casey carried the pizza while Anne carried the wine, as they went through the living room and out through the glass door to the small terrace overlooking the Willamette River.

"Hey, this is great!" Anne commented as she went to the balcony and looked out at the river. "Nice view."

"I know, it's a pretty good deal, living here. Seven hundred and fifty bucks a month, with a view of the river. Hard to beat."

"Well, you can thank Bud Harley for that. It would easily be twice that much if he hadn't worked out a special deal for the players."

Casey set the pizza on the small metal table in the center of the cement terrace, and they each took a seat on one of the two metal and plastic chairs. Casey, dressed in jeans and a Gonzaga U T-shirt, grabbed a slice of pizza and took a bite, while Anne did the same.

They were both sitting with their backs to the patio door and their chairs facing the river, which winded silently below. The table was in between them, and a slight breeze blew in from the river. Anne sat upright in her jacket, one hand on her glass, looking like a professional businesswoman, while Casey leaned back in her chair, with one leg casually crossed at an angle over the other, and her hand resting on a leg.

"So, how was the road trip?" Anne asked. She already knew how the road trip went, but was asking out of courtesy, and out of friendship.

"Ah, it sucked," Casey responded, using her left hand to tuck her short hair behind one ear. "Or should I say, I sucked. I was one for nine, another error. Morris reamed me in front of everybody, then gave me a big talking to after the game. Half the team hates me, and my confidence is at an all-time low. Other than that, I'm doing great."

Anne took a sip of wine as she looked at Casey. "Oh, come on, it couldn't have been that horrible. What did Morris say?"

"Well, it wasn't all bad, I guess. He basically said he thought I was just trying too hard, and to settle down a bit. Easy for him to say."

"Well, maybe he's right. I mean, I don't claim to know a lot about baseball, but during our last home stand, Chris and I were in the owner's box, and even I could see how tight you were. But it's completely understandable, it being your first series with the team and all."

Casey finished a bite of pizza, wiped her mouth, and took a sip of wine. "I guess, but you gotta understand. Up until now, it's come fairly easily to me. I mean, I've had to work at it, of course, but there's never been any doubt in my mind that I could compete at whatever level I'm at. But this is different.

"I've gone from playing with an independent Class A minor league team to a Triple A affiliated team, and even though the guys on the Richmond Tigers were good, these guys are really good."

"Hey, wait until you get to the majors, then they'll be, like, really, really good," Anne laughed, dipping her head to the side and applying her best Valley Girl accent, trying to add some levity to the conversation.

Casey was chewing on a bite of pizza, and almost choked on it, and had to quickly wash it down with a swig of wine. Then matching Anne's accent, "Yeah, like, that would be, like, *way* cool."

Once they got over that, Anne continued, "No, seriously, you have to believe you can make it."

"What, to the majors? I don't know. That still seems so far away. I'm only one week out of Single A, although it feels like a month. Right now, I'm just trying to concentrate on making it at this level, then we'll see what happens."

Anne waved her hand casually. "Ah, you can do it."

Casey looked at her. "Why do you seem so sure?"

Anne turned to face Casey squarely. "You don't even realize how special you are, do you?"

"What do you mean?"

Anne shook her head, pushed her chair back and walked around to the front of the table, motioning for Casey to stand. "Go ahead, stand up for a minute."

Casey looked at her warily, but stood up anyway, facing Anne. "What's this all about?"

Anne looked up at Casey. "Just do it. Don't worry, I'm not going to kiss you or anything." Casey laughed as she looked down at Anne, who continued, "Look at you. You tower over me, probably outweigh me by twenty pounds. I know you're twice as strong as me and you'd kick my butt in a second."

Casey chuckled, and started to interject something, but instead, Anne continued with her speech. "No, seriously, you have these superhuman genes from your mother and father; you've been coached all your life, and you're used to playing with guys. No reason you can't go all the way."

Casey held her hands up in front of her. "Okay," she said, "I get it. But you have to understand, as much as I 'tower' over you, as you said, that's how much bigger and stronger the guys who I play with are over me. It's not that easy." She paused, then gestured to where the two of them were standing. "By the way, are we done here?"

"Oh, sorry," Anne laughed as they both sat back down in their chairs. "I was just trying to make a point. I get carried away sometimes. But I still think you can do it. You have to do it."

Casey looked at Anne, admiring her conviction. "I *have* to do it? Why?"

"Because we're all pulling for you, that's why."

"Who's we?"

157

Anne took another sip of wine, and smirked. "Oh, only every woman in the entire state of Oregon, that's all."

"Right."

"No, I'm serious, everyone's talking about you," Anne said, looking intently at Casey. "Not only the women in the team office, but everyone I talk to is asking about you, pulling for you.

"But why so much attention on me?"

"People need heroes, Casey, someone to root for. Especially young girls and women. They want you to do well; they need you to do well, to become their hero."

"Heroes don't bat .062," Casey returned with a scoff. "Besides, I don't want to be a hero; I just want to play baseball."

"Sometimes the two go hand in hand."

Casey's head tilted back slightly as she laughed. "Hey, that's great. All I need is more pressure." Then with a more serious look, she continued, "But seriously, Anne, I appreciate everything you're saying. I know I have a gift and some special talents and all that, but I just don't know how far that can take me yet. This past week, with my poor performance and all, was the first time I've ever had any self-doubts about my abilities. It's a weird feeling, one I'm not used to."

Anne finished off her glass of wine and glanced at her watch. Rising from her chair, she said, "Well, I need to get going, but like I said, I think you can do it. You know you can do it. So just do it."

"Hey, shouldn't that be some kind of slogan or something?"

"I think it's already been used."

They laughed as Anne helped Casey clear the table. As they made their way back into the kitchen, Casey said, "Hey, we spent so much time talking about me, I didn't even ask about you. How's it going with Chris?"

"It's going great. He's working late tonight, but then we're going to hook up for a night cap after that."

"Well, I can't wait to meet him. So, thanks for coming over, and thanks for the wine."

"Don't mention it," Anne said as Casey escorted her to the door. "Just get a good night's sleep and kick some butt tomorrow."

They gave each other a brief hug, as Casey shut the door behind Anne.

The next morning, when Casey woke up, she flipped on the radio. It was set to KSPT – or *K-Sport*—the all-sports talk radio station for the greater Portland area. The morning segment was hosted by Richey Moore, and the show was called *Moore or Less*. Richey would typically pick a few current sports topics, and start off the show by introducing each topic with a short narrative, including some of his own opinions. Then he would invite his listeners to call in and offer their comments.

The station was just coming out of a commercial, and Casey's ears perked up when she heard the topic being discussed. She sat up in bed as Richey Moore performed the transition.

"So, if you want quality tires for the lowest price, come to Tire Town."

"Welcome back to K-Sport, the all-sports radio. If you're just joining us, this morning's topic is women in sports, specifically women in men's sports. We're talking about Casey Collins, the young female right fielder for the *Portland Power* who was called up from Single A Richmond about two weeks ago.

"Well, she's played in six games now, and she's batting .062, with one hit in sixteen official at bats. She has one stolen base and has made two errors in the field. The Power is two and four in those six games, not to imply that there is necessarily a correlation there.

"So, here's some of the questions we're putting to our listeners this morning. Do you think Casey Collins, or any woman, can play men's baseball at this level, or even at the next level, in the majors? Do you think this move by *The Power* is good for baseball, or does it somehow cheapen the sport? Do you think Bud Harley is doing this strictly as a publicity stunt in order to sell more tickets? Or is it time for men's baseball to be opened up to women?

"If you want to make a comment or ask a question, give us a call at 1-800-THE-SPORT. The lines are open. Let's take some calls."

After a few seconds, "Okay, we have our first caller. We've got Robert from Hawthorne on the line. Hello, Robert, you're on the spot at *THE SPORT.*"

The voice of an older gentleman came through the radio. "Hi, Richey, thank you for taking my call. I'm a longtime listener and I love your show."

"Thank you, sir. What's your comment?"

"Well, I'm sixty-six years old and I've been watching baseball almost my whole life. I saw Don Drysdale play, Hank Aaron, Willie Mays, Ted Williams, Willie Stargell..."

Richey interrupted, "So what's your question?"

"Well, not a question really, just a comment. I mean, well, it was bad enough when baseball added the designated hitter. Then they added a wild card, then interleague play. And now a woman playing men's baseball? It's too much. It's like it's not even baseball anymore."

Richey countered, "I don't know, they still play nine innings, there's still nine players on either side, it still takes three strikes to make an out, each team still gets three outs in an inning. Still seems like baseball to me."

"Well, you know what I mean. It's just not the same."

Richey responded, "Sounds like you're a traditionalist. Nothing wrong with that. But look, I'm not saying we should automatically go to all-coed baseball or anything. It just seems to me that if an individual, regardless of sex, race, nationality, religion or whatever—if they can meet the physical requirements, then it seems like they should get a fair shot.

"But that's just my opinion, and it sounds like you disagree, which is fine. Let's take another call. All right, we've got Ellen from Laurelhurst on the line. Hello, you're on the spot with THE SPORT."

"Hello, Richey, this is Ellen. First, I just wanted to say I love your show, and I also appreciate how you always seem to be objective. I listen to it every morning at work."

"Well, thanks Ellen, I certainly try to be objective, although I do have my opinions like everyone else. So, what's your comment?"

"Well, the last gentleman talked about all the changes that have occurred in baseball in the last few years, and, if you ask me, everything he mentioned has added more excitement to the game. And, it seems to me that baseball, like everything else, needs to evolve over time. Maybe this is just the next step in the evolution of baseball. If a woman has the athletic talent and has gotten to the level where she can compete with guys, then why not let her play?"

Richey complimented Ellen. "Now those were some intelligent comments, and I thank you. I agree with you that the sport does need to evolve. But I'm sure that there are those out there, like our last caller, who want the sport to stay exactly as it was back in the days of Ruth and Gehrig."

Ellen countered, "Well, don't forget that back in the days of Ruth and Gehrig, blacks weren't permitted to play either, so should we go back to that? I don't think so."

"Excellent comment again. And look, let's put some things in perspective here. It's not like all of a sudden we've got hundreds of woman rushing in to play men's baseball. Let's not forget here that we are talking about one woman, and that we are still talking about the minor leagues. As much as we love our team here in Portland, we are only Triple A, and no one even knows yet if this woman, Casey Collins, can make it at this level, let alone the majors.

"Maybe this can serve as a test case and we'll see how it goes. I'm thinking that this will resolve itself. If Casey Collins goes another couple of weeks or so and continues to bat .062, then it would probably be hard for Bud Harley to keep her here. But if she turns it around and starts to produce, then it would be hard to argue to get rid of her.

"But let's get back to the phones, and take another call. Hello, Dave from Beaverton, you're on THE SPORT."

"Hey, Richey, love your show, man. Hey, about this Casey Collins thing. Well, the way I see it, is that it's first and foremost a business, right? I mean, it seems like every time you see an interview with a player or an owner, they're always talking about how baseball is a business.

"And if it's like any other business, it's about making money, right? Well, I read in the *Portland Times* yesterday that they sold an extra ten thousand tickets over the first three-game series with Collins in the line-up. If we say that the average ticket price is what, around eight bucks? That's an extra eighty grand that they made already just from having her on the team. Seems like a smart decision to me. It's all business, man, just like anything else."

Richey took over again. "All right. That was Dave from Beaverton. So, Dave thinks that it's all about the business side of it. If the Power can sell more tickets, then that justifies having a woman on the team. Well, that's certainly an angle that deserves some consideration. But, winning games is also part of the business, and if it gets to the point where this woman is hurting the team's chances – and I'm not saying that she is, I'm just asking what if — then that needs to be considered also.

"All right, let's take a break for a commercial and we'll continue this conversation. It seems like a lot of people have opinions on this subject so we'll keep it going when we come back."

Casey had been listening intently, sitting forward on the edge of her bed with her legs on the floor and her arms crossed. As the radio station cut to a commercial, she moved over to an easy chair beside the bed stand, plopped down and shook her head in bewilderment. She was amazed that she, coming from a small town like Richmond, could be the focus of a major radio call-in show.

This was way beyond anything she had experienced before. Here were all these people she didn't know calling in to make comments about her life. She almost felt violated, like a layer of her privacy was being stripped away. She had always heard that many professional athletes didn't read the sports pages or listen to sports talk shows, and now she knew why.

It was hard enough on her that she was experiencing her own level of introspection and self-doubt, but to have a group of strangers do it publicly on the radio was something else.

As the radio station came back from the commercial, she turned up the volume, as Richey Moore again took over. "All right, we're back. You're listening to K-Sport, KSPT radio. I'm Richey Moore and the show is called *Moore or Less*. We were taking comments about the new right fielder for the Portland Power, Casey Collins, and in case you've been out of the area or on another planet or something, Casey Collins is a woman – the only woman playing men's professional baseball. And she happens to be playing for our beloved Portland Power, which is why we're talking about her this morning. We've got time for a few more callers, so let's get back to it. Hello, you're on the air with K-SPORT."

"Hey, Rich, this is Chad Jeffries from Portland. I wanted to comment on this Casey Collins thing."

"Okay, go ahead."

"Well, I played minor league ball for two years with Oklahoma City. I'm six feet two and two hundred and five pounds, and a pretty good athlete, but I never got any further than Double A. I don't see how some woman at five feet ten inches and what, one hundred thirty-six pounds, can have the strength to fight off these guys throwing the ball in the middle nineties. There's just no way she's going to make it."

Richey responded, "Well, Chad, thanks for your comments, but I'd have to disagree on that particular angle of your argument. You seem to be making it all about size and strength, and as even Casey herself said at her press conference, this is not football we're talking about. I think baseball, more than any other sport, with the possible exception of golf, is as much about physics as anything else.

"I mean, let's reduce it to the ridiculous. Let's give this woman a twenty-ounce bat, and have her start her swing while the pitcher is still winding up. Then she would be sure to catch up to the pitch, right? Obviously, she's not doing that, but she has seemed to find that confluence point where timing and physics and speed, come into play. I mean, look at Ichiro of the Mariners. He's not a big strapping guy who's powering out tons of homers, yet he's at the top of the majors in batting. We'd have to check the actual stats, but something like one-third of his hits are infield hits. He generates his offensive success from bat control and speed, and from what I hear, if he and

Casey Collins were to run in a foot race, I'm not sure that Ichiro would win."

Chad tried to object. "Yeah, but Ichiro is special."

"So is Casey Collins. She has to be, to have gotten this far. Granted, she hasn't shown us anything yet here in Portland, and maybe she never will. Who knows? But I do disagree with you that someone has to be big and strong in order to be successful in baseball, and I think if we called up David Eckstein from the Angels, he might disagree with you also. But thanks, I do appreciate your call, and let's get to the next caller."

"Hi, Richey, this is Cathy from Vancouver, and I'm the mother of three wonderful daughters, ages seven, eight and ten. All my girls play youth league soccer, and the two older girls also play little league baseball."

"Oh, a soccer mom, eh? Okay, what's your comment?"

"Well, being the mother of three daughters, I think they need more positive role models, and I really like the way this Casey Collins handles herself. My husband and I took our girls to the Power game on Sunday, and she took the time to sign autographs for all three of them. I think it takes a lot of courage to do what she's doing and I just want to say that I respect her for it, and I wish a lot more of the players, not only in the minor leagues but in the majors also, were like her."

"Well, thanks for those comments, Cathy. I agree that we need more positive role models, and not just for women, for both sexes. But, we're running out of time here so let's try to get another call or two in.

"Here we go. Tom from Raleigh Hills, you're on THE SPORT."

"Yeah, I got a comment for this Casey Collins. Four words – Hasta La Bimbo, Baby! Ah-ha-ha," he laughed as he hung up.

"Oh man, that was harsh. Well, we get some intelligent comments and some not-so-intelligent comments. Maybe we need to get Ellen back on the phone."

"All right, one last caller. We've got Steve from Alameda. Go ahead, Steve."

"Hello. Thanks, Richey. I'm a longtime listener. Love your show. My question is, would we be having this argument if this lady was batting .300? Maybe. Maybe not. But why don't we just let the natural dynamics of baseball take their course? She's only had, what, sixteen, at bats? I'm not sure that's a good enough indicator of whether or not she can make it at this level. Why don't we let Butch Morris make the decision? That's what he gets paid for. If she can play, she stays; if she can't, then we won't have to worry about it."

Richey responded, "Well, I think that's a pretty good comment, Steve, and I'd have to agree with you. What was it that Bud Harley said at the press conference, something about the word 'baseball player' not being a gender-specific term? Why don't we just treat her like any other player and let the laws of baseball decide? If she can play, she can play, if she can't, then she can't.

"But we're not going to settle this issue here, and we're also not going to let this story go. We'll continue to follow the saga of Casey Collins as she makes her bid to stay with the Portland Power.

"Well, folks, I'm afraid that's all we have time for today. But thanks to all of you who called and offered your opinion. We'll be back tomorrow at the same time, and don't forget, you can hear the Power live on KSPT starting tonight at 7:05."

Casey turned off the radio and sat in the chair in silence, staring out the window and thinking to herself. She didn't want to become a topic of conversation or a political issue. She just wanted to play baseball. What she didn't realize was that this was only the beginning. She didn't know that three other radio stations from Pacific Coast League cities were discussing the same topic—her.

She pondered her situation as she sat there in the chair. The way she saw it, she could do one of two things. She could be intimidated by the publicity and the athletic hurdles that faced her, and retreat into oblivion, or she could treat it as a challenge and rise to the occasion.

Casey knew what she had to do. There was only one answer. She had to produce. It was like some of the callers had said – why not let the dynamics of baseball decide – if she could play, then she deserved to stay. If she couldn't play, then she didn't deserve to stay. Just like any other ballplayer. It was as simple that. Casey quickly got out of her chair, picked up the phone from the nightstand, and dialed.

After a few rings, a groggy-sounding Mooch Moran answered the phone. "Yeah, hello?"

"Oh, hello, Mooch?" Casey said apologetically, "Sorry, this is Casey. I woke you up, didn't I?"

"Oh, no, not at all," Mooch answered. "I'm just back from my five-mile run and I was doing some pushups."

The guy is amazing, Casey chuckled to herself. *He even wakes up joking.* "Well, sorry to interrupt your workout, but I need to ask you a favor."

It was obvious that Mooch was trying to sound alert, even though he was still half asleep. He sat up in his bed, holding the phone up to his ear. "Sure, anything," he said. "What is it?"

"Will you pitch to me?"

"Pitch to you?"

"Yeah. Look, I really need some work, and just taking a few extra swings at batting practice isn't going to do it. I need some help. Will you do it?"

"Uh, yeah, I guess. I mean, sure. When?"

"How about this morning, in about a half an hour? I'll buy you breakfast and then we can head out to the stadium."

"How about an hour, instead?"

"Okay, sure," she laughed. "I'll see you in the lobby at ten."

Casey was waiting in the lobby with her athletic bag when Mooch came out of the elevator, carrying his. He was wearing gray sweat pants and a red Oklahoma Sooners T-shirt, and he had a Chicago Cubs baseball hat on, slightly askew. He looked like he was still half asleep.

Casey greeted him as he came over to where she was standing. "Hi, Mooch. Thanks for doing this. I really appreciate it."

"No problem," he said. "Happy to do it. Where to?"

"I thought we would just grab a quick fast-food breakfast somewhere so we can get to the field sooner. I'll drive."

"Hey, that works for me. As long as I get some coffee in me, I'll be ready to go."

After a quick breakfast at a local fast food establishment, Casey pulled into the stadium parking lot. They checked in with the security guard at the main gate, and headed into the team facilities under the bleachers. They were surprised to find Pop in his office, and they stopped in to say hello.

Casey knocked on his door, and Pop was also surprised to see someone in so early in the day. "Yes, hello?" he said upon hearing the knock on the door.

Casey poked her head in and said, "Hi, Pop, how are you?"

Pop was seated at his desk, wearing his reading glasses. He had been reading over some charts from the last series, and he looked up at Casey. "Casey. What are you doing here?"

Casey took a step into his office. "I came in to get some extra BP. I figure I need the work."

Pop put his paperwork down and removed his reading glasses. "Well, that's great Casey, but I'm a little old to be pitching batting practice."

Casey smiled, and then said, a little uncomfortably. "Uh, that's okay Pop. I brought a pitcher."

"Oh?"

Just then Mooch took a step in to the office. "Hey, Pop," he said.

Looking back at Casey, Pop smirked, "Moran? He's your pitcher? What do you need, dodge ball practice?"

Mooch protested, "Oh, c'mon Pop. I'm not that wild."

"Yeah, right," Pop said. Then, looking back at Casey, he said, "Maybe you should wear Grunt's catcher's gear while you're batting."

Casey laughed. "I'll think about it. So, Pop, is the equipment room open? We want to grab a couple of ball bags."

"Sure," Pop said. "Go ahead and help yourselves."

They both thanked Pop, then stopped by the equipment room. Casey grabbed her bat as Mooch grabbed two mesh bags full of baseballs, and they made their way out onto the field. After putting on their spikes and throwing a few warm-up tosses to each other, Mooch headed out to the mound with the baseballs as Casey grabbed her bat and took her position in the batter's box.

Mooch called in from the mound. "You want the stretch or a full wind–up?"

Casey called back. "Let's start with a full windup first."

"Fastballs or sliders?"

"Mix them up, and don't tell me what you're going to throw."

"Okay, here we go." Mooch picked up one of the baseballs, took his position on the mound and went into his windup.

Casey was in her batting stance as she watched Mooch windup and release the ball. The first pitch went 3 feet over Casey's head and slammed into the backstop with a resounding "thud".

She watched the pitch sail over her head. "What the hell was that?" she called out with a laugh.

"Ah, sorry," Mooch apologized.

She laughed again. "Look, just relax and throw normally, okay?"

"All right," Mooch answered. "Here we go."

He wound up and delivered a fastball down the middle of the plate, which Casey stepped into and smacked into left center field.

"Good one," Mooch called in from the mound.

"Thanks," Casey said. "That felt good. Was that your fastest?"

Like most pitchers, Mooch had gotten a pretty good feeling as to what speed he was throwing at, by turning around to look at the scoreboard radar readout after his pitches. "No, that was only around ninety," he answered.

"Go ahead and pick it up if you want. And don't forget to throw in some sliders."

"Okay, here we go."

Mooch mimicked everything he did in a game situation, pitching from a full windup, then the stretch, even pretending to take the signal from the catcher. As he did in game situations, he also fiddled with his hat in between every pitch. The next three pitches that Mooch delivered were way out of the strike zone. Casey stepped out of the batter's box and called out to Mooch. "Hey, can you do me a favor?"

"What's that?" Mooch called back.

"Can you just straighten out your hat and leave it there? It's driving me nuts."

Mooch smirked as he straightened his hat out with an emphatic motion and pulled it down firmly on his head. "How's that?"

"Much better," Casey replied as she stepped back into the box.

Mooch settled down after that, and for the next 30 minutes, he pitched to Casey. She gradually got comfortable with his delivery and the speed of his pitches, and she spread her hits around the field. He had pitched both from the windup and from the stretch, throwing her a mixture of fastballs and sliders. She even spent about ten minutes trying different types of bunts.

She could see that Mooch was starting to get tired, and she didn't want to give him a sore arm, so she called out, "All right, Mooch, just a few more."

Mooch called back, "No problem. Here's another one." He went into his windup and delivered a slider that started as an outside pitch and then curved right down the middle. He completed his throw, and his follow-through had him facing Casey squarely.

Casey had picked up the spin on the ball, saw it was a slider, and adjusted her swing. She swung through the ball and connected with it solidly, sending it zinging straight back at Mooch.

Mooch did not have enough time to react, and the ball hit him squarely in the groin. He let out a loud "umph" as he tumbled to the ground, curling into a ball and holding his groin.

"Oh, my God," Casey exclaimed as she dropped her bat and went running out to the mound. "Mooch, are you all right?" She dropped to her knees beside Mooch, who continued to roll around in agony. His face had turned bright red.

"I'm so sorry," she said with concern. "Are you all right?"

"Not really," he grimaced. "Nice shot."

"Sorry," Casey repeated. "I didn't mean to do that." She put a hand lightly on the side of his leg in sympathy, but knew there wasn't much else she could do.

Then, with a slight grin, she asked Mooch. "You're not wearing a cup, are you?

"No," he moaned. "Didn't have time."

Casey laughed, and Mooch looked at her. "Why do people always think it's funny when a guy gets cracked in the nuts?"

Casey tried to show a straight face, but still let out a giggle. "I'm sorry," she said. "I didn't mean to laugh. I can see you're in pain. Listen, why don't you relax for a minute and I'll go retrieve the balls."

Mooch was still curled up in a ball, and holding his groin with his hands. "Great," he mumbled. "I might need a couple of them for myself."

Casey laughed again as she rose to her feet. *Always joking,* she thought to herself. She grabbed the two empty bags and trotted out to the outfield to pick up the baseballs that she had scattered around the field. It only took about ten minutes to retrieve all the balls, and she jogged back in toward the pitcher's mound with the full bags.

Mooch had managed to sit up by now, but his face was still a little flushed. Casey stood beside him, put a hand on his shoulder and said, "How are you doing, Mooch?"

"Oh, I'm all right. I think I'll live." He started to get up.

Casey extended a hand. "Here, let me help you."

Mooch took her hand and managed to stand. Casey gabbed the two bags of baseballs and they gathered up their gloves and Casey's bat, and headed back towards the locker room.

Leaning up against the tunnel door with his arms crossed, Dale "Turk" Roberts watched the last ten minutes of the interaction between Casey and Mooch. He had forgotten his favorite shirt in his locker and had stopped by to pick it up for a big date tonight. He had heard the cracking of the bat out on the field and went out to see what was going on.

He saw Casey put her hand on Mooch's leg, and scoffed at the scene taking place on the mound. *This is getting out of hand*, he mumbled to himself, *Something's got to be done.* He smiled perversely as he retreated unnoticed back down the tunnel.

Casey drove herself and Mooch back to the team's apartment building, and pressed the elevator button 3 for Mooch's floor, and 5 for hers.

As the elevator arrived at the third floor, and the doors opened, Mooch prepared to get off. Casey was standing at the front of the elevator, and placed her hand over the slot for the doors in order to keep them from closing.

"Are you going to be okay?" she asked.

"Oh, yeah," he said. "I think I'll just go and put some ice on my, uh, my…"

"Leg?" she said with a sly smile.

Mooch laughed. "Yeah, that's it."

As he walked by Casey on his way out of the elevator, on an impulse, she grabbed him lightly by the arm, stood up on her toes and kissed him on the cheek.

"Thanks again, Mooch, I really appreciate it."

"Don't mention it," he said, trying to be nonchalant. "It was no problem, really."

The elevator doors closed, leaving Mooch standing in the hallway. He put his hand up to his cheek where Casey had kissed him, and wondered, *Could this be the start of something?*

171

Nineteen

That afternoon, Casey was in a pretty good mood on the way to the stadium. She felt good about the batting practice session with Mooch earlier in the day. He had thrown her his best fastballs and sliders, and she had handled them well. Admittedly, it wasn't a game situation, but at least she felt better about the timing of the pitches. She felt a new resolve within herself, and had the feeling that, starting tonight, she was going to start turning things around.

She was still reflecting on those thoughts as she pulled through the gate into the parking lot. As she got out of the car, she noticed that a van from a local television station was parked near the walkway to the stadium, and that a crowd of several hundred people had gathered outside the player's entrance. The van had KPTL printed on the side in big letters.

She parked her car and grabbed her bag out of the trunk, and started walking over to where the crowd had gathered. The TV crew was the first to notice that she had arrived, and one of them called out, "There she is."

A woman with a microphone came running over to Casey, followed by a man with a television camera hoisted on his shoulders. The woman shoved the microphone in Casey's face and said, "Casey, Melinda Burk from KPTL TV. Can we ask you a couple of questions?"

As the attention of the crowd swung towards Casey, several kids of varying ages came running over, and surrounded her in a few minutes. "Can I have your autograph?" they were all yelling, as they held out their autograph books for her to sign. Their parents had filled in around the outside of the circle which had formed around Casey, and she was now totally surrounded.

The woman television reporter hadn't waited for Casey's response to her request to ask some questions, and instead went right into the interview.

"How does it feel to be the only woman baseball player in the minor leagues?" she asked, as the kids continued to thrust their autograph books at her, shouting all the while. Casey felt totally overwhelmed, and trapped. She looked around in desperation, but all she could see was the crowd all around her.

"Ms. Collins?" Melinda Burk asked again.

"Yes? Oh, um, fine, I guess." Casey felt disjointed as she grabbed one of the autograph books that was being thrust at her, quickly scribbled *Casey Collins*, and gave it back. She did this for a few others, but as soon as she signed one there were five others to take its place.

"Do you think you can make it at this level?" the reporter continued.

Casey was trying to split her attention between the autograph seekers and the reporter, all the while looking around for a means of escape. She tried to collect her thoughts and respond to the reporter, "Well, yes, I think I can. I'm just off to a slow start, that's all."

"How much time do you think they'll give you to prove yourself?"

Casey was getting more and more frustrated as the crowd continued to push in around her. She was looking around helplessly, when suddenly the shrill sound of a whistle pierced the air. A portion of the crowd nearest the stadium started to part, as the whistle blew loudly several more times.

Casey turned her head in the direction of the whistle, and saw that it was being blown by Pop, who was being followed closely by a security guard.

"All right! Break it up! Break it up!" Pop ordered loudly.

"Let us through, folks, let us through," the security guard added, as he moved firmly through the crowd. The crowd had turned to focus their attention on the two men making their way towards Casey. After a few minutes, they reached her.

"Pop!" Casey said as she let out a sigh of relief. "Boy, am I glad to see you."

"It seems like you've gotten yourself into a little pickle here," Pop replied as he eyed the crowd warily.

173

"I'll say," Casey said as Pop grabbed her by the arm.

The security guard stepped forward and grabbed Casey lightly by the other arm, positioning her slightly behind him. "Miss, Collins, follow me, please."

"With pleasure," Casey replied. She hunched in behind the security guard and grabbed the back of his belt with one hand, as he and Pop made their way back through the crowd with Casey in tow, heading toward the stadium entrance.

When they were finally inside the stadium, Casey let go of the guard's belt, let out a deep breath and said, "Wow, thank you guys so much. That was incredible. I've never seen anything like that before."

Pop was breathing heavily from pushing his way through the crowd. "Young lady," he said between breaths, "you sure know how to draw attention to yourself."

"I'll say," the security guard echoed.

"I don't know what happened. All of a sudden they were just all around me."

"Well," Pop said, "It's clear we're going to have to make some adjustments around the entrance." He looked at the security guard. "I'll talk to Mr. Harley first thing tomorrow."

"Okay," the guard responded. "Are you two going to be all right?"

"Yeah, we'll be fine, now that we're inside," Casey answered. "Thanks again."

"No problem," he replied. "If you like, I'll come around after the game to walk you to your car. Just in case."

Before Casey could object, Pop interjected. "I think that might be a good idea. Thanks."

Casey went to her private locker room, still a little shaken by the scene that had just taken place outside the stadium. First, the radio show, now this. She just could not get over the fact that she was the cause of so much attention. As she changed into her uniform, she vowed not to let it get to her. Looking in the mirror, she reaffirmed her resolution to play better, starting tonight.

She'd had a great batting practice session with Mooch in the morning, the minor accident notwithstanding, and she felt like she was seeing the ball much better now. She finished changing and made her way out through the short tunnel to the dugout. There were already a few players arranging their bags under the bench, and a few more were out on the field going through their warm-up routines.

Casey took her turn in the batting cage, willing her body to remember the morning's successful practice. It definitely felt like it helped, as she scattered the pitches around to all three fields. She barely even noticed how many fans were filing into the stadium, the beginning of what would be the largest crowd so far this year for the Power – 23,700.

After both teams had taken their batting practice, and the national anthem was played, Portland prepared to take the field. Pop was standing at the top of the steps at the outfield end of the dugout, and he sensed that Casey was feeling nervous. As she ascended the stairs to pass by him, he grabbed her lightly by the arm, indicating he wanted to talk to her.

"Casey," he said as he pulled her aside and positioned himself in front of her. "I wanted to talk to you about Sunday's game. You know what happened?"

"Yeah," she said, expecting another lecture. "I got yelled at by Skip, but I understand why now. I ran on my own and he didn't like that."

"No, that's not it, exactly," Pop said with a smile as he looked into her eyes. "He yelled at you, *just like he would any other player.*" Pop said the last part with added emphasis. He put his hands on her shoulders as he continued. "He didn't back off for fear of hurting your feelings because you're a woman, or anything like that, did he?"

Casey looked back into his eyes, not quite sure what he was getting at.

Pop continued, "If he didn't say anything to you, all the other players would have noticed, and they would have seen that you were getting special treatment. Instead, you got the exact same treatment that any other ballplayer—that any *man* would

175

get. It's a sign of respect. And all the other players saw that. *He's helping you.* You understand?"

Casey's face brightened up as Pop's words sunk in. She removed her ball cap and ran her hand front to back through her hair. "Wow, I had no idea," she said. "I guess I can be pretty slow sometimes."

"That's okay," Pop said with a wink. "That's why they keep us old guys around." He nodded his head towards the outfield and said, "Now, get on out there. You're holding up the game."

Casey placed her hat back on her head and jogged out to her position in right field. A careful observer would have noticed a little extra spring in her step and a grin on her face.

The home umpire yelled "Play Ball" and the first batter for Calgary stepped into the box. On the third pitch, he smacked a low line drive about 20 feet towards the right field side of the center fielder, James Johnson, who immediately broke towards the ball. "I got it!" he called out, as the ball was clearly his and appeared to be an easy catch. But as he got about five feet from the ball, he slipped, and both feet suddenly went out from underneath him. "Dammit!" he cursed, as he realized the ball was going to skip by him. He made a feeble wave at the ball with his gloved hand as he fell on his bottom. The crowd let out a collective "Ohhh" as they saw what happened.

The ball landed only about two feet from his outstretched arms, skidded by him, and headed for the fence. He immediately scrambled to his feet and prepared to chase the ball down. But he stopped after taking one step, shocked to see that Casey was standing there, stooped over, and was fielding the ball.

She gathered the ball to her glove, came up into a throwing position and rifled the ball towards the second baseman, who had come running out to take the relay throw. The base runner, seeing the ball get by the center fielder, was preparing to round second base and head for third, thinking that he was going to get a triple, or maybe even more.

But as he got to second, he saw that the third base coach had both arms raised up in a "halt" position. A bit surprised, he took a glance towards the outfield and saw that Casey had backed up the play. He had to suddenly put on his brakes, and he half slid, half stumbled, awkwardly, into second base.

The crowd, recognizing that Casey had saved an extra base and maybe even a run, clapped loudly in acknowledgement of her hustle on the play.

"Nice backup. Thanks," Johnson commented, recognizing that Casey had not only saved the team a possible run but had also saved him some major embarrassment.

"No problem," she responded with a wink.

As she was jogging back to her position, she heard a male voice call out from the crowd. "Nice play, number nine," he yelled, referring to the number on the back of her jersey. Fans may not make or break your game, but it was always nice to get some positive recognition.

Casey resumed her position over in right field and glanced briefly towards the Power dugout. Butch Morris was standing at the top of the stairs, leaning against the fence with his arms crossed. He looked out at her, gave a simple nod of approval, then spat some tobacco juice on the ground. From a man like Morris, it spoke volumes.

The Turk, Dale Roberts, was on the mound for the Power. He did not acknowledge Casey's good play, but he did strike out the next batter on three pitches, got the following batter on a groundout to the shortstop, and got Calgary's clean-up hitter on a pop-up behind home plate. The Power survived the top half of the first inning, but more importantly, so did Casey.

The Power managed to get one man into scoring position in their half of the first inning on a line-drive double by the designated hitter, Juan Garcia, but he was left stranded as the last batter flied out to center field.

The second inning saw no threats from either team, and the Turk again sat Calgary down in order in the top of the third. It was now bottom of the third, and Casey was scheduled to lead off the inning.

She grabbed her bat and was heading out to the batter's box, preparing to take a few practice swings. Just as she was halfway to the box, she heard Butch Morris's voice from the top of the stairs. "Collins, wait a minute." The words froze her in her tracks.

Oh God, what does he want, Casey thought to herself. *He's not going to yank me again, is he? And not right in front everyone like this.* She looked back at Morris, who had taken a few steps out of the dugout towards her. She walked up to him with a perplexed look on her face.

"Yes, Skip?" she asked warily.

He spat some tobacco juice on the grass as she approached. Butch Morris was not one with which to discuss the evils of chewing tobacco. He walked up close to her and said, "Look, this guy has a hitch in his windup, and he's telegraphing his moves to first base. You see it?"

The question took Casey by surprise. "Uh, yeah, he drops his shoulder more when he's going home." She had been watching the pitcher closely for any telltale signals that could give her an advantage, either at the plate or on base. She noticed that he had a habit of dropping his left shoulder and arm lower to the ground when he went home than he did when he threw to first base. Apparently, the skipper had noticed it also.

He continued, "You get on base, you've got the green light. You see an opportunity, you take it. Okay?"

Casey tried to hide her excitement by showing a serious face, but a slight grin slipped out nonetheless. "Sure thing, Skip. Thanks."

"Don't thank me. Just get on base," Morris mumbled as he turned and walked back to the dugout, resuming his stance at the top of the dugout.

Wow, that was amazing, Casey thought to herself. *That was about the last thing I expected. Now all I have to do is get on base!*

The public announcer's voice came over the speakers, reverberating off the concrete pillars of the stadium. "Now batting, the right fielder, Casey Collins."

There was a loud noise from the crowd, but Casey knew that it didn't all come from cheers. She distinctly heard a few boos in the mix, but tried to block it out and concentrate on the task at hand, which was to get on base.

Six–foot-four-inch-tall Todd Harrison, a left-hander, was on the mound for Calgary. He had a fastball, a slider and a curve, and had only given up one hit and one walk so far. Casey clicked her bat against her spikes, and stepped in and took her stance, as Harrison wound up and prepared to deliver the first pitch. It was a fastball which got to the plate very quickly, zinging over the outside corner for a called strike one.

Casey glanced out at the radar gun readout on the center field scoreboard – 94 mph. She choked up on the bat a little, took a couple of practice swings, and prepared for the next pitch.

She focused on the pitcher's release point, which she had been watching closely ever since the game started. As soon as he released the ball, Casey focused on it as it left his hand. She saw the ball spinning wildly, and she heard the pitcher grunt heavily as he released the pitch. Too much effort for a curve ball; it was a slider. She shifted her weight forward and swung into the ball, connecting with it solidly as the bat made a loud cracking sound.

The ball rocketed over the third baseman's head, but curved foul at the last second. Strike two, with the count now at 0 and 2. Casey was already halfway down to first base when the umpire called "Foul Ball", and she had to retrieve her bat and step back into the batter's box.

She heard Crush Davis yell from the dugout, "Good wood, Casey. Straighten it out."

A woman fan sitting behind home plate yelled, "Come on, Casey, you can do it," as the opposing team yelled their encouragement to their pitcher.

Casey resumed her batting stance and watched as the third pitch, a fastball, came right down the middle of the plate, but at her eye level. She let it go by, and the umpire called "Ball One." The count was now 1 and 2 as the catcher threw the ball back to Harrison. He caught the ball and walked around on the mound a little, tugging at his jersey before stepping back onto the mound. He glared towards home plate as he took the signal from the catcher.

Casey choked up another half inch on the bat, and watched him closely as he went into his windup. Again focusing on his release point, she saw that this ball was also spinning, but that the pitcher eased up a little at the last moment. A curve ball.

She honed in on the ball to determine the breaking pattern, then stepped into it and swung with authority. Again, there was a loud crack of the bat, but this time, the ball went sizzling about two feet over the pitcher's head, heading straight towards center field.

Casey broke out of her batting stance and was heading towards first, as Harrison jumped up and stabbed at the ball, which caught the top part of his glove. But he couldn't hold on to it, and the ball popped out of his glove and landed about three feet behind him. He scurried after the ball, picked it up, spun around and fired it to the first baseman.

Casey was running full speed down the base path by now, and beat the ball to the base by a full step. The umpire called "Safe!" as the crowd cheered loudly. The Power now had a runner on first with nobody out.

Casey had run several feet beyond the bag, and after turning around, made a slow jog back to first base. Pop was clapping his hands, and he had a broad smile on his face, like his own daughter had just taken her first step. His eyes twinkled, and he gave her a pat on her back as she stepped on the bag. "Nice hit, kid. That was solid."

"Thanks, Pop. It felt good."

Pop, dressed in full uniform, had his hat pulled intently down to shade his eyes. His pushed his hat back on his head a little, then took a few steps back and assumed his coaching position. "Okay, we got nobody out," he said. "Check your signs."

Casey nodded as she looked over to the third base coach, who started going through the signs. She watched closely as he made a few meaningless gestures meant to throw off the other team, then touched the bill of his hat. That was the indicator saying that now the gestures he made would include the real signs. He made a few more gestures, then touched one finger to his chin. This was the signal to the base runner that they had the green light to steal, and the signal to the batter that he should let the base runner attempt to steal until he had one strike.

Casey slowly took a few steps off the bag, watching the pitcher closely. Harrison now changed his windup to go from the stretch, and Casey took one more step towards second base. She was now about six feet from the bag, just far enough that, if she had to, she could take one step and then dive into the bag and reach it with one hand extended.

Harrison had taken the signal from the catcher, and he first looked towards home plate, then over at Casey. He looked back at home plate and kicked his leg high like he was going to throw home, but he stepped towards first base and threw the ball over to the first baseman, who was holding Casey on.

"Back!" Pop yelled to Casey, as he had picked up on the fact that the pitcher was throwing over to first instead of to home. But it wasn't necessary, as Casey had already picked up the signal a second earlier and shuffled safely back to first.

The first baseman returned the ball to the pitcher as Casey took another lead. Harrison went into his stretch again, looking over at Casey and then at home plate. *Come on pal, drop the arm, drop the arm*, Casey muttered to herself, as she watched him closely. Again, the pitcher gave the high leg kick, and this time, he dropped his arm low and behind him, giving Casey her signal that he was throwing home. She broke for second as soon as she saw it.

"She's going!" the first baseman yelled in to the catcher. The ball was high and outside, and James Johnson took the pitch for "Ball One". The catcher sprang up from his crouching position and fired the ball down to second, where Casey was just beginning her slide. It was close, but she beat the throw by a split second, with the umpire spreading his hands out with his palms down, calling Casey safe.

The crowd cheered as Casey dusted herself off. Now, there was some pressure on the defense, as the Power had a runner on second with nobody out. Casey checked the third base coach for the next set of signs, and saw that he gave the signal for a bunt, wanting Johnson to bunt Casey down to third.

As the pitcher wound up and delivered the pitch, Johnson went into a bunting position, as Casey went about a third of the way towards third. She saw the bat connect with the ball, but also saw that Johnson did not square around properly, and he popped the ball up to the pitcher. Seeing this, Casey reversed her direction and sprinted back to second, as the pitcher wheeled around and pegged the ball to the shortstop covering second. Casey beat the throw to the bag, and was safe, but now they had one out.

The number two batter, Bobby Turner, popped up to the third baseman, and Casey was in danger of being stranded on second base. Two outs, and up to the plate came the third baseman, Scott Wilson. The first pitch was a high fastball and "Stud" jumped all over it, hitting the ball high and long to left center field. With two outs, Casey was off at the crack of the bat, but could tell by the sound that it was going to go a long way. She looked over her right shoulder just in time to see the ball sail over the fence for a home run.

Up in the press box, Stan Marx made the call. "Harrison set to deliver the first pitch to Wilson, with two out and a runner on second. He winds up, delivers a high fastball. Wilson swings, and he hits it deep! Conners, the left fielder going back, back, back. Hasta La Baseball Baby! It's a two-run home run for Scott Wilson, his tenth of the year. The Power leads it two to zero."

Stan's partner, Gunner Thomas, spoke up, "Wow, Wilson really got all of that one, Stan. He jumped on the first pitch from Harrison and drilled it right over the left center fence. For a minute there, I thought we were going swimming."

Stan replied, "Well, it would have meant a free year's lease of a Mitzua Motors EX 5000 for Mary Simpson, who predicted that a Power player would hit the fountain in tonight's game. Unfortunately for Mary, she doesn't get the car, but the Power leads it two to zero nonetheless."

Down on the field, the players were standing at the top of the dugout to meet Wilson and congratulate him on his home run. Casey crossed the plate and took a high five from the on-deck batter, then turned around to greet Wilson. She gave him a high five as he crossed the plate, and said "Nice hit, Stud."

"Thanks," he replied. "Way to be on base." He trotted past Casey on his way to the dugout, where Butch Morris was waiting at the top of the dugout to greet him. He was clapping his hands and nodding his head.

"Nice stroke, big fella. That's just what we needed." He gave Wilson a big smack on the butt as he walked by. Casey was trailing Wilson, and was the last to get to the dugout. Morris clapped his hands a couple of times as he looked at Casey. "Good job, Collins. Way to get on," he said.

"Thanks, Skip," she said as she walked by. Then, without thinking, Morris gave her a big smack on the butt, just like he had done with Wilson. A soon as he did it, a look of panic came over his face, like he had just done something horribly wrong. He was about to mutter an apology when Casey noticed the look on his face and laughed.

"Relax, Skip. I'm just one of the guys, okay?"

Morris still looked uncomfortable, and muttered a faint, "Uh, sure. Right." He quickly turned his attention back to the field.

Casey felt great as she walked through the dugout and took a seat on the far end. *One inning doesn't make a turnaround,* she told herself, *but it's a start. I just need to keep it up.*

After flying out to the left fielder in the fifth inning, Casey came up again in the bottom of the seventh. There were two outs when she came up, and nobody on base. The infielders were playing back at their normal depths, and Casey took notice of this as she surveyed the field.

On the very first pitch, a fastball on the inside corner, Casey broke out of her stance and executed a perfect drag bunt down the first base line. The first baseman was caught completely by surprise, and realized he couldn't possibly field the ball and throw Casey out. He stood there watching the ball roll down the line, hoping that it would go foul. It didn't, and Casey was on board with her second hit of the game.

Pop was at his coaching position, and again congratulated her as she took her place on first base. "Perfect bunt!" he exclaimed. "Perfect!"

"Yeah, nice bunt," the first baseman echoed with a frown.

"Thanks," Casey replied.

She took her lead off of first, and once again, two pitches later, saw the signal that the pitcher was going home. She stole second easily, and called time out to brush herself off. Butch Morris was right. Harrison was definitely telegraphing his moves to home plate.

Like taking candy from a baby, Casey smiled to herself as she took another lead off of second. On the very next pitch, she took the candy again and slid in safely to third base. The catcher, caught by surprise, threw the ball high and wide, and the third baseman had no chance. On the next pitch, James Johnson hit a sharp single over the first baseman's head, and Casey scored the Power's third run.

In the top of the eighth inning, Butch Morris pulled the Turk out of the game with one out and a runner on first, and brought in Mooch Moran. Mooch jogged in from the bullpen to choruses of *"Moooooch"* from the fans, and on the second pitch, got the batter to hit into a double play to end the inning.

The Power didn't score in their half of the eighth, and Mooch Moran prepared to take the mound for the ninth, with the Power leading 3-0. As he grabbed his glove and started walking out of the dugout, the players voiced their encouragement.

"C'mon, Mooch, do your thing," Casey winked at him.

"Nothing but strikes, dude," Grunt said, as he laced up his shin guards and grabbed his catcher's mask.

"You're the man, Mooch," Crush Davis added.

"Come on, Moran, preserve my shutout," Turk Roberts said selfishly.

Mooch fidgeted with his hat a little as he took the mound, and struck out the first batter on three pitches. Then he got into trouble, walking the next two batters and bringing the tying run to the plate for the Cowboys. One out and runners on first and second.

Turk Roberts paced in the dugout, his face twisted in anger. "What the hell is he doing out there?" he raved. The rest of the players in the dugout ignored him, as did the coaches. Pop chose, instead, to shout encouragement out to the mound. "Come on, Mooch, bear down now, you can do it."

Mooch got the next batter on a foul-out to Eric Davis, and then struck out the final batter to end the game, preserving the win and Turk Robert's precious shutout. Mooch had wavered a little, but he got the job done.

Later, during the post-game wrap-up, Stan Marx was commenting to his partner, "Well, the Power pick up a full game on Calgary as they go on to win three to zero behind the strong pitching of Dale Roberts, and a shaky but scoreless performance by Michael Moran. And how about Casey Collins, Gunner?" he said. "It looks like she turned things around a bit tonight with two hits, and she had three stolen bases, giving her four for the year. Is that all just a matter of speed?"

"Well, not completely, Stan," Gunner answered. "Speed has a lot to do with it, of course, but just as importantly, the runner has to be able to read the pitcher's moves in order to get a good jump. I don't know for sure, but I'd have to guess that Collins picked up on something tonight, and used it to her advantage."

"What would that be?"

"Well, it could be a number of things. It could be in the way Harrison was kicking his leg, or how he's turning his head. I did notice that he seems to be dropping his left hand very low when he goes to the plate. I'm just speculating, but it could be something like that."

Stan continued the query. "Boy, you would think the Calgary pitching staff would have picked up on that and tried to fix it."

"Well, they probably have, Stan. I'm sure they're working with him on it. But remember, that's why they have the minor leagues –– to prepare the players to play in the majors."

"Good insight as always from my partner, Gunner Thompson. Well, folks, we're just about out of time. We'll be back tomorrow night for the second game in the series between the Portland Power and the Calgary Cowboys. For Gunner Thompson, Suzanne Miller and all of us here at KSPT, I'm Stan Marx saying good night, and good baseball."

The next morning, when Casey read the newspaper, she was greeted with a much better headline than her last one:

Portland Takes First Game from Calgary; Collins Contributes

Last night the Portland Power took on the Calgary Cowboys at the Powerhouse, and the Power got off to a good start, winning the first game of the series, 3 to 0. Power Pitcher Dale Roberts got his fourth victory of the year, and got offensive help from third baseman Scott Wilson, who hit a two-run home run in the third inning.

Right fielder Casey Collins, who had been struggling offensively since she joined the Power, turned in a strong performance, going 2 for 4 with 3 stolen bases, and scoring two of the Power's 3 runs. She also contributed defensively, making a smart backup play in the outfield that saved a possible run, and a diving catch in the fifth on another ball hit into the gap in right-center.

When asked after the game if this was the turnaround point for her, Collins replied, "Well, this was only one game. I'm just happy I was able to help the team any way I could. We're still in third place, and we just need to concentrate on the game tomorrow night."

On a related issue, Power team owner Bud Harley announced that the team would be erecting chain-link fences around the team entrance to the stadium, in response to a situation that occurred before the game. Apparently, some over-zealous fans seeking autographs had surrounded Ms. Collins, and Mr. Harley expressed concern for her safety.

"We understand that many people are anxious to see Casey Collins, but her safety and that of the team comes first. She will still be signing autographs before the games, and she has agreed to arrive to the ballpark early to give fans every opportunity to see her. We just wanted to put up these fences as a precautionary measure."

Casey folded the paper and put in back on the table. No one had asked her to come out to the stadium early, although that was no big deal. She suspected that Bud Harley was using this as another publicity play, but she did feel a little better knowing that the fences would be there as a buffer from the fans. She had never really felt threatened, but it made her feel a little better just the same.

More importantly, she had finally contributed, and could hold her head a little higher. As she had commented to the reporter who had asked her the question, it was only one game, but she did feel like it was the start of a turnaround.

Sitting in his apartment five floors above Casey, Turk Roberts slammed the newspaper paper shut and threw it on the floor. *The bitch is stealing my headlines*, he cursed to himself. *No one asked me for any comments. I go 7 1/2 innings, strike out nine batters, and all they can talk about is how she gets a couple of hits. It's bad enough that I'm still stuck in this damn league, without her stealing my press. Something definitely has to be done about this.*

A few days later, during a game against the Phoenix Vipers, the Power had just shut down the Vipers in the bottom half of the second, and the players jogged in to the dugout for their turn at bat. Casey was scheduled to bat second in the inning, behind Julio Perez, who was already making his way to the plate.

But when she prepared to head out to the on-deck circle for her first at bat, she encountered a problem. She went to grab her bat out of the bat rack at the front end of the dugout, but it wasn't in its normal slot. She looked at the two adjoining slots to see if she misplaced it by mistake, but they were filled with other player's bats. Feeling concerned, she quickly went down to the end of the bench where her bag was sitting, to grab her backup bat. But it wasn't there either. *What is this? I just used my bat in batting practice thirty minutes ago.*

By then, Perez had just hit a double, and the umpire was calling for the next batter. She had to hurriedly grab another bat from the rack, and was too frazzled to notice that Turk Roberts was grinning to himself.

Every professional baseball player had their own bat, in fact, usually more than one, weighted and sized exactly to how they wanted it. With hitting being such an exact science, anything that threw off their timing could drastically affect a hitter's performance at the plate. Taking a player's bat away from them was equivalent to breaking one of their arms, and it was a dirty trick.

Casey tried to shake it off as she hurried out to the plate, with Perez standing out on second base. The signal from the third base coach was for a sacrifice bunt, and she was thankful that she only had to place the bat in front of the ball, and not worry about timing a full swing with a new bat. She took a strike before laying down a perfect sacrifice bunt.

The next inning, after the Power had retired the Vipers in order, Casey rustled through the dugout looking for her bats. She finally found them at one end of the bench, lying down against the wall and hidden under the ball bags. There was no way they got there on their own, and it was obvious that someone had intentionally hidden them. She knew instinctively who it was, and she glared at Turk, who smirked at her as if to say, *You got something to say to me?* Not wanting to start something in the middle of a game, Casey let it go, but filed it in her memory as something that had to be dealt with.

Twenty

Two weeks later, Casey was sitting on the end of the bench after an afternoon game with the Fresno Bears. The Power had won the game, and she had performed well, going 2 for 5 with a stolen base. She should have been in a good mood, but something was gnawing at her.

She had completed her first full month with the Power, and her performance had improved considerably. Her batting average was rising almost every day, and she was now up to .281. She was playing well in the field and was now a contributing and important member of the Portland Power.

But something was causing her not to feel like part of the team. She couldn't quite put her finger on it, but she felt like she wasn't completely accepted by her teammates. Most of the players were cordial enough, with some notable exceptions, but other than Mooch, Grunt and Eric Davis, she really hadn't made a lot of friends on the team.

It was a combination of a lot of little things. The separate locker room situation at home contributed to her feeling of alienation, and some of the players still complained when they were on the road that they had to wait for Casey to shower. She also knew that many of the players often went out for drinks and didn't invite her. Several times, she had come upon a small group and they stopped talking and broke up when she approached. Not quite ostracized, yet not quite accepted, either.

She was reflecting on this when Pop came over, sat down beside her and said, "Hey, what's on your mind, Casey?"

"Oh, nothing," she responded with a sigh.

Pop smacked her lightly on one leg and said, "Ah, come on, girl, I can tell something's bothering you. What is it?"

Good old Pop, Casey thought as she looked at him. *Can't get anything by him.*

"Oh, I don't know," Casey started, as she looked down at the dirt. "I'm just not feeling like part of the team too much. I can't explain it, really. It's just a feeling, like I don't really belong."

Pop smiled, his eyes crinkling as he looked at her. "Well, look," he said, "I think that's to be expected. I mean, if you think about it, these guys played half the season without you, and then you join amidst all this publicity and everything. Plus, it's the first time any of them have played with a woman. I'm not surprised if they are a little slow in accepting you."

"I know, but I've been here a month now, and I've been playing fairly well, haven't I?" Casey looked at him for approval.

"You've been playing great," Pop said. "No doubt about that. Even Skip is happy with your play, and that's saying something. But, hey, if you want, I'll say something to the guys, but I think you just need to give it some more time."

Casey gave Pop's hand a light squeeze and said, "No, don't say anything to them, please. I'll take care of it. But I appreciate the talk, Pop, as always. Thanks."

Pop stood up and said, "Anytime. Don't mention it." He turned and headed towards the locker room tunnel.

Casey sat there contemplating Pop's words. *He's probably right*, she thought, but she didn't feel comfortable just letting things take their natural course. She felt like she didn't have that much time. They were three quarters of the way through the season, and who knew what was going to happen once the season was over? Even though she had been playing well, maybe next year they would decide that she didn't fit into their plans. They were approaching the playoffs, and she wanted to be able to focus on her performance and prove her worth to the team.

She felt like she had to make some kind of statement, and as she walked by the men's locker room and heard the voices coming from within, she bit her lip, and decided what she was going to do.

Several of the players were in the shower room, laughing and joking with each other, when Darnell Jenkins turned toward the entrance of the shower, and froze. The other players followed his gaze, and the entire shower room suddenly went silent as they stared at the entrance of the shower.

Casey stood there naked, as jaws dropped. She walked by one of the players who was holding a bar of soap and grabbed it out of his hands, then continued on over to an open showerhead, turned on the water, and started to shower like nothing was out of the ordinary.

As she let the water run over her body, she turned and confronted the group, which was still staring at her in amazement. "What, you guys got a problem?" she asked. "Am I part of this team or not?"

One of the stunned players managed to utter a few words. "Uh, yeah, sure, I suppose so." A few of the others managed to mumble various forms of agreement.

"Then, what's the problem?" she asked again, looking them in the eye.

"Nothing," a few of them muttered, as she turned around and went back to showering. Gradually, they also went back to showering. After Casey thought enough time had passed, she turned off the shower nozzle and started to walk out of the shower, grabbing her towel off the rack by the door. She calmly wrapped it around her body and walked out of the locker room and back to her private room.

She closed the door and plumped down on her bench. Her heart was racing at what seemed like a thousand beats per minute. She had *never* done anything like that before, but although she had been terrified, she refused to let it show. And ten big, macho men had all backed down. It worked. She smirked as she though about what she just had done.

It wasn't a sexual encounter; it was a declaration of rights. She was not asking to be accepted; she was telling them she belonged. *Sometimes you just have to make a statement.*

The next day, after she dressed for the game, Casey was a little later than usual in getting out to the dugout, and most of the players had already assembled. As she entered the dugout, everyone looked up at her, and five players jumped out of their seat to make room for her.

Later, as they were running out to take the field for the start of the game, James Johnson, the center fielder, jogged alongside Casey as they headed out to the outfield. "Hey, what you did yesterday. That was something. It took guts."

"Yeah, well, don't get used to it," she said jokingly in return. *Men*, she laughed to herself. *They were so easy.*

Twenty-One

Early one afternoon the following week, Casey was making herself a sandwich before getting ready for that night's game. It was the last game of a three-game series with the Spokane Steam, and the Power had won the first two games. She finished making her sandwich, grabbed a Diet Coke from the refrigerator, and plunked down on the easy chair in the living room. She opened the *Portland Times* to the sports section, spread it out on the coffee table, and went immediately to the standings page.

PACIFIC COAST LEAGUE STANDINGS

NORTHERN DIVISION	W	L	PCT.	Games Behind
Calgary Cowboys	65	65	.500	----
Portland Power	65	65	.500	----
Spokane Steam	62	68	.478	3
Vancouver Lions	60	70	.462	5

SOUTHERN DIVISION	W	L	PCT.	Games Behind
Sacramento Sting	70	60	.538	----
Phoenix Vipers	62	68	.480	8
Las Vegas Gamblers	60	70	.462	10
Fresno Bears	59	71	.454	11

CENTRAL DIVISION	W	L	PCT.	Games Behind
Omaha Chiefs	68	62	.523	----
Salt Lake Racers	64	66	.492	4
Colorado Pioneers	62	68	.477	6
Iowa Blizzard	61	69	.469	7

EASTERN DIVISION	W	L	PCT.	Games Behind
Memphis Hawks	68	62	.523	----
Orlando Sharks	68	62	.523	----
Oklahoma Thunder	62	68	.477	6
Birmingham Bulls	60	70	.462	8

It was now August 15, and she had been with the team for about six weeks. The Power had made significant headway since she first joined. They had now pulled even with Calgary, with a couple of weeks still remaining in the regular season. Whichever team won the division would face the winner of the Eastern Division in the semifinals of the League Championship. Casey took a sip of her Diet Coke as she continued to study the standings.

It was a toss-up between Memphis and Orlando for the Eastern Division title, but it looked like it would most likely be Sacramento and Omaha in one of the semifinal series.

The winners of the two semifinal series would then go on to play each other in a best-of-five League Championship Series, starting September 1.

Casey flipped to the Portland Power Team Statistics section, and reviewed her personal stats. She had raised her batting average to .289. Not great, but respectable. And although the chart in the paper didn't show it, Casey knew that about one-third of her hits were infield hits. She continued to put pressure on the defense, which was one reason why Butch Morris had moved her up to bat seventh in the line-up. But the one statistic she was most proud of was not the fact that she had 15 stolen bases, but that she had 15 stolen bases in 15 attempts. She had not been caught once.

She paused briefly to reflect, attributing her success at stealing bases to her father Rip. Not so much to the many hours of practice in the backyard, and not so much to him teaching her the various signs to look for. It was more the way that he always taught her to look for her own angle –– any edge she could get that would tip her off as to when a pitcher was going to throw to home plate.

And she had found one. One that she was sure no one else knew about. She discovered it in a pickup game way back in junior high school, on a hot summer day when the guys she was playing with weren't wearing any shirts. It was the reason she was 15 for 15, and, she thought, was probably the major reason why she had made it to where she was today. So far, she had kept it a secret.

She finished her sandwich, grabbed her athletic bag from the hallway, and left for the stadium. After going through the now familiar routine of signing autographs, answering a few questions from a newspaper reporter, and getting dressed for the game, Casey was reading the line-up card which was posted outside Butch Morris's office.

It was the last game of the series with the Spokane Steam, and Morris had told her he was probably going to move her up in the line-up to bat behind Grunt. Grunt had been hitting well lately, and Morris wanted Casey behind him so she could bunt him along if he got on. The line-up card confirmed that Morris had, in fact, made the move.

It wasn't that big of an adjustment for her, and in the second inning, with Grunt on second base, she laid down a perfect sacrifice bunt to the third baseman, making him field the ball, and enabling Grunt to move to third. He then scored on a deep sacrifice fly by Crush Davis, and it had given the Power a one-run lead.

It was now the bottom of the seventh inning, with Portland leading 3-0, and the Steam had just completed their turn at bat.

As the two teams were changing positions in between innings, the center field scoreboard was showing a film clip that had become very popular among Power fans. It was a scene from a 1960s-era science fiction movie, and it featured a mad scientist dressed in a white lab coat hovering over an operating table. As the scientist was trying to bring the creature on the table to life, he turned his face to the camera and commanded, "MORE POWER! WE NEED MORE POWER!"

As the fans started cheering the clip, the scoreboard graphics took over. The screen transformed into a colorful gauge that looked like a big thermometer. A line representing the power level started at the bottom section of the thermometer. The line gradually started rising out of the bottom section, which was colored yellow, into the next section, which was colored green. As the bottom of the screen flashed the words "MORE POWER!" in silver glitter, the gauge rose out of the green section to the top section of the thermometer, which was colored red.

But instead of stopping at the top of the thermometer, the line pushed at the very top, as the thermometer starting shaking back and forth, until the top finally exploded as the line burst through. The entire scoreboard then erupted into one large MORE POWER! sign in silver glitter. It was another Bud Harley idea, and it always seemed to get the crowd going.

Tonight was no different. The crowd was still cheering as Jason "Grunt" Taylor walked out of the dugout on his way to the plate. As the on-deck batter, Casey was right behind him.

"Come on, Grunt, get us started," she said to him as he made his way to the plate.

Grunt was having a great game so far. Not only had he thrown out two base runners tonight, he was two for two at the plate. In the second inning, he hit a double off the wall in right center field. In the fourth inning, the pitcher had brushed him back with a pitch high and inside, and Grunt responded by hitting the next pitch over the left field wall for a two-run home run.

Now the pitcher glared at Grunt as he made his way to the batter's box, pushing his batting helmet firmly down on his head. He paused, tightened up each of his batting gloves, then took a firm grasp of the bat as he stepped into the box.

Casey watched from the on-deck circle as the pitcher wound up and proceeded to throw a fastball right at Grunt's midsection. Grunt started to back away from the plate, but then realized he could not avoid the pitch. He dropped his left arm to protect his ribs, as the ball slammed into his elbow. The crowd let out a collective "Ugh!" as they imagined the pain that Grunt must have felt.

Stung, Grunt dropped his bat and squared around to face the pitcher, his temper flaring. Casey, standing in the on-deck circle, saw what was in his eyes.

"No, Grunt. Don't!" Casey warned, but it was too late. Grunt ran directly at the pitcher, as the pitcher threw down his glove and prepared for the attack. The catcher raced after Grunt as the stunned crowd looked on.

By instinct, the players in both dugouts prepared to file out and rush on to the field. But the coaches from both teams, well aware of league president Huey Jacobs' penalties, stood at the top of their respective dugouts and blocked the players from rushing to the field.

Butch Morris, standing at the top of the Power dugout, held out his hand in a "halt" position. He issued a one-word command to his players: "Don't."

Grunt had reached the pitcher by now and had tackled him by placing his face in his chest and driving him backwards off the mound. The two rolled around in the dirt at the back of the mound, each trying to establish a superior position, as the catcher arrived two seconds later. The Spokane infielders, seeing Grunt attack their pitcher, all rushed towards the mound and pounced on him.

Grunt was badly outnumbered as the catcher grabbed him and pinned both of his arms behind his back. The shortstop was holding his legs down as the pitcher positioned himself on one knee over Grunt. "Hold him still!" he commanded as he raised a fist high in the air, preparing to drive it into Grunt's face.

Totally helpless, Grunt cringed as he prepared for the blow. As the pitcher's hand started to come forward to deliver the punch, Casey Collins came flying into the pile. She hit the pitcher broadside with a cross body block, knocking him backwards three feet and taking the catcher with them. The pitcher rolled over a couple of times, and ended up on top of Casey. Shocked, he tried to hold her down as she struggled against his superior weight.

As this was happening, Casey thought she heard a large "Boooo" coming from the crowd. But it was actually "Mooooch," as Mike Moran had raced in from the bullpen bench to join in the fray. As he approached the mound, he was swinging wildly and yelling, "Leave her alone, you assholes!"

By this time, the other Power players had overrun the coaches, ignoring their admonitions, and swarmed out on to the field to help their teammates. The Spokane players had done the same, and now the entire infield was one big melee.

In the midst of it all, Casey was pinned beneath a pile of players, some from Portland and some from Spokane. In the scramble, one of the player's knees connected solidly with the side of Casey's head, and she blacked out.

Twenty-Two

It was early the next afternoon, and Casey awoke in her hospital bed to find a middle-aged nurse standing over her, holding a clipboard and looking at her chart. As Casey struggled to regain consciousness, she became aware of how sore she was. Her head was pounding and it felt like someone was sitting on her chest.

Her head was propped up on some pillows, and her hands were folded over each other and resting on her stomach. She reached up to her chest with one hand to see what was restraining her breathing, and discovered that she was wrapped in gauze and tape. She was feeling around to see how much of her was covered when the nurse noticed that she had awakened.

"Well, hello there, Miss Collins," she said as she looked up from her clipboard. "Glad to see you're awake. How are you feeling?"

Casey tried to lift her head, but it started to throb so she let it fall back on the pillow. "I feel lousy," she said. "What happened?"

"Well, it seems like you got yourself a nice little concussion and three bruised ribs."

The previous night's events gradually started to come back to Casey. The brawl on the field, the trip to the hospital. "How long have I been here?"

The nurse placed her clipboard into a plastic holder at the foot of Casey's bed, and walked over to a small night table by Casey's side. "They brought you in last night, along with two other players. I'll tell you, you sure looked a sight, bleeding from your head, with your uniform all torn."

It was only then that Casey noticed that her head was also wrapped in a bandage. She raised a hand to feel around the bandage. "Wow, how bad is it?" she asked with a concerned look.

The nurse had picked up a small paper cup filled with water and two blue pills from the night table. "Oh, relax, dear, it's not that bad. It was a mild concussion. You had a nice little gash on your head that required a few stitches, but it was above the hairline so you won't see a scar or anything. The stitches will dissolve in a couple of days. She handed Casey the pills and the paper cup of water. "Here, take these," she instructed.

Casey took the cup of water and eyed the pills. "What are these?"

"One's a painkiller and the other's a mild sedative to help you sleep. Go ahead, dear, drink up."

Casey put the pills in her mouth, washed them down with the water, and handed the paper cup back to the nurse. "How long do I have to stay here?" she asked.

The nurse tossed the paper cup into a small wastebasket in the corner. She looked at her watch while she held Casey's wrist, checking her pulse. "You should be able to leave tomorrow. The doctor just wants to keep you one more night. You'll be sore for a few days but within a week, you should be fine."

"A week?" Casey asked in dismay as she made an effort to get up, but again the tightness around her chest and her aching head caused her to fall back on the pillow. "But we're playing Calgary tonight and…"

The nurse interrupted as she tucked the sheet in close around Casey's side. "Now, now, we'll have none of that. You're not going anywhere tonight. You just relax and get better and let the rest of those things take care of themselves."

"But…" Casey started to object again when there was a knock on the door. The nurse walked over to see who it was, and then took a step out into the hallway. Casey heard her say, "But visiting hours don't start for two more hours yet, and I just gave her a sleeping pill."

The other person apparently objected, and there was a few more minutes of conversation, which Casey couldn't quite make out. Finally, she saw the nurse step backwards into the doorway and heard her say, "Oh, all right, but keep it short. You've got ten minutes."

Casey saw Mooch walk through the doorway, sporting a purplish bruise under his left eye, swinging one arm by his side and holding the other behind his back. "Hey, tough guy," he said with a smile as he walked over to the side of the bed. "How are you doing?"

Casey's face brightened. "Mooch, what are you doing here?"

"What do you think?" he asked. "I came to see you. And to bring you this." He brought his hand around to the front and Casey saw that he was holding an empty flower vase.

She sat up a little in her bed, wincing at the pain that it caused. "You brought me an empty vase?" she asked.

A large grin came over Mooch's face. "Well, not exactly," he said. He turned to the door, put two fingers to his mouth, and let out a low whistle, causing the nurse to frown. Casey looked on in astonishment as one by one, the members of the *Portland Power* filed through the doorway. Each of them was carrying a single rose.

"Oh," Casey sighed as her eyes started to well up. "That's so sweet. I can't believe it."

Mooched smiled and said, "Well, I couldn't very well carry all those flowers by myself." He set the flower vase on the table as each player walked up and added his flower, then took a place around Casey's bed.

James Johnson placed his flower in the vase and came over to the side of the bed. "Uh, look, Casey," he muttered. "We all sort of realized that we've been treating you like crap since you got here, and we just wanted to say we're sorry."

"Oh, you just realized that, did you?" Casey asked mockingly.

"Hey, we're a little slow sometimes," Stud Wilson joked.

"Speak for yourself," Julio Perez chuckled, as he elbowed Wilson in the ribs.

Casey looked around the room, and saw that Jason Taylor wasn't there. "How's Grunt?" she asked.

TJ Morrison, one of the starting pitchers, answered. "He's got a broken nose. Funny thing is, we think it was Mooch that hit him. Hey, Mooch man, you swing like a girl." Then, looking at Casey, he quickly added, "Oh, sorry."

Casey laughed again. "No, that's okay. He does swing like a girl."

"And he runs like one, too," James Johnson chimed in.

The guys erupted in laughter, as Mooch accepted the good-natured ribbing. He spread his hands and pretended like he was insulted. "Hey, what did I do?"

Then, Darnell Jenkins, dressed all in black, walked up to Casey. "Hey, seriously, girl, what you did last night took real guts. I'd go to war with you anytime." He stuck out his clenched fist towards Casey and she responded by touching her fist to his. A show of solidarity.

"Yeah, anytime," several of them echoed.

"And you probably saved Grunt's life," Crush Davis said. "Although, we're not sure that's a good thing."

Casey grinned as she changed the subject. "So, who's going to play right field tonight?" she asked.

Mooch spoke up. "Oh, yeah, you probably haven't heard. There was a fight in Omaha last night also, and Huey Jacobs suspended the season for one week. We don't play now until next Tuesday night."

"Wow," she said. "That's drastic." Then her face brightened as she realized that it meant she probably wouldn't have to miss any games.

The nurse had been standing over by the wall, taking this all in, and she interrupted. "All right, gentlemen," she said officially. "We need to wrap this up. Miss Collins needs to get some rest."

Casey said, "Hey, thanks for coming, guys. This really meant a lot to me. And thanks for the flowers."

The players had surrounded the bed. One by one, they said their goodbyes, each touching fists with Casey and wishing her a fast recovery. Mooch was the last to leave, and Casey took his hand.

"Thanks, Mooch," she said as she looked into his eyes. "I know this was your idea."

Mooch smiled back at her. "Ah, it was all of our idea. I just happened to get the flowers."

Casey knew better but let it slide. "Well, thanks anyway."

"Don't mention it," Mooch replied. "But I guess I should go. Take care and get well soon, and I'll call you tomorrow." He bent over and gave her a kiss on the cheek, then turned and walked towards the door. "First time I ever kissed another ballplayer," he joked over his shoulder, as he disappeared into the hallway.

After the nurse finished ushering everyone out the door, she took a minute to arrange things. "Well, you sure are a lucky lady to have so many friends," she said.

The sleeping pill was starting to take effect, and Casey's eyes started to close. "They're more than my friends," she muttered. "They're my teammates."

The nurse tucked the sheets in around Casey, turned out the lights, and started to leave the room. Before she closed the door, she turned around and took a final look at Casey, and noticed that she had a slight grin on her face as she dozed off to sleep.

Casey slept straight through until the next morning, when the sunlight coming through the window woke her up around six o'clock. A doctor came in a little after that, and following a brief examination, cleared her for release. He gave her a prescription for some painkillers for her ribs, and gave her instructions for their use.

Hospital policy stated that anyone who checked in for at least one night's stay had to be escorted out in a wheelchair. Although Casey was still pretty sore around her rib area, she felt she could walk, but reluctantly accepted the wheelchair ride to the lobby.

Anne Ross had called earlier to check on Casey and offer her a ride home from the hospital, which Casey accepted. She was waiting in the lobby when the elevator door opened and Casey was wheeled out by the nurse.

Anne rose from the chair on which she was sitting, and came over to greet Casey as she was being wheeled into the lobby. She gasped as she saw how Casey looked—with a large bruise under her right eye and the bandages around her ribs showing under her shirt. "My God!" she exclaimed. "Look at you. You look like you've been through a war."

"Yeah, that's about how I feel." Casey put both hands on the armrest and let out a small grunt as she struggled to get out of the wheelchair.

Anne put a hand on the back of her arm to help her up. "So, how *do* you feel?" she asked with concern.

"Oh, I'm all right," Casey answered. "I just had a mild concussion, which has cleared up, and some bruised ribs, which are still pretty sore. I just need to go home and rest for a while."

Anne escorted Casey out to the parking lot, and again held her arm as she slowly got into the car. As they were driving to the Riverside apartments, Casey told Anne how her teammates had come to visit her, and about the flowers.

"Was that Mooch's idea?" Anne asked as she looked over at Casey sitting in the passenger's seat.

Casey returned the look. "Yeah, how'd you know?"

"He has a thing for you, doesn't he?" Anne said, as a smile crossed her lips.

"I told you, I don't date baseball players," Casey countered. But she also was smiling.

"Yeah, right," Anne laughed as she turned the car onto West Burnside street. "Besides, I don't see anything wrong with it. Mooch is a nice guy. A little weird and quirky, and I don't know why he can't figure out how to get his baseball hat on straight. But he's not like most of the other ego machines walking around here."

Casey shifted slightly in her seat to face Anne more directly, which caused her to grimace as her rib cage tightened. "I know, he really is a nice guy, and he seems to be interested in me as a person, and not just some freak woman baseball player."

Anne smiled, "Casey, you're not a freak."

"I know, I know," Casey said with a wave of the hand. "It's just that I've always had to be extra careful because of my situation. Dating a guy on my own team is just asking for problems."

"Well, it's not like you guys are having sex in the locker room or anything." Then she narrowed her brow as she faked a serious look. "You're not, are you?"

"No, of course not," Casey chuckled. "I mean we haven't even...well, you know..."

"Hit a home run?" Anne said, causing them both to burst out in laughter. Casey had to hold her ribs with both hands to keep them from hurting. They were both still laughing as Anne pulled the car into the apartment parking lot, found a space, and pulled in.

As they got out of the car—Casey with a little more effort—they walked around the back to the trunk where Anne had put Casey's bag. As she handed the bag to Casey she said, "You know, Casey, it's really none of my business, but if you like the guy I say go for it."

Casey took the bag from Anne. "Easy for you to say, lady. You don't have to deal with the consequences." Then, with a smirk, she said, "But I'll give your recommendation some serious consideration."

They gave each other a brief hug as Casey thanked Anne for the ride and made her way back to her apartment. She called her mother to see if she heard about the fight, and to tell her she was okay. But good old Pop, again, had thought ahead and called Sue the night before to tell her that her daughter was bruised but would be all right.

Casey took a couple of the painkillers that the doctor had prescribed, and washed them down with a glass of water. Feeling very sore, she crawled into bed and pulled the covers over her. Lying in bed, she reviewed the conversation with Anne regarding Mooch.

She didn't quite know what she was going to do yet. She was falling for him, and she thought it funny that out of all the studly guys she had met during her travels, she felt herself attracted to a guy who definitely wasn't. It seemed wrong, but it felt right. She was still pondering the issue when she drifted off to sleep.

Twenty-Three

Casey spent the next couple of days resting, and her soreness was gradually subsiding. With four days still left until the season resumed, the players had some free time on their hands. It was late Wednesday afternoon, and she was sitting on the couch watching the news when there was a knock on her door.

She got up from the couch, went over to open the door, and saw that it was Mooch. "Oh, hey, Mooch," she said as she swung the door open. "What's up?"

"Hey, Casey." Mooch looked a little uneasy, as he looked down at the ground, then tentatively up at Casey. "Uh, look, I was wondering if you wanted to go grab dinner tonight, or some drinks or something?"

Casey's face showed a slight grimace. Although she was attracted to Mooch, and had even kissed him once, she still felt that dating a teammate was too risky. "Uh, look Mooch," she said, also feeling a little awkward. "I like you. I really do. But I told you, I don't date baseball players."

Mooch tried to laugh it off. "Yeah, but I'm a relief pitcher. We don't really count." Casey laughed, and Mooch continued. "Besides, it's not really a date. We can just grab some dinner or something. So, what do you say?"

Hmmn, what do I say? Casey thought to herself, as she looked at Mooch. *He's so funny, and he was such a sweetheart bringing me those flowers, and pitching to me and everything.* The alarm bells in her head were going off, telling her to close the door, literally and figuratively, and put an end to it right there. But instead she responded, "Oh, all right. Give me and hour and I'll meet you in the lobby."

"Cool. See you then."

Casey closed the door, so she didn't see Mooch skipping back to his room. Sixty minutes later, he was waiting in the lobby when the elevator door opened up and Casey walked out. She was wearing black dress pants with black heels, and a white V-neck top, and she was clutching a small black purse.

Mooch beamed as she walked over to him. "Wow," he said. "You look great."

"Thanks," she replied with a slight blush.

"Nice cleavage, too."

Casey laughed out loud. "Boy, you just say whatever's on your mind, don't you?"

Mooch laughed back, "Oh, did I say that out loud?"

As they walked out to the parking lot, Casey asked, "So where are we going?"

"Well, there's a couple of choices. There's some seafood places down by the river, and there's a great steakhouse right up the road. You choose."

"I love seafood, and I keep hearing how Portland has so many great restaurants. Let's do that."

"All right. You got it," Mooch said as they reached his car. Like most guys on a first date, he held the car door open for Casey, a routine that usually lasted until about the third date.

Since Casey was still relatively new to the Portland area, Mooch narrated as he drove, pointing out places of interest, until they arrived at McCormick and Schmick's Harborside Restaurant on SW First avenue. Mooch parked the car, opening Casey's door for her, and they went inside and got a table for two. It was a weeknight so they were able to get a table along the window, looking out at the water.

They ordered their drinks – a Full Sail beer for Mooch, and a glass of white wine for Casey. "This is nice," Casey said, looking out the window, at the water.

"Yeah, I like this place, and I love their halibut," Mooch said, taking a swig of his Full Sail.

Casey took a sip of her wine and placed her glass back on the table. She smiled. "That's funny. You don't strike me as a halibut-eating kind of guy."

"I wasn't until I got here. I was mainly a meat-and-potatoes man, but Portland has so many great seafood restaurants that I've changed my habit. And my colon really appreciates it."

Casey laughed again at his candor. "Well that's good to know, Mooch. Thanks for sharing that with me."

"No problem, I'm full of wisdom."

"Well, you're definitely full of something."

They were both chuckling when the waitress came to take their order. Casey decided to take Mooch's recommendation and ordered the halibut, and they each ordered another drink.

After their food was delivered and they were eating, Casey said, "So, isn't it right around here where one of us says something like 'Tell me a little more about yourself?'"

"Oh, yeah, I guess we should do that routine. You want to go first or you want me to?"

Casey finished a bite of her halibut and waved her fork at Mooch. "No, you go ahead. You probably know more about me than I do about you." She leaned forward and looked at him. "As a matter of fact, I'm not even sure what color eyes you have. They look sort of blue-grayish."

"I prefer to call them steely blue."

Casey chuckled, "Steely blue, huh?"

"Yeah. You know how you always read in those novels how the lead character had 'steely blue' eyes that drove the women wild?"

"That's you, huh?"

"Absolutely," Mooch said, grinning as he took another drink of beer.

"Okay, Mr. Steely Blue, what's the rest of your story?"

"Well, it's a short and boring story really. I grew up in a small farm town, Rangeville, Oklahoma – population eight hundred forty-six. My parents are farmers, still live there. They're simple people but the greatest parents in the world. They scraped and saved to put me through college, which I got through by the skin of my teeth, but got through, nonetheless. It gave me a chance to play college baseball and to get drafted. So here I am, handsome young relief pitcher for the Portland Power, in my third year."

He paused, and took another swig of his beer. "I'll tell you, though, if I ever do make it to the majors, my parents are going to have the biggest farmhouse in all of Oklahoma."

"That's not a bad story. But I do have to ask you one question?"

"Yeah, what's that?"

"What's with the whole 'hat' routine? How come you can never keep that thing on straight?"

Mooch was finishing up his last bite of halibut, and washed it down with a swig of beer. He leaned back in his chair a little and looked at Casey. "Well, to tell you the truth," he said coyly, "you're not the only one who looks for an angle."

Casey leaned forward and looked at him intently. "What, are you saying you do it intentionally?"

"Well, sure. You think I'm some kind of idiot who can't figure out how to keep his hat on straight?" Casey tilted her head slightly to one side, causing Mooch to quickly add, "Don't answer that."

Casey smiled as he continued, "Yeah, I do it on purpose. It drives batters crazy. Totally distracts them. Don't you remember how it threw you off when I was throwing to you?"

"Yeah, sure. It really *was* distracting."

"Well, there you go. That's my angle." He leaned back in his chair with a slight look of triumph.

Casey also sat back, and clapped her hands together lightly a couple of times. "Bravo," she said, an approving smile on her face. "Bravo."

Mooch nodded his head in appreciation, and did a not-too-bad Elvis impersonation. "Well, thank you. Thank you very much."

After a little more conversation, they finished their meal, with Mooch paying the check over Casey's objection, and they drove back to their apartment building.

Mooch's room was on a lower floor, so they walked to his room first. As they approached his door, Mooch said, "So, you want to come in for a drink or something?"

Casey was enjoying Mooch's company, and wasn't ready for the night to end. "Well, I might have *one* drink," she replied.

A little later, as they were sitting on the couch next to each other, both sipping a beer, Mooch finished his and got up to go to the refrigerator. He turned to Casey and said, "You want another one?"

"No, thanks," she replied. "I'm fine. Actually, I should probably get going." She rose off the couch and smoothed her pants out with her hands.

Mooch was visibly disappointed to lose her company, but said, "Oh, sure. Okay, well, I'll walk you to the door."

Casey reached the door first, and turned around to face Mooch, who was a few feet behind her. She looked at him coyly and said, "You know, Mooch, I think I might be a little too tired to make it all the way back to my apartment."

Mooch started to respond. "Oh, that's okay, you can sleep on my couch…" Then he stopped when he finally realized what she was really saying. "Oh," was all he could manage to say.

Although Mooch and Casey were not power hitters, together that night they hit a home run.

Twenty-Four

Two days later, the players were summoned to batting practice. It had been five days since the big fight, and there were two days left until the season resumed. Butch Morris wanted the team to be sharp as they tried to nail down the divisional title. The players, except for Casey, were in the locker room dressing, and the typical banter was in full swing.

Grunt Taylor was bent over a bench, lacing up his baseball spikes. Both of his cheeks were bluish purple, and he had a white plastic bandage covering his broken nose. "Did you take her home or not?" he asked Stud Wilson.

"Of course I did," Stud replied with a smug look.

"Man, she was hot," Crush Davis chimed in.

"You have no idea," Stud replied, causing chuckles from the other two.

On the other side of the locker room, Turk Roberts was talking with the two reserve players that he had taken to hanging around with. He had just removed his street clothes, including his underwear, and was pulling his jock strap out of his locker, and pulled it on. He followed that by putting his practice sweats on, and then took a seat as he prepared to put on his socks. The other two players were on either side of him, and the three were talking about what they did during the one week layoff.

One of the reserves was talking, when Turk started fidgeting. It was minor at first, as he shifted a couple of times on the bench. Then he started to pull and tug at his crotch, then wildy began scratching it.

"What the hell's the matter with you?" one of the players asked, as they both looked at Turk suspiciously.

"Ah, shit! Oh, my God, owww!" Turk screamed as he jumped up and began hopping around and frantically scratching his crotch with both hands. The entire team turned to look at him as he danced around, screaming, finally tearing off his clothes and running into the shower room.

The players howled as they heard the moans continue to echo from the shower room, as Turk desperately tried to wash away the irritation. Evidently, someone had put some sort of itching powder in Turk's jockstrap. An old practical joke, but an effective one nonetheless.

Turk remained in the shower for twenty minutes, while the rest of the players finished dressing and headed out to the field. The last one out of the locker room, other than Turk, was Mooch Moran, who paused when he reached the door. Looking around cautiously, he quickly reached into his bag and pulled out the empty can of Doctor John's Magic Itching Power, then tossed it into the trash can by the door. He laughed to himself as he joined the team on the field.

Butch Morris and Pop were discussing line-ups and strategy as they were walking through the tunnel together on their way up to the field. As they reached the dugout, they saw a small group of players huddled around the pitcher's mound, with Casey Collins in the middle.

"Hey, what's going on?" Butch muttered.

"I don't know. Let's check it out," Pop responded as the two walked towards the pitcher's mound. Two of the other coaches were standing about ten feet inside the first base line, with their arms folded, watching Casey as she positioned players around the field.

"Okay, TJ, you get on the mound. Crush, you take first base, and James, you pretend you're the base runner. The rest of you guys stand here."

"What's going on?" Morris asked the pitching coach, Manny Rodriguez.

Rodriguez had his arms crossed, and he kept his eyes on Casey while he spoke over his shoulder in Morris's direction. "Casey is giving a base-stealing clinic."

Morris grunted while Pop gave a proud smile. "Well, I'm glad these guys finally realized they can learn something from her."

"Sshhh," Rodriguez said. "I want to hear this."

They all turned their attention to the mound. Casey had positioned the players where she wanted them, and spoke up loudly. "Okay, James, take your lead off of first. Crush, hold him on." James Johnson responded by taking a few steps off of first, and Eric Davis pretended he was holding him on.

"Now, TJ, go into your stretch, in slow motion. First, I want you to pretend you're going to throw to first; then I want you to pretend you're going to throw home. Everyone watch closely."

"Okay," TJ responded. He simulated both situations in slow motion, as Casey had instructed.

When he was finished, Casey spoke up again as she looked at the group. "Okay, so who can tell me what the differences were?"

James Johnson was the first to speak up. "His leg kick was higher when he went home."

"Was not," TJ immediately countered.

"Relax, TJ," Casey said. "You're not on trial here."

"He didn't look at the runner long enough," Julio Perez offered.

"No, that's not it, either." Casey looked at the pitcher, as the coaches looked on with interest. "Okay, TJ, let's try it again, but this time describe what you're doing every step of the way. First, the throw over to first."

"Okay," TJ responded, as he described each phase of his windup. "First I look in to get the sign, then I look over to check the runner. I look home again and give a high leg kick to make the runner think I'm going home, then I step quickly towards first and throw over." He made a short throw over to Davis, and Johnson mimicked a retreat back to first.

Casey didn't seem satisfied with the description, but instructed TJ to continue. "All right. Now describe going home."

TJ again described his routine, and acted out each step. "I look in to get the sign. I look over at the base runner as I give a leg kick. I continue to look over at the base runner to freeze him, and then I look to home at the last second before I make the pitch." He looked to Casey for approval.

"Fine, but that's not it," she said. She paused for a moment, then remembered the junior high school game when she had first figured it out. "All right, TJ, she said. "Take your shirt off."

"What?" he asked, not quite sure he heard her correctly.

"You heard me. Take off your shirt. And this time, I want to hear you describe everything you are seeing, thinking and doing."

The players, as well as the coaches, all looked at each other as they wondered what it was that Casey was driving at. TJ dropped his glove and took off his shirt. Feeling a little foolish, he picked up his glove and continued to describe his move to first.

"I look in to the catcher to get the sign. It's for a curve ball so I know I need to freeze the runner an extra second because the pitch takes a little longer to get to the plate. I look over at the runner. I look home and give a high leg kick to make him think I'm going home, then I step towards first and make a snap throw."

The players watched as TJ, bare-chested, threw over to first, his stomach muscles contracting quickly as he made the throw.

"Okay," Casey continued the instruction. "Now describe your move home. And remember to describe every little action."

By this time, everyone was watching and listening intently, convinced that the lesson would soon come to a point, but clueless as to what that point was.

TJ, getting a little tired of the game, nevertheless again started to describe his move home. He sighed. "I look in to get the sign from the catcher. It's for a curve ball so I know I need to freeze the runner an extra second because the pitch takes a little longer to get to the plate. I look over to first to freeze the runner. I take a deep breath as I..."

Casey immediately jumped in to interrupt. "What was that?" she asked loudly.

TJ stopped his motion and looked at her with a puzzled look, not sure which portion she wanted him to repeat. "Uh, I look over to first to freeze the runner. I take a deep breath as I give a high leg kick..."

Again Casey interrupted. "Why do you take a deep breath?" she asked.

"Because I'm going home and I'm going to throw a lot harder..." He suddenly grasped what Casey was driving at, and threw his hands out in astonishment. "Ah, come on," he said. "Are you telling me you're looking at my *breathing*?"

"Nahh," Casey said with an elongated drawl. "I couldn't tell you that. That would be giving away my secret." She grinned and walked towards the dugout, leaving the stunned group standing there with bewildered looks on their faces.

She later explained to the team that you could tell by the rise and fall of someone's chest and shoulders, even with their shirt on, whether they were taking a short breath or a deep one, and that a pitcher taking a deeper breath more often than not meant they were going to throw to home plate. It was a better indicator than a leg kick or head positioning, because you can't disguise taking a deep breath.

Casey had been considering whether or not to give one of her secrets away, but after the hospital scene, she decided to do so in a gesture of team loyalty. Besides, she had many more base-stealing tips that she could use at any time.

As the base-stealing practice was breaking up, Dale "Turk" Roberts was finally making his way out to the field. His face was still flushed, and he was walking a little gingerly as Casey passed him on her way to the dugout. Mooch had proudly told her what he had done, and he took great pleasure in describing Turk's reaction in the locker room.

"Hi, Dale," Casey said with a big smile, in mock friendliness. "How're they hangin'?"

"Bite me," was all he could manage.

Twenty-Five

The next night, with the season set to resume the following day, Casey called her mother to chat. Sue was at home, and answered the phone on the third ring.

"Hello?"

"Hi, Mom, it's me."

"Hi, Casey, how are you, sweetheart?"

"I'm fine, Mom," Casey replied. "Just checking in. The season's getting ready to start back up tomorrow, so I'll probably be busy again."

"How are your ribs feeling?"

"They're okay, Mom. Most of the soreness has gone away and I have full range of motion. Nothing to worry about."

"I just didn't think things would be so rough up there," Sue said with concern. "I'm worried about you."

"It's all right, Mom, really. It was just one of those things. It hardly ever happens, and this time, I just got caught in the middle of it, that's all."

"Well, I certainly hope you'll be more careful," Sue said, then added. "That Luscious Brown fellow sure seemed nice."

Casey paused as she thought to herself, *Luscious Brown? – Oh, right, Pop.* "Yeah, Mom, he's great. The players all love him. We call him Pop."

"That sounds appropriate. He really seemed to care about you."

"He does, Mom, and he's helped me out a lot since I've been here."

"So, it does sound like you've made some friends there."

"Well, sure, Mom, I have a few friends. I already told you about Anne…"

Sue shifted into the mother role again. "I know, but I was thinking more along the line of boys. Have you met anyone yet?"

Casey pondered whether or not to tell her mother about Mooch. They had slept together the last few nights, and she was developing strong feelings for him. At first she thought not to tell her mother, but she knew it would come up again eventually, anyway, and figured that it would make her mother happy, so she decided to proceed, but carefully.

"Well, Mom, now, don't get all excited, but I have been seeing this one guy."

There was immediate excitement in Sue's voice. "That's great, dear. What does he do?"

Casey fumbled for a second. "Uh, well, he pitches for the Power." She cringed at the reaction she knew was coming.

"A pitcher? You mean a baseball player? Why, Casey Lee Collins, what about your famous credo of not dating baseball players?" she said, ribbing her daughter.

"Come on, Mom, give me a break. I didn't plan it this way; it just sort of happened."

"That's usually the way love works, dear."

"Now wait a minute, Mom. I'm not sure it's love yet, exactly. I mean, it could be, I just don't know yet."

"It's okay, there's no rush. So what's his name?"

"It's Moo…uh, Michael. Mike Moran."

"That's a nice name. What's he like?"

"Well, he's kind of hard to explain. He's tall, kind of cute, a little quirky, but a really nice guy. He helped with my hitting and we've been out a few of times, and well, I don't know. We'll just have to see."

"Well, that's great dear. I'm happy for you."

Then came the other question Casey feared, but also knew was coming. "So, when do I get to meet him?"

"I don't know, Mom, we'll see. Maybe you can come to Portland for one of the playoff games or something, if we make it."

"I'd love that. You know I'd be at every game if I could."

"I know you would, Mom, but you've got the restaurant. It's okay. Look, I'll let you know the playoff schedule and we'll talk about it."

"All right, dear," Sue replied. She heard her daughter slurping her drink. "Goodbye, and don't drink so much Diet Coke."

"Yes, Mother," Casey said dutifully, as she hung up.

Twenty-Six

When the season finally resumed a full seven days after the big brawl, the Portland Power came out on fire, sweeping their first series on the road against Omaha, while the Calgary Cowboys had lost two out of three to the Spokane Steam. The Power was now leading the Northern Division of the Pacific Coast League by two games, and it was looking like they would win the divisional title.

The morning after they returned home from their successful road trip, Casey was lying in bed watching the morning news. The phone rang, and she flipped off the television and picked up the receiver. "Hello?" she answered.

"Casey, it's Anne. Have you seen the paper today?"

Casey could tell by the tone in Anne's voice that something was wrong. "No. Why, what's the matter?"

"Just get the paper. I'll hold on."

Starting to feel concerned, Casey put the receiver down and got the newspaper from outside her front door. She walked back over to the phone and picked up the receiver, cradling it between her ear and her shoulder while she looked at the paper.

The headline on the front page jumped out at her, as she quickly skimmed the article:

Allegations of Sexual Misconduct within the Portland Power

By Ken Riley

A source within the Portland Power professional baseball team, speaking on condition of anonymity, claimed yesterday that Casey Collins, the right fielder for the Portland Power, has committed acts of lewd behavior in the locker room, including a striptease in front of the other Power players. In addition, the source claims that the romantic involvement between Miss Collins and one of the other players is a constant source of distraction for the team as they strive to qualify for the playoffs.

Team officials have declined to comment, but have pledged to open an internal investigation.

"Oh, my God!" Casey exclaimed. "Where did this come from?"

"I don't know," Anne replied, "But Mr. Harley wants to see you in his office right away. *Right away, Casey.*"

"Wow. Okay, I'll be there." Shocked, Casey put down the phone. Someone in the organization, or worse, someone on the team, obviously said something. And she had a pretty good idea who it was. *Turk. That bastard.*

She went into the bathroom, splashed some water on her face and put on some jeans and a blouse. She grabbed her purse and car keys and rushed out of the apartment. As she drove to the Power offices, she became more and more convinced. It had to be Turk. Who else would do something like this?

Casey entered Bud Harley's office to find him, Butch Morris, Pop, Mooch and Anne waiting for him. As the team's marketing and PR person, it was going to be Anne's responsibility to help control the story.

Harley was sitting behind his desk, and the others were scattered around the room. They all looked up as Casey entered, looking like a grade-schooler being called into the principal's office, which was exactly how she felt.

As he came around to the front of the desk, Harley motioned for Casey to take a seat in a chair, and without any kind of preamble, got right to the point. "I'm assuming you saw this?" he said through gritted teeth, as he held the paper in front of him, folded so the headline was visible.

"Yes, sir, I saw it. But..." Casey protested.

"But what? Do you know what this does to us? It shoots our family image all to hell. Now, I want to know if there is any truth to these allegations?" Bud leaned against the front of his desk with his arms crossed, glaring at Casey. His face was turning red, and Casey could now see why Anne had described him as intense.

Casey was sitting straight up in her chair, at full attention. "No, there's no truth to the allegations. I mean some things were taken out of context, but there's nothing bad going on."

"What about this locker room striptease thing? That seems like a pretty major thing for someone to make up. Did that happen?"

"No, sir. I mean, not exactly. I mean…" Casey was stumbling, not sure what to say. How could she explain the shower scene, and the fact that it wasn't really *a shower scene*?

"Not exactly? What the hell does that mean?"

Mooch stood up and tried to come to Casey's aid. "Look, Mr. Harley…" he started, but Harley cut him off.

"You just sit back down. We'll get to you in a moment," Bud commanded as he pointed a finger at Mooch, who sheepishly plopped back down in his seat.

It was Pop's turn to come to Casey's defense. "Look, Mr. Harley," he said. "This whole thing is a big misunderstanding. We had a mix-up in the shower one time, but that's all it was. Someone is trying to blow this way out of proportion."

"Why would they do that? *Who* would do that?"

Butch Morris spoke up, "I don't know, but I'd sure like to find out. Whoever it is, they're doing more damage to this organization than anything else, and I don't want him on my team."

"Correction—my team," Harley said. Then he turned his attention to Casey and Mooch. "What about this thing between you two. Is there something going on there?"

Casey shifted uncomfortably in her chair as she shot a quick glance over to Mooch. "Well, sort of. I mean there is, but…"

"Jesus Christ! We've got players dating each other now? What the hell is going on here? This is not what I had in mind when I brought you to this organization. This has got to stop—right now."

It was Mooch's turn to object. "Look, Mr. Harley, Casey and I haven't done anything wrong, and we've never done anything in or around the locker room or even anywhere near the stadium. And, well, sir, the way I see it, what we do on our time is our business."

Bud stared at Mooch coldly. "Not when it threatens this organization, it isn't." He again turned his attention to Casey. "Look, Casey, I've stood behind you since the beginning, and I'll stand behind you again. But I don't want to hear any more about any of this stuff again. Am I understood?"

"Yes, sir," Casey responded, feeling that she was being treated unfairly, but not sure what else she could say.

Bud pointed to Butch Morris and Pop in succession. "And I'm looking to you two to make sure that nothing like this happens again. Got it?"

"Yes, sir," they responded in unison.

"Good. Now everyone get out of here. Anne, you stay behind. We need to figure out how to spin this and issue some kind of a statement."

Butch and Pop were the first to leave the office, and walked down the hall muttering to each other. Anne had a helpless look on her face as Casey and Mooch walked out into the hall. Mooch looked at Casey and was about to say something, but Casey spoke first. "Look, Mooch, I don't think we should see each other for a while."

Mooch's face twisted in objection. "What, because of this bullshit? Come on, Casey, we're stronger than that. And what do you mean by a 'a while'?"

Casey looked tentatively up at Mooch, then down at the floor. "I don't know. I just need to think about things. I knew it would cause problems if I dated a baseball player. Just leave me alone for the time being. All right?" She turned and walked away, leaving Mooch standing there, bewildered and dejected.

Two nights later, Casey was at home when her phone rang, and she answered it. "Hello?"

"Casey?"

"Oh, hi, Mom." *Shit! Mom! She must have heard the news, Oh, God.*

"Casey, honey, what's going on?"

"Mom, you must have heard the news. Look, nothing happened, okay? Some things just got blown way out of proportion, and the press got a hold of it. But nothing happened, okay?"

"I know, sweetheart, you don't have to explain it to me. I trust you. I just don't like to see you getting hurt like this, especially when it's so public."

"I know, Mom. Look. There's this guy on the team who hates me, and I'm pretty sure he's behind all of this. I think he made up some things and went to the press, and, well, you know the press, if they can create a scandal and sell more papers or air time, they'll do it."

"But what about you and Michael?"

"Well, we're taking a break from each other right now. It was my decision, and I think it's the right to do. Now you know why I had a rule against dating baseball players. It just causes problems."

"Well, if it's like you say and this guy on the team just made some things up, is that really being fair to Michael, and is it being fair to you? It sounds like you really liked this boy."

"I do, Mom. He's great and he has tried to be understanding. But I need to focus on baseball right now, especially heading into the playoffs. This is my big shot, and I can't let anything threaten that."

"But you need to have a life also, you know."

"That's the thing, Mom. Baseball is my life."

Twenty-Seven

Over the next couple of weeks, as the regular season came to a close, the playoff picture unfolded. It was now the Portland Power versus the Memphis Hawks in one semifinal series, and the Sacramento Sting versus the Omaha Chiefs in the other. The winners of each series would go on to face each other for the Pacific Coast League Championship.

During this period, the life and times of Casey Collins received national attention. News organizations that at one time or another had made only casual reference to "The only woman playing men's professional baseball", took on added interest as the Power qualified for the playoffs, and even more interest when the "sex" scandal surfaced. It had been discussed in newspapers and on radio stations nationwide, and even Jay Leno had made a few cracks about it on *The Tonight Show*.

Meanwhile, Casey's performance on the field had caught the attention of the national sports media, and the speculation of whether or not she could play at the Triple A level had now turned to whether or not she could make it to the major leagues. The debate was even the subject of a baseball focus group on ASN's *The Minor League Report*.

The number of interested parties grew on both sides. The baseball purists were against Casey, as were many male athletes from baseball and other professional sports who feared that it would negatively impact their particular sport. Even the religious right came out publicly after the sex allegations and claimed that allowing men and women to play together would not only ruin sports but would eventually bring about the downfall of society in general.

But the number of groups that came out in support of Casey was overwhelming. She received support from some obvious places—the soccer moms and the young girls playing little league all across the country. Women athletes from all sports. The Girl Scouts of America. And from some not-so-obvious places—Mothers Against Drunk Driving, The National Organization of Women, even the Breast Cancer Survivors Association.

They were all heralding Casey as some kind of role model, even heroine—a notion which Casey dismissed outright. She thought about real heroines like Krista McCauliff, the flight attendants on Flight 495, and the first woman soldier killed in the fight against terrorism. All Casey did was play baseball for a living.

Within the Portland area, things had changed as well. A Portland Power home game was now a hot ticket, especially among women. In the minor leagues and in major league baseball, women made up about 46 percent of the attendance, but in Portland, the figure was 68 percent. A Power home game had replaced Tupperware and cosmetics parties, or cocktails at a local restaurant, as a favorite girls' night out activity. The right field bleacher section, behind where Casey played, was occupied almost entirely by women, and they vocalized their support whenever Casey came to the plate or made a play in the outfield.

Bud Harley, of course, was laughing all the way to the bank. They were now consistently filling the new stadium to its full capacity, and he was licking his chops over the money he was going to make from the upcoming playoff series. At the same time, he was regularly sending the Power attendance figures to the Major League offices, as he continued to court a baseball franchise for Portland.

He seemed to have benefited from both sides of the coin. Not only was Casey Collins helping him sell more tickets, it turned out she really *could* play, and she was a major factor in the Power's push into the playoffs.

Casey had watched it all in amazement, and again, was astounded at the level of attention she was receiving. Somehow, a woman playing minor league baseball in Portland, Oregon, had captured the attention of the entire country. She felt like she was running for political office, instead of running around the bases.

She was constantly hounded for autographs and interviews, and now understood why sports people used so many clichés. After answering the same questions over and over again, it was much easier to just give pat answers. In Casey's case, the questions were always the same:

What's it like to be the only woman baseball player in the minor leagues?

Do you think you can make it to the majors?

Do the other players treat you any differently because you're a woman?

Do you see yourself as a role model?

Throughout Casey's whole ordeal, Anne Ross had proved to be a real godsend. She fielded all the requests for interviews and filtered out many of them to protect Casey, only approving the ones from credible interviewers. She also helped Casey develop some standard answers that made the interview process less of a strain.

But the biggest thing that Anne had done for Casey was to confirm that it was, in fact, Turk Roberts who had gone to the press about Casey. Anne was dating the public relations director for one of the Portland area radio stations, and he knew the reporter at the *Portland Times* who had written the story. Over a few drinks, the reporter had let it slip that it was a pitcher, and Anne's boyfriend had narrowed it down after that. Anne took the information to Bud Harley, who vowed that he would take action.

But for Casey, one of the most amazing events occurred when her phone rang one Sunday night.

"Hello, may I please speak to Miss Collins?"

"Yes, this is Casey."

"Please hold one moment."

Casey looked at the receiver, then raised it back to her ear. *Who the hell is this?* This time a different voice spoke from the other end of the line.

"Hello, Casey?"

"Yes, who is this?" Casey asked, somewhat rudely.

227

"This is Katherine Hayes."

Katherine Hayes, Casey thought to herself. *That name sounds familiar, but do I know her?* She answered with an uncertain tone in her voice. "Uh, yes?"

"I'm Robert Hayes' wife."

Casey snapped to attention. "You mean President Hayes?"

"Yes, I'm the First Lady."

"Wow! How are you, Ma'am? I mean, Your Honor, uh." Casey wasn't sure how to address her.

The first lady laughed lightly. "Relax, it's just Katherine, okay? Sorry about the personal assistant calling. They won't let me make my own phone calls anymore. Anyway, I've been following your story, and I'm just calling to tell you what a wonderful role model I think you are, and I just wanted to offer my support."

Casey was overwhelmed. "Wow, thanks, I mean, you know none of that stuff was true."

The First Lady was very reassuring. "I never thought it was. It's not consistent with the way you carry yourself."

"How do you even know about me?" Casey asked.

"Well, besides reading the papers, one of the autographs you signed was for my niece, when you were in Memphis, and you made a huge impression on her and my sister. You probably don't even remember, but you took the time to take a picture with them. My sister had it blown up into a poster and it's hanging on my niece's wall.

"Anyway, I have to go. I just wanted to wish you good luck and say keep up the good work."

"Thank you, Mrs. Hayes. Thank you very much for calling. Goodbye."

Casey was thankful for the support, not only from the First Lady and the many groups that supported her, but also from her teammates who stuck by her. Mooch, of course. But "Grunt", "Shaft", "Stud" and most of the others had declined to comment on the allegations, even when prodded by aggressive reporters. Butch Morris, Pop and Bud Harley all vehemently denied any improprieties within the organization. For the most part, the team was presenting a united front.

Although the story had started to fade somewhat, the scandal continued to hang in the air, thanks to the press, until it was finally put to rest by Eric Davis. It happened while he was being interviewed before a game by a reporter from a local Portland television station.

The reporter was Brad Smiley, and he was the one who had made the crack at Casey's press conference about her wearing her high heels when she was batting. He was called *Squirrelly* behind his back, because of his small wire-rim glasses and the way he hunched his shoulders over in front of him as he talked.

Smiley was interviewing Eric Davis outside the stadium before the game. Crush was a favorite interview candidate for the press, because of his good nature and willingness to talk to reporters.

Smiley had a cameraman standing beside him, and he held a microphone in front of Crush as he began the interview. "Good afternoon, folks, I'm Brad Smiley reporting live from outside Portland Stadium, as the Power prepare to take on the Fresno Bears in the first game of a three game series. We have with us today Eric 'Crush' Davis, the big first baseman for the Portland Power. Eric, thank you for spending some time with us before the game."

"No problem."

"Tell us about the mood of the team as you wrap up the season and head into the divisional playoffs."

"Well, we're pretty upbeat. We've been hitting the ball well, playing good defense, and getting some strong pitching as well."

"And what about the allegations of sexual misconduct on the part of Casey Collins? What kind of impact is that having? No one else seems to have any comments on the incident, but what about you, do you have any comments?"

"Yeah, it never happened."

Smiley looked a little confused as he held the microphone up to Davis. "What do you mean?"

Crush crossed his arms and looked at him coldly. "What part of that didn't you understand?"

"Squirrelly" took a step back, surprised by the harsh reaction by the normally cordial Eric Davis. "Uh, well, everyone has been talking about this striptease thing she supposedly did in the locker room."

Crush took two steps towards the reporter, who physically recoiled from his glare. "I'm telling you it never happened." he said.

"But..."

"But nothing. Were you there?"

The reporter was now totally flustered. "No, but we were told..."

"Well, I *was* there. And let me tell you what happened. Casey asked me to guard the door while she took a shower, and that's exactly what I did. No other players went in or out of the shower during that time, and that's the extent of it. That's all that ever happened.

"I'm sick and tired of you sleazeballs trying to make something out of nothing. Casey Collins is a good person, and one of the best baseball players I've ever played with, and you jerks better back off if you ever want an interview from any of us ever again! You got that?" Crush pointed a finger in the reporter's face for emphasis, then turned and walked away.

Smiley was left standing there, quivering, obviously shaken by the hostility of Eric Davis. He tried to elegantly wrap up the interview, but it didn't work.

The interview made the rounds in the local Portland area, and even got picked up by ASN, which used it as a lead in to their *Minor League Report*. Crush got his fifteen minutes of fame, and Casey had her vindication. The story was dead, and Casey gave Crush a big hug and a kiss on the cheek the next day in the tunnel on their way to the field. "You're my new hero," she joked.

The only negative that Casey had in her life currently, other than Turk, was her relationship, or rather lack thereof, with Mooch. Ever since her request that they didn't see each other for a while, things had been awkward between the two of them. Fortunately, Mooch was usually out in the bullpen dugout in center field, so during the games they didn't have that much interaction.

Mooch had approached Casey a couple of times, wanting to talk, but Casey stuck to her decision to maintain a distance between the two of them for the rest of the season. She had tried to make it clear that she wasn't ready to call it quits between the two of them, that she really did like him, they just couldn't be the way they were while the season was still in progress.

To Mooch's credit, even though he was obviously upset at the situation, he tried to be understanding, which made Casey all the more attracted to him. In her mind, it was something she would deal with after the season was over, and hopefully, their relationship would not suffer too much damage in the meantime.

With the scandal behind her, and the situation with Mooch somewhat tabled for now, Casey was happy that now she could concentrate on baseball and the next task at hand, which was beating the Memphis Hawks in the first round of the playoffs. Memphis had a better regular season record than Portland, so the first two games were in Memphis, the second two would be in Portland, and if necessary, the final game of the best-of-five game series would be played back in Memphis.

Twenty-Eight

Two days before the Power was scheduled to leave for Memphis, Butch Morris called a team meeting, with batting practice to follow. After the players had dressed, he had them assembled in the locker room, and Casey had joined them. The players were sitting on the benches or leaning up against the lockers, when Morris called their attention.

"All right, guys, listen up," he said loudly, and the conversations subsided. "You all know we head into Memphis on Wednesday. We need to get a couple of good workouts in before then so we're sharp.

"Before we head out today, though, I have an announcement to make, regarding two personnel moves." Every player was now at full attention, looking around the room at each other, wondering what those moves were and who was involved.

Morris showed a rare smile, as he continued, "It seems that one of our own has been called up to the show, and if I must say so, it's well deserved..."

Before he could continue, Turk muttered, "Well, it's about time," assuming it would be him. He had no idea what a fool he was making of himself, but then again, he never did.

Morris let the comment pass as he walked over to Eric Davis. He had already informed him earlier, but wanted to make the official announcement in front of the team. He reached out his hand to Crush, and said, "Congratulations, big man."

The team let out a collective cheer as they all high-fived Davis and slapped him on the back. Then the noise subsided a bit as an important question dawned on the players. *Did this mean they would be without Crush for the playoffs?*

Morris preempted their concerns. "Now, Eric has asked to stay with the team through the playoffs, and upstairs has given their permission." This brought on another loud cheer from the team.

That is, from everyone except Turk, who said, "That's it? What's the other move?"

Morris wheeled and looked at him. "You've been traded to Montreal."

A shocked look came over Turk's face, as some snickers rose from around the room. "W-what? Montreal? What the hell?" he stammered.

"That's right," Morris said emphatically. "You're to report immediately."

"But, but what about the playoffs?" Turk asked, a pathetic look on his face.

"We'll be fine without you. Clean out your locker, and go see Bud Harley's secretary. She's got your travel itinerary."

Turk jumped up, his face turning red. "What kind of bullshit is this?" he screamed, looking like he was ready to go after Morris.

Crush Davis and Darnell Jenkins stepped in front of Turk. In his best Shaft imitation, Jenkins put his sunglasses on, pointed at Turk's chest and said, "Take a hike, pal. You don't work here anymore." This brought more chuckles from the other players.

Totally flustered, Turk slumped back down on the bench. Just then the locker room door opened and one of the stadium's security guards entered, and walked over to where Turk was sitting. "Mr. Roberts," he said, "I'm here to escort you out of the stadium. I'll wait until you gather your things."

Morris spoke up again, addressing the team as a whole. "Okay, guys, that's it for the meeting. Let's hit the field and get some good BP in."

Normally, a professional baseball manager would not humiliate a player in front of an entire team like that, but Butch Morris was sending a message. Team unity was everything. Either you're part of the team or you're not, and Turk had demonstrated through his actions that he wasn't. Now it was official.

Pop was standing beside Butch Morris, and he caught Casey's eye and gave her a wink. *Justice served.*

Team spirits were high as the Power headed into Memphis for the best-of-five series. They won the first game, but lost the second, returning to Portland with the series tied at 1-1. The Power won the first game in Portland by a score of 2-1, and then, vowing not to have to return to Memphis for the final game, turned on the offense to win the third and decisive game, 8 to 3. They would now play for the Pacific Coast League Championship.

At the same time, Sacramento was locked in a 2-2 series tie with the Omaha Razors, with the final game scheduled in Sacramento in two days. This gave the Power a real edge, as they would now have at least 4 days' rest before the start of the championship series.

Butch Morris gave the team two days off, with each player spending them in his or her own way. Grunt went fishing off the Oregon Coast with Scott Wilson, while Eric Davis, James Johnson and Darnell Jenkins spent their time golfing. Mooch Moran, TJ Morrison and two other pitchers went on a road trip to Seattle to watch the Mariners play the Yankees, while the coaches spent their "days off" working — scouring scouting reports for both Omaha and Sacramento. They worked out line-ups and game plans against both teams so they could be prepared regardless of which team won.

Casey had one commitment in Portland, so she decided to stay in the area. Anne had arranged for her to speak at a breakfast meeting of the Portland Women's Association, for which Casey was to be paid $500. It was part of an ongoing public relations arrangement Casey had made with Bud Harley. Bud agreed to pay her an additional $2,500 if she would make certain public appearances on behalf of the Power.

She had already appeared at two different grade schools in the Portland area, as well as one Girl Scout meeting and a women's high school softball team pep rally. For those appearances, Casey had worn her full Portland Power uniform, and she had had a great time with the kids.

The meeting with the PWA was different, however, and Casey was feeling apprehensive about it. This wasn't a meeting with eight-year-old girls who wanted to know how far she could throw a baseball. These were grown women—professional women who were successful in business, and Casey had no idea what to say to them. The meeting was to take place in two days, and Casey was extremely nervous.

Again, it was Anne Ross to the rescue. An accomplished public speaker, Anne coached Casey on how to open, what topics to cover, and if necessary, how to appear to answer certain questions without really answering them. Anne's main advice to Casey was for her to be herself. She was the celebrity after all, and Anne told her that the audience would be thrilled just to have her there.

It sounded good in theory to Casey, but it didn't stop her palms from sweating as the president of the Portland Women's Association, Margaret Haines, introduced her to the audience. Margaret was at the podium, with Casey standing by. Unlike her other appearances, Casey was not wearing her Power uniform, but instead was dressed smartly, a la Anne Ross, in dark blue slacks and a matching jacket, with a light blue blouse. She wore a small silver Portland Power pin over her left breast pocket, and forced a smile as Margaret Haines performed the introduction.

"Good morning, ladies, may I have your attention, please?" Margaret Haines said firmly into the microphone. She paused a few seconds as she waited for the background chatter to cease, before continuing. "Today, we are pleased to have with us a real-life example of a woman succeeding in a man's world. Please welcome the starting right fielder for the Portland Power, Casey Collins."

There was a loud round of applause as Margaret Haines motioned to Casey, who took the podium as Margaret stepped aside. Casey looked out at the audience of over 200 women, and said "Thank you," a couple of times while the applause gradually subsided.

Anne had taught Casey to open up with some humor to get the audience on her side and to calm herself down, so she started out with a baseball analogy. "Good morning, and thank you, Ms. Haines, for inviting me here today. I have to tell you though, I think I could come up to the plate in front of twenty thousand people, with two outs in the bottom of the ninth and I wouldn't be half as nervous as I am about speaking in front of a live audience."

The audience laughed, and it had the desired effect on Casey. She felt a little more comfortable already, as she continued. "And even though I'm a lot better at running bases than I am at public speaking, Miss Haines asked me to address you today, because while talking with her, we both realized there are a lot of parallels between my job and yours.

"And yes, even though I play baseball, it is still a job. I have a salary, bosses and coworkers, and I have to perform in my job just like you have to perform in yours, or I'll lose that job. And I think a lot of the situations that we face are probably similar."

Casey now had the audience's full attention, and she could feel herself getting stronger. "For instance, I constantly have to prove that I have my job because I perform, not because I happen to be a woman." This brought a light round of applause, as well as many nodding of heads.

"And I'm sure, like some of you, sometimes I feel like I have to perform better than others, just to be considered equal." More applause, more heads nodding in agreement.

"When I was first called up to Triple A, I immediately wondered if I was being called up because of my baseball skills, or to be the token woman so they could sell more tickets. It caused me some anxiety for a while, but then I decided that regardless of the reason, I was going to prove myself on the field, and that's what I focused on. Fortunately, in baseball, we have published statistics, so I have something concrete to point to that says, 'Yeah, I do belong here.'"

Casey paused, then continued. "But not being a businesswoman myself, I won't pretend to know what's important to you, and I don't think you all came here just to hear me ramble on. Maybe what we should do is just open it up for questions."

The first question was from a woman seated at one of the front tables, and she asked Casey who her role models were when she was growing up.

Casey thought about it for a few seconds, then answered. "Well, not surprisingly, many of my early heroes were male baseball players, for the way they played the game. Pete Rose for the way he always hustled, Tony Gywnn and Rod Carew for their great bat control, Lou Brock for his aggressiveness on the base paths, Cal Ripkin for his sheer love of the game.

"I needed someone to model my style after. But as far as role models go, my two biggest were my father and my mother. My father, not only because he taught me how to play baseball, but more importantly, because he taught me how to look for an advantage. I mean, everyone in my league is bigger and stronger than me, so I've always had to try harder to find an edge.

"My mother because rather than just taking my father's insurance settlement and living off of it, she invested in a restaurant, and she built it into a great business that has provided for the both of us. She's my true hero, and also my number one fan."

Another woman from the audience asked, "What's the hardest part about playing on a team with all men?"

Casey responded with more humor. "Well, I just can't curse as well as they can." This brought a round of laughter, and she quickly added, "No, I mean it, some of these guys can be really creative. You wouldn't believe some of the things I hear."

Once the laughter died down, Casey waved her hand as she continued, "Seriously, I was kidding of course, but actually that is part of the real answer. I mean, there are the physical challenges, of course, but I have been blessed with some skill which lets me play at this level and I thank God for that. But probably the hardest thing for me is to maintain a balance between trying to be one of the guys, while at the same time retaining my femininity. I mean, in order for me to be accepted by my teammates, I have to play hard and be willing to get down and dirty like they do, and I can't very well do that and then turn around and blush when somebody curses. I can't expect twenty-three guys to change their behavior just because I'm around.

"But I'm also not going to sit around and belch and scratch myself like some kind of a cowboy out on the range, either. I am a woman and I'm damn proud of it and I will maintain my dignity."

This brought another big round of applause, and even a few cheers. The next question was from an African-American woman with short hair, dressed in a business suit. "Yes, Casey. I've always heard that baseball, and sports in general, is the great racial equalizer. Do you think it's the great gender equalizer also?"

"Great question. First of all, I do think that sports is the great racial equalizer. I mean, there are exceptions, of course, as there are everywhere, but you don't see a Puerto Rican shortstop field the ball and then pause because he has to throw it over to the white guy playing second, who wonders if the black guy playing first is going to catch it. It's player to player to player. If a person can play, it doesn't matter where they came from or what color they are or what kind of music they listen to; when you're on the field, that stuff goes away. So there's no reason why we shouldn't be able to plug a woman in at any of those spots, and there's no reason why nothing should change. If she can play, she can play."

The next question, from the back of the room, was, "How do you want to have people view you?"

"Well, right now, I think the main thing is that I'd like to be referred to as a baseball player without the 'woman' modifier. I mean, you don't hear people refer to Edgar Martinez as 'The best Latino designated hitter' in the game. Or, hey, Roger Clemens sure is a great white male pitcher. No, they're simply great baseball players. Someday, although I'm not there yet, I'd love to see a write-up that just says, Casey Collins was a great right fielder, or a great baseball player. Then I'll know I've made it."

The final question was, "How do you motivate yourself?"

"Well, first of all, I love the game of baseball, so for me, just walking out on the field and smelling the grass, or the Astroturf, whatever the case may be, is motivating enough. And at this stage of my career I'm still trying to see how far I can go, so I'm constantly trying to make myself a better ballplayer. But I also get motivated when people tell me I can't do something.

"For instance, a couple of weeks ago, when we were playing in Omaha, there was a man outside the stadium who was holding a sign that said, 'A woman's place is in the home.'" This brought on some boos and several looks of disgust from the women in the audience."

Casey continued, "And I thought to myself, you know, he's right. A woman's place is at home." She paused, as the audience went dead silent, with a few looks of bewilderment, wondering if they heard her correctly. That was when Casey continued, and delivered the punch line.

"At home plate, that is. And at first, and at second…"

The audience erupted in laughter and gave Casey a standing ovation, as she took that opportunity to end on a high note. She thanked them, said her goodbyes, and left the podium.

Twenty-Nine

Casey got home from her speech at the Portland Women's Association, to find that the Sacramento Sting had beaten the Omaha Razors to take the series, 3-2. The stage was now set for the Pacific Coast League Championship series. It was the Portland Power versus their archrivals, the Sacramento Sting, winners of the league championship three years in a row.

The first game was played in Portland, with the Power winning 2-1 on a dramatic ninth inning home run by the designated hitter, Juan Garcia. The next two games were to be played in Sacramento, and the Power had just arrived in town the night before the first game. The local newspaper, *The Sacramento Scene*, had featured Casey in their article about the series:

Woman Professional Baseball Player to Visit Sacramento.

This Friday night, the Sacramento Sting take on their archrival in the Pacific Coast League, the Portland Power, in the second of a league playoff series that will determine who is the 2003 PCL champion. The first game of the five-game series was played in Portland on Wednesday evening, with the Power outlasting the Sting 2-1.

This series is sure to generate extra excitement as Portland brings with them Casey Collins, the only woman baseball player in the minor leagues. Miss Collins has generated local and national attention as the center of the debate of whether or not a woman should be playing in a men's professional baseball league. The on-going discussion is whether Ms. Collins can continue to make baseball history by going on to become the first woman ever to play major league baseball.

Miss Collins plays right field for the Power, and batted .293 during the regular season, with 21 stolen bases even though she has only played half the season with the Power. She was

2 for 4 on Wednesday evening, with two stolen bases and a run scored.

There are still tickets available for this weekend's games, but they are going fast as many people are anxious to see a part of history being made.

The next day, the team boarded their Greyhound bus for Sacramento's stadium. As the team bus pulled into the parking lot, the bus driver pulled even with the security gate. When the bus came to a stop, a policeman came out of the security station and gave a rap on the bus doors. The bus driver opened the door and the policeman came up the stairs. The players, who had been chatting amongst themselves, went quiet as they saw the officer enter the bus.

"Good afternoon," the officer said loudly with a curt nod. He looked around the front of the bus and asked, "Mr. Morris?"

Butch stood up to greet the officer. "Yes, I'm Butch Morris." He stuck out his hand towards the officer.

The officer took his hand and said, "Hi, I'm Officer Gentry. I'm here to escort Miss Collins into the stadium."

"Do you really think that's necessary?" Butch asked with raised eyebrows.

"Well, I don't want to alarm anyone," the officer responded. "But the stadium office has received some threatening phone calls." He held up his open palms in front of him as he continued. "Now, usually these things are just crank calls, but we don't want to take any chances. We'd rather be safe than sorry. Is Miss Collins on board, sir?"

"Uh, sure, she's right back there," Butch answered, turning to point towards Casey.

Casey rose uneasily and said, "I'm Casey Collins."

The officer took a few steps towards her and extended his hand. "Hi, Miss Collins, it's a pleasure to meet you. We've heard a lot about you around here."

Casey took his hand, and watched as the officer, like everyone else, took notice of her strong grip. "Thank you, but call me Casey, please."

241

"All right, Casey, why don't you just have a seat and once we're parked I'll escort you inside."

"Okay, thanks," Casey said uneasily as she slowly took her seat. Some of the players around her began kidding her.

"Ooooh, Miss Bigshot, with her own personal escort," chided Grunt.

"Hey, can I get your autograph?" James Johnson added.

"Maybe you should wear a disguise," Crush joined in.

Casey accepted the good-natured ribbing from her teammates, and turned around in her seat. "Shut up, you guys," she said in mock reprimand.

In a situation that was tailor-made for wisecracks, Mooch Moran, sitting two seats behind Casey, was strangely quiet.

As the bus slowly pulled in to the stadium lot, Casey saw that a large crowd was assembled in two lines along chain-link fences that had been erected to keep them away from the players. Some of the people were waving signs and Casey read a few of them as the bus made its slow progression to the player's entrance. Some were directed at the team, but many revolved around her.

"Portland Sucks—Go Sacramento," one of them read.

"No Power Available Here," another one said.

"Go back to Portland, Collins," from yet another.

Still others read, *"Casey Go Home"*; *"Casey, You're not so Mighty"*; and *"Keep Baseball Pure—No women!"*

Casey continued to read the signs as the bus moved slowly into the lot. A short round man with a big belly held up a sign that said, *"Marry Me, Casey,"* next to a tall lean man holding a sign that said, *"Baseball is a Man's Game."*

One woman was holding her four-year-old daughter high in her arms. The little girl was holding up a sign that said. *"Girl Power! Go Casey."*

Another woman was holding a *"We love you Casey"* sign, right in front of a man holding a sign saying, *"Collins, You're Ruining Baseball"*.

A tall skinny man with a long beard, wearing beads and sandals, held a sign that read *"Harlot, Get Thee Out!"* right next to one that said *"#9 You Go Girl."*

As Casey read the signs, she told herself that she should be used to this by now, but again, she was surprised at the level of emotion—both positive and negative—directed at her.

When the bus finally pulled to a stop, Officer Gentry stood up and said loudly, "Folks, can I have your attention, please? I would like everyone to file out first, and then I'll follow with Miss Collins."

Pop stood up at the front of the bus and yelled towards the back, "All right, guys, you heard the officer. Let's do what he says and let's get it done quickly." He clapped his hands a couple of times for emphasis.

The players started gathering up their gear, cracking jokes all the while. The bus driver opened the rubber-lined doors, and one by one the players started filing out. The coaches followed the last of the players down the stairs and out the doors, and then the police officer motioned to Casey. "All right, Miss Collins, let's go. Just stay close to me, please."

Casey grabbed her bag and followed Officer Gentry down the stairs and out onto the pavement. As soon as she exited, a loud roar went up from the crowd, and people started waving their signs wildly in the air and shouting a mixture of jeers and encouragement. People were jammed against the two chain-link fences on either side of the aisle that had been made for the players to walk on. Those closest to the fences were holding out autograph books and pleading for Casey to sign.

The rest of the *Power* players were walking up the artificial walkway, and were looking around at the crowd, marveling at both its size and its intensity. Casey was walking behind officer Gentry, and she put a hand lightly on his arm.

"Excuse me, Officer Gentry," she said over the roar of the crowd.

He stopped and turned around. "Yes, Miss Collins?"

"Do you mind if I sign a few autographs? There's a lot of kids here and I'd like to sign some of their books."

Officer Gentry surveyed the crowd, frowned, then reluctantly agreed. "Well, okay, but don't get too close and don't let anyone grab you."

"I'll be careful, I promise."

Casey walked over to one side of the fence, and went down the line, taking autograph books from people one at a time. There was no time to personalize the autographs, so she just signed, *Casey Collins # 9* in each of the books, and gave them back to the owner.

She was halfway down the second side of the fence, and was in the process of signing a young girl's book, when a man shoved his way to the front of the crowd and threw a raw egg directly at Casey's chest. "Hey, Collins, take this!" he yelled.

"Ahh!" Casey expressed in dismay as the egg splattered all over her shirt and part of the girl's autograph book. She looked up to see who had thrown the egg, but the man had already disappeared into the crowd.

Officer Gentry immediately stepped forward and took Casey by the arm. "All right, that's it!" he commanded. "Let's get out of here."

"Yeah, okay," a stunned Casey replied.

They hurriedly walked through the rest of the gauntlet until they were safely inside. The officer was apologizing profusely as Casey was trying to brush the gooey egg off her shirt. "I'm so sorry, Miss Collins. I shouldn't have let that happen."

"Don't worry about it," Casey said. "It wasn't your fault. There was nothing you could have done about it anyway. I'm all right."

"Are you sure?" he asked.

"Yeah, it's only an egg. I just can't believe people can be such jerks."

Butch Morris and Pop had seen Casey and the officer hurrying into the stadium, and they saw the egg on Casey's shirt. They both came rushing over and asked her if she was all right.

"I'm fine," she assured them. "Let's just get to the game."

Vowing not to let the incident bother her, Casey followed the police officer to a women's bathroom that had been closed off for Casey. Although the Sacramento Sting were the archrivals of the Portland Power, they were a professional organization, and they had even moved a bench and a vertical clothes locker into the ladies room especially for Casey. Officer Gentry took his post outside the door, and assured Casey she would not be disturbed.

Casey dressed quickly, focusing her mind on the coming game, and joined her teammates as they proceeded through the player's tunnel and out to the field.

That night, in the first game in Sacramento, which was the second of the series, the Sacramento pitcher, who was 14 and 2 in the regular season, proved to be too tough for the Power, going the full nine innings and shutting them out 3-0.

In the third game of the series, also in Sacramento, the Sting won the game 4-3, on a grand slam home run in the eighth inning, giving them a 2-1 edge in the series, as the two teams headed back to Portland for game four.

After initially having the advantage by winning the first game in Portland, the situation had now flipped, and with the Power now behind in the series 2-1, they had to win both of the games in Portland in order to win the league championship. The pressure was on as the two teams returned to Portland, and took the field for game number four.

Eric "Crush" Davis demonstrated how he got his nickname, and also why he was being called up to the majors, as he hit two home runs and drove in 5 runs, leading the Power to a 5-2 victory in game four. Casey Collins was on base both times, scoring 2 of their 5 runs. She had also stolen 2 bases, giving her 7 for the series, which led both teams.

An interesting statistic that probably went unnoticed by the average fan was that, in the series so far, the Power, as a team, had gone 14 for 14 in stolen bases.

Thirty

With the Power's victory in game number four, the series was now tied, and it all came down to this: Nine innings of baseball to determine the Pacific Coast League Champion. Game five was completely sold out, as were the other playoff games in both Sacramento and Portland.

Casey jogged out to right field for the pre-game warm-ups. It was still an hour before game time and the stands were already almost full. Over 35,000 people had seen the last game in Portland, which was a minor league attendance record. The championship game was also being televised by a local TV station, and special attendees included league president Huey Jacobs, major leagues scouts from every team, Bud Harley, three executives from Mitzua Motors of Japan, the mayor of Portland and the governor of Oregon.

Casey nodded to the fans behind the right field fence. They had become regular attendees at Power home games, and they dropped a sign that said "Casey's Corner" over one of the railings. Then Casey blew a kiss and waved to a special group that was in attendance tonight in the right field bleachers. Sue Collins, accompanied by Uncle Mike, Burt Drivers and some of Sue's friends, had made the road trip from Richmond to see her play in the final two games.

Butch Morris had moved Casey up to leadoff batter for the championship series. He had moved her up to the number two spot before the division series with Memphis, mainly because she was such a good bunter. Then he realized that she was much more than a capable sacrifice bunter; she could also bunt for base hits with regularity, and she was now the leadoff hitter for the Portland Power.

As the playing of the national anthem came to an end, the Power took the field for the top of the first inning. The stadium was now fully packed, and a hearty cheer rose from the crowd as they greeted their hometown team.

After the Power had completed their warm-up tosses, the umpire yelled "Play Ball!" and the championship game was underway.

Casey felt a surge of adrenaline as the game was ready to begin. Her normal level of excitement and jitters were intensified by the added pressure of this being the championship game.

Still, it was nothing like the nervousness she had felt in her first game with the Power back in early July. It seemed like a lifetime ago. The uncertainty and self-doubt that came from her poor performance in those early days were now replaced by confidence and pride.

She had gone from being a replacement player, batting ninth, to a team leader and batting leadoff. She had turned her personal numbers around and had helped the team improve its position. Now, here they were, in what was, without a doubt, the biggest game of Casey's career. This was what it was all about.

She focused on the batter's box as the leadoff hitter for Sacramento stepped up to the plate. His name was Darious Jones, and he was fast, leading the Sting in stolen bases with 32. A right-handed batter, he swung at the very first pitch and hit it solidly back up the middle for a leadoff single. Thirty seconds into the game and the Power defense was already under pressure.

Casey assumed her ready position as the second batter for Sacramento came to the plate. The Sting had established a pattern of playing for one run at a time, and therefore everyone was expecting the batter to attempt a sacrifice bunt. Knowing this, TJ Morrison, on the mound for the Power, threw the first pitch intentionally high, hoping to get the batter to pop up. It worked, as the batter tried to bunt the high pitch, but instead popped it up directly to the pitcher.

T.J. Morrison took a few steps off the mound to make the easy catch, then swung around towards first to try to double up the runner. But the speedy Jones had seen the pop-up and slid safely back in to first. Now there was one out and a runner on first.

The next batter, the number three hitter for Sacramento, took the first pitch for a called strike, trying to give Jones an opportunity to steal second. But TJ did a good job of holding him on, and he remained on first with a count of 0-1. On the very next pitch, though, Jones took off towards second, as the right-handed batter swung and connected with the outside pitch, causing the ball to shoot over the second baseman's head for a base hit.

Casey was off at the crack of the bat, and ran in quickly to field the ball. Darious Jones, who already had a big jump from running with the pitch, saw the ball sail over the second baseman's head, and made a wide turn at second, heading for third base.

Casey came up with the ball and saw that there was no way she could make a play for Jones at third. The correct play was to throw the ball into second base, in order to hold the base-runner at first and preserve a possible double play scenario. Everyone knew this was the play, including the batter, who made a wide turn at first and looked over to second. If Casey's throw went errant at second, he might be able to advance another base.

Yes, everyone knew the correct move was to throw the ball to second, which is exactly why Casey did what she did. As she fielded the ball, she took a couple of strong steps towards third base, and wound up with an emphatic motion as if she was going to try to throw the ball all the way to third. The shortstop, covering the bag at second, saw what was on Casey's mind, or at least thought he did.

"No," he yelled, "Come to me!"

The runner on first, having made the wide turn, also saw Casey's big windup, and as she looked towards third base, he took another couple of steps towards second base, ready to advance once Casey threw to third. But halfway into her windup, Casey changed her pivot foot and turned her body towards first base. She grunted loudly as she threw the ball as hard as she could on a straight line to first, where Eric Davis was covering.

The base runner was caught completely by surprise, and was too late in recognizing what Casey was doing. He lost his footing as he tried to suddenly reverse his direction and turn back towards first. The ball arrived on a line drive to Eric Davis, who caught it and easily tagged out the runner trying to scamper back to the bag.

Darious Jones, now on third base, took a couple of steps towards home, acting like he might make a break for it. But Davis turned to face him with the ball, and a look that said, *Go ahead and try it pal, you'll be dead*, and Jones walked harmlessly back to the bag. Now there were two outs and a man on third.

The home crowd cheered wildly, especially those in *Casey's Corner*, as shouts of "Great play, Casey!" and "Wow, what a throw!" echoed from the stands. In the Power dugout, Pop smacked his hands together a couple of times as he yelled encouragement out to Casey, while Butch Morris simply nodded and smiled.

Up in the press box, Stan Marx commented to Gunner Thomas. "Wow, what a play by number nine. How many times have we seen that this year, Gunner? A heads-up play by Casey Collins turns the situation around in favor of the Power."

"Well, we've seen it a lot," Gunner responded. "You get the feeling that there's no end to the amount of tricks that this young lady has up her sleeve. Maybe we should call her *The Magician*," he chuckled.

"That's right. *Magician* is a gender-neutral term also, isn't it?" added Marx, as they both laughed. Throughout the season, the two announcers had congratulated themselves on coming up with new terms to describe ballplayers that didn't specifically imply either male or female. They had picked up on Bud Harley's comment at the press conference about the term "baseball player" not being a gender-specific term, and had added to the list the terms—right fielder, base stealer, teammate, hitter, and winner.

TJ Morrison, pumped up by Casey's play in the outfield, bore down and struck out the next batter on three pitches. Again the crowd cheered, as the Power ran off the field to prepare for their first at bat. Pop watched his team head in towards the dugout, and he noticed that Casey had paused on her way in and had an exchange with one of the fans.

He was standing at the edge of the dugout as she approached. "What was that all about?" he asked with concern.

Casey descended the stairs and tossed her glove on the bench. "Ah, some guy called me a bimbo."

"What did you do?" he asked anxiously.

"Well, I wanted to flip him off, but then I thought about what you said before about how you handled those situations. So, I waved at him and gave him my warmest, most affectionate smile," she said, as she repeated the look she had given to the fan.

Pop's eyes were wide open in anticipation. "Yeah, then what happened?"

"You were right, he didn't know what do. He just kind of shrugged, looked at me sheepishly and sat back down."

Pop slapped his knee and laughed. "That's my girl."

"Even better," she said, also laughing. "His wife was sitting next to him, so I blew him a big kiss, and now she thinks we have something going. I think he's in trouble."

Pop roared in laughter. "I love it!" he howled.

They were both still laughing when Butch Morris broke in from the other end of the dugout. "Collins, you're up," he shouted. "That is, if you two are done cracking jokes down there."

Casey tried to suppress her laughter as she started to make her way through the dugout to where the bats were stored.

"What the hell was so funny down there, anyway?" Morris asked as she approached the bats.

"Oh, nothing," she smirked as she picked up her bat, "We were just laughing about a fan."

"Well, let's try to concentrate on the game," he said, not really angry but just being the manager. "We need base runners."

"No problem, Skip," Casey said, a slight smirk still on her face.

As the Sacramento Sting took the field and completed their warm-ups, Casey grabbed her bat and took a few practice swings with the doughnut. The crowd was still buzzing from the first half of the inning, and the scoreboard was flashing POWER UP!

The umpire yelled "Batter Up" as the PA announcer's voice came over the loudspeaker. "Leading off for the Portland Power, number nine, Casey Collins."

A hearty round of applause came from the crowd as Casey stepped up to the plate. As she did so, the catcher grunted at her, trying to get her goat early. "Hey, Butch," he said.

"Hey, Mary," Casey returned, not missing a beat.

She clicked the bat on each of her heels, surveyed the field, and watched as the infielders all took ten steps to the left side of the diamond. The third baseman was almost standing on the third base line, and the shortstop was playing in the hole between shortstop and third. The second baseman was standing on the third base side of second base, and the first baseman was standing on the infield grass, and had also taken a few steps towards second.

The center fielder came running in and took up a short fielder's position behind the shortstop, like you would see in a softball game, and the right fielder was playing in the gap in right center field.

Stan Marx described the scenario for his listening audience. "Wow, it looks like Sacramento is putting on a big shift for Casey Collins. What do you think of that, Gunner?"

"Well, it looks like they've done some homework and are making some adjustments. We know that about a third of Casey's hits are infield hits, and we also know that the majority of her hits are to the left side of the diamond. It looks like they know it, too."

"What do you think of the strategy being employed by the Sting?" Stan asked.

"Well, I think it's smart. You can see how the first and third basemen have moved in to take the bunt away from her, and how they're playing a short fielder to compensate for her slap hits over the infielder's heads. I think it's very smart."

"But doesn't it leave a big gap in right field? I mean, look where the right fielder is playing. He's almost playing center field, and he's leaving right field down the line almost completely open. What if she pulls the ball?"

"Well," Gunner continued. "She's pulled very few balls to right field this year, and the Sting is just playing percentages. I'm sure that they will be pitching her outside just to make it even more difficult for her to pull the ball. The strategy does have a little risk, but we'll just have to see what happens."

Back down on the field, Casey stepped out of the box as she saw the shift taking place. No team had ever done that against her before, and she pondered what her strategy should be.

"What's the matter, sweetheart?" the catcher wisecracked. "Never seen a shift before?"

"Well, I've seen how we all move in whenever you come up to the plate, but nothing like this," Casey retorted.

The umpire laughed at Casey's remark. The catcher did not.

Casey stepped back into the box as the pitcher looked in to get the signal. He wound up and delivered the first pitch, a fastball that missed the outside corner by an inch, and she let it go for a called ball one.

As the pitcher delivered the second pitch, Casey slid her left hand down the end of the bat, and took two steps toward the first base line. She waved at the pitch like she was attempting a drag bunt, although she had no intention of trying to hit the pitch. The umpire called "Strike One," as the catcher laughed. The first and third basemen, who had taken a few steps in at the sign of the bunt, patted their gloves and grinned at each other. They had the bunt covered.

On the next pitch, a curve ball over the outside corner, Casey swung hard, and hit it about five feet to the left side of the third base line, foul, for strike two. The count was now one ball and two strikes.

Casey stepped out of the batter's box briefly and again surveyed the field. The first and third baseman both took several steps back towards their bases. With two outs, batters don't try to bunt, because if they attempt to bunt and the ball goes foul, they are automatically out.

Casey stepped back into the box, and on the next pitch, opened her stance while sliding her left hand down towards the fat end of the bat, and dragged the ball along with her down the first base line. Stunned that someone would attempt to bat with two strikes, especially a drag bunt which is a higher risk, the first baseman froze for a few seconds, as Casey raced down the first base line.

By the time the first baseman recovered and ran in to get the ball, Casey was almost at first base, and all he could was watch the baseball rolling down the base line, hoping that it would curve foul. It didn't, and instead came to a stop halfway down the base line and two inches inside the foul line. A perfect bunt.

"Wow! Did you see that?" Stan Marx exclaimed into the microphone. "Casey Collins executes a perfect drag bunt, with two strikes, no less! That was just amazing, wasn't it Gunner?"

"Wow, it certainly was, Stan. Talk about having confidence in your bunting ability. That move was perfectly executed, and it caught the defense flatfooted. Now the Power have a runner on first with nobody out. This is already shaping up to be a great game."

Down on the field, Casey accepted the congratulations from Pop at first base, and listened to the roar of the crowd. She looked over to the third base coach for the sign, which was for the batter to lay down a sacrifice bunt. They were playing for a one-run lead.

Casey took her lead off of first base, as the pitcher went into his stretch. He threw over to first twice in a row, before finally throwing home. James Johnson, now batting second, put down a perfect bunt to the third baseman, forcing him to throw over to first, and allowing Casey to advance down to second base.

Johnson accepted his high fives in the dugout for a job well done, and Casey looked over at the third base coach for the signals, as she took her lead off of second. He clapped his hands a few times while looking at the batter, the signal for him to hit away.

Casey was thinking about stealing third base, but on the first pitch, Scott Wilson hit a towering fly ball to left field, and Stan Marx made the call from the press box.

"Collins takes her lead off of second base, with one out and Scott Wilson at the plate. Rogers goes into his stretch, checking Collins at second, winds up and delivers. Wilson swings and connects with a high-towering fly ball to left field. Miller goes back, back, back. Hasta La Baseball Baby! It's a two-run shot for Scott Wilson!"

Casey jumped in the air as she rounded third base and smacked a high five to the third base coach. The Power players emptied out of the dugout to congratulate Wilson. Casey crossed the plate for the first run, and turned around to greet Wilson. He crossed the plate a few moments later as the team swarmed to the top of the dugout to meet him.

The scoreboard was flashing "POWERSHOT!!!" as the crowd roared its approval. The next two batters for the Power grounded out to the shortstop, and the first inning was complete. The score: Portland Power, 2, Sacramento Sting, 0.

The two teams battled for the next four innings, with neither of them able to score, until it was the bottom of the fifth, and Casey came up to the plate with no outs, and Julio Perez on first. Casey looked down at the third base coach, and he tugged on his left ear — the sign for the sacrifice bunt.

Again the defense went into their shift, with the first and third basemen moving in close, expecting the sacrifice bunt. This time though, the shortstop stood closer to second, and the second baseman stood closer to first, so they could cover their respective bags if the sacrifice bunt came. As the pitcher prepared to deliver the first pitch, Casey squared around to face him, giving the bunt away early. But she pulled her bat away as the first pitch slid over the inside corner for a called strike one. Again, she wanted to see how the defense was playing the bunt, and again she had an idea.

The pitcher began his windup for the second pitch, and delivered what he thought was a perfect pitch in this situation – a high fastball. He could not have known that this was exactly what Casey wanted.

As she squared around to bunt, she faced the third baseman, who had moved in several steps in front of the bag in anticipation of the bunt. When he saw Casey square around and face him, he took another step closer.

As the ball reached Casey, she firmly bunted the ball high in the air towards the charging third baseman, but at the last moment she gave it an extra push, and it went sailing high over his head. The crowd let out a groan, and the Power coaches both yelled "Back!" to Julio Perez, as they all thought that Casey had mistakenly popped up to the third baseman.

But then they all suddenly yelled "Go! Run!" to Perez, as the ball landed ten feet behind the surprised third baseman, and fell with a thud onto open dirt. Perez scurried safely to second base, and Casey crossed the bag at first with her second bunt base hit of the day.

Again Stan Marx made the call in amazement. "The oh-one pitch to Collins as she squares around to bunt. It's a high fastball. And she pops it up to the third baseman –- No! It's over his head! It's over his head! It's going to be a base hit, and everyone is safe. What a break for the Power, Gunner."

"Well, it was no break Stan; that was an intentional move by Casey Collins. What an amazing display of bat control, and yet another trick from up her sleeve. I can't wait to see what she pulls next. Maybe we *should* call her The Magician."

The centerfield scoreboard sign flashed "POWER PLAY!" as the number two hitter for the Power, James Johnson, came up to the plate, while up in the owner's box, Bud Harley was explaining to his Japanese guests how he had handpicked Casey Collins.

With runners on first and second and nobody out, the third base coach again flashed the bunt sign. The first pitch to Johnson was high and inside, but the umpire called it a strike, and it put him in the hole with a 0 and 1 count. He squared around and bunted the second pitch towards the third base side, but it went foul for strike two. The bunt sign was taken off, and on the next pitch, Johnson hit a ground ball to the second baseman. It was a tailor made double play ball.

Casey was off and running at the ground ball, as the shortstop came running over to second base to receive the throw from the second baseman. The second baseman fielded it cleanly and made a perfect throw to second, where the shortstop caught the ball and slid his foot over the bag for the first out. Then, stepping towards right field and facing first base, he prepared to make the relay throw for the double play.

But he misjudged how quickly Casey would get down the baseline. She slid into him hard, knocking him off his feet and causing the throw to go high, over the first baseman's head. Julio Perez was just getting to third when he saw the throw go high, and he scampered home as Johnson stopped at first.

The shortstop was upset as he picked himself off the ground. Casey had also risen and was dusting herself off, preparing to head back to the dugout. The shortstop walked over to her aggressively and put his face directly in front of hers.

"What the hell are you doing, bitch?" he screamed at her.

Casey shoved him in the chest and looked him in the eye as she tried to walk around him. "Just playing baseball, pal."

The managers from both teams, as well as Bud Harley, held their breaths as they feared another confrontation on the field. But the second base umpire jumped in front of the shortstop and said, "Hey, back off. That was a legal slide. Get back to your position or I'll throw you out of the game." He glared at the shortstop until he grunted in disgust and walked back to take his position.

Casey got back to the dugout, where Pop greeted her. "You okay?" he asked.

"Yeah, I'm fine, the guy was just being a jerk."

"Well, great slide. You got us another run."

After the next two batters flied out, it was now 3-0 in favor of the Power, as they took the field for the top half of the 6th inning. TJ Morrison continued to pitch well, getting the first two batters to ground out to the infielders, but gave up a solo home run before finally getting the third out on a pop up behind second base. The score was now: Portland Power 3, Sacramento Sting: 1.

Another two innings passed without further scoring, until it was the top half of the eight inning. Casey's teammates were feeling pretty confident, knowing that all they had to do was to hold Sacramento for two innings and the championship was theirs. Unfortunately, that would prove to be easier said than done.

TJ Morrison had been going strong up until then, giving up only three singles and the solo home run in the sixth inning. As he faced the first batter of the eighth inning, he ran the count to 3 and 2, and then lost him on a questionable call for ball four.

Butch Morris had been watching the pitch count closely, which was now at 108 pitches. As soon as ball four was called, he motioned out to the bullpen, and Mooch Moran got up to throw. TJ walked the next batter on four straight pitches, and it was clear that he had run out of gas.

Morris called time-out and walked out to the mound, tapping his right arm a couple of times. He wanted Moran. Morris took the baseball from TJ, shook his hand and smacked him on the butt. The crowd gave the pitcher a standing ovation as he walked back to the Power dugout, where he was congratulated for a job well done. Butch Morris stood on the mound holding the baseball as the outfield fence opened up and Mike Moran, his hat slightly askew, came jogging through on his way to the mound.

The crowd was still on their feet when they saw Moran enter, and shouts of "Mooooch" reigned down on the field. Mooch reached the mound and took the ball from Morris, who said simply, "It's up to you, big man."

Mooch took his warm-up throws as Morris returned to the dugout, and Casey looked on from right field. *He looks a little wild*, she thought to herself as she watched him complete his warm-ups. The umpire called "Play ball", and play resumed.

With runners on first and second, Mooch went into his stretch. On the very first pitch, he was trying to throw inside to the batter, but came too far inside and hit the batter right in the middle of the arm. There was no danger of altercation however, as everyone in the stadium knew that Mooch would not throw at a batter in this situation.

However, now, Sacramento had bases loaded with no outs. Mooch wound up and delivered a slider as the first pitch to the next batter, and it curved over the outside corner for a strike. On the next pitch, a high fastball, the batter swung hard and connected with the ball, but got under it so that it went almost straight up into the air about 30 feet. Grunt whipped off his mask, got under the ball and made the catch for the first out of the inning. The batter slammed his bat into the ground as he walked back to the dugout in disgust.

Now, with one out and bases loaded, a ground ball could lead to a double play and get Portland out of the inning. Mooch stood on the mound, playing with his hat and shuffling it around on his head. He looked in to get the signal from Grunt, then wound up and threw the first pitch 2 feet over the batter's head. The crowd groaned as the ball hit the backstop with a loud thud, and the runner from third came sprinting in towards home plate.

Mooch ran in to cover home plate, but by the time Grunt retrieved the ball and threw it to him, the runner had already crossed the plate, and it was now Portland 3, Sacramento 2. The other base runners advanced, and the Sting now had runners on second and third with only one out. Again Mooch paced on the mound, moving his hat into another off-center position, preparing for the next batter.

Mooch worked him to a full count, and then blew a fastball by him for strike three, and the second out. The Power was still up 3-2, and now a strikeout, fly-out or ground ball would get them out of the inning.

Up to the plate came Larry Thomas, Sacramento's clean-up hitter. He was already 2 for 3 in the game, with the solo home run in the sixth. Mooch pitched around him carefully, until the count was 2-2, then wound up and delivered a slider which was intended to be inside, but got out over the plate. Thomas stepped into the pitch and laced a shot right over the shortstop's head into left center field.

The runner on third base scored easily, as Darnell Jenkins jumped on the ball quickly. With two outs, the runner on second was off at the crack of the bat, and as he approached third base the coach was waving him around towards home plate. Jenkins scooped up the ball and fired it on a line drive right towards home plate.

Grunt whipped off his catcher's mask as he took a couple of steps out in front of home plate, standing on the third base line, waiting for the throw and blocking the plate. The ball came in on one hop and Grunt caught it just as the runner came barreling into him, knocking him back two feet and creating a huge cloud of dust. Grunt rolled over a couple of times in the dirt as the umpire watched closely. He held up his catcher's mitt to show that the ball was still in the webbing, and the umpire pointed at the runner as he jerked his thumb in the air, yelling "You're out!"

The crowd cheered at the great throw by Jenkins and the gutsy play by Grunt at home plate, but the noise subsided quickly as they realized that their team had blown the lead and the game was now tied.

As the Power reached the dugout, there were a few high fives for Darnell Jenkins and Grunt, and a few "Don't worry about it, Mooch, we'll get 'em back," comments for Moran. It didn't help Mooch feel any better, as he threw his glove against the dugout wall, and slinked down into a seat on the bench.

Casey was scheduled to bat third in the inning, and as she made her way down the dugout past Mooch, she slapped him lightly on the bill of his hat. "Hey, don't worry about it Mooch, we'll get it back."

"Yeah, sure," was the dejected reply.

Casey empathized with Mooch. Every ballplayer at every level had their screw-ups; it was just unfortunate that Mooch had his at this particular time. And she felt bad about the current awkward state of their relationship, although that was not uppermost in her mind at this point.

Even though it was only the bottom of the eighth inning, the crowd was on its feet, cheering as Darnell Jenkins, who had just made the good defensive play, came to the plate. It was one of those interesting occurrences in baseball where it seemed that so many times when a player made a great play in the field to end the defensive half of the inning, he also led off the offensive half of the inning. It had absolutely no significance; it was just one of those baseball-isms.

The centerfield scoreboard flashed "POWER SURGE!!!" as the pitcher wound up to deliver the first pitch. Jenkins swung hard and connected solidly with the ball, hitting a searing line drive right at the third baseman, who caught it more out of self-defense than anything else, but caught it nonetheless.

This brought up the shortstop, Julio Perez, who took the count to 3 and 2, but struck out on a wicked curveball right at the knees. It was now Casey's turn to bat in the bottom of the eighth with two outs. She was two for three so far in the game, with two bunts for base hits. She had hit a solid line drive over the shortstop's head in the fourth inning, but the special shift that the defense put on for her worked, and the short fielder made the catch of what otherwise would have been another base hit.

Now she stepped into the batter's box and surveyed the field, looking around for any edge she could find, any opening where she could hit the ball. She looked around the infield. Even with two outs, the first and third basemen were up on the grass, guarding against the bunt. The shortstop was shifted over almost behind the third baseman, guarding against one of Casey's special "pop-up" bunts, and the second baseman was playing in a few steps closer than normal, making the infield very tight.

The outfield still had its shift on as well. The short fielder strategy had worked in the fourth inning against Casey, so, again, the center fielder ran in to take up the short fielder position, as the right fielder came over to play a right-center position. It looked almost like Casey had "closed" right field. In fact, she hadn't.

After a one-ball and two-strike count, Casey again surveyed the field as the pitcher looked in to take the sign. He had thrown the first two strikes over the outside corner and he was going to try and fool Casey by coming in tight. She watched the pitch he delivered, a fastball, coming in very close to her body.

She took one step backward with her right foot, opening up her stance so she was almost facing the pitcher. The first baseman, seeing this move, thought she was going to try another drag bunt, and he broke out of his ready position and started to take a few steps in towards the plate.

But Casey swung away instead, connecting solidly with the baseball, which almost took the first baseman's head off. He flailed at it wildly in self-defense, then watched in panic as it rocketed over his head and bounced ten feet behind first base.

Casey was off at the crack of the bat, and was halfway down the first base line when she saw the ball hit behind first base and bounce towards the right field corner. The second baseman turned and started to sprint after the ball, while the right fielder, playing all the way over towards center field, madly did the same.

"That's three! That's three!" Pop shouted to Casey at the top of his voice, indicating that it looked like a sure triple. Casey swung outside of the foul line as she prepared to make the wide turn at first, which she did at breakneck speed. She watched the ball rolling steadily towards the right field corner as she neared second base, and looked at the third base coach for the signal to stand or slide going into third base.

Instead, the third base coach was swinging his arm in a cartwheel motion, and screaming "Take four! Take four!"

Surprised by this, Casey swung her head around to see that the second baseman had just reached the ball, and he was preparing to throw it to the first baseman, who had come running out to take the relay throw. The crowd was on its feet as Casey rounded third.

There was going to be a play at the plate.

As Casey rounded the bag at third, the first baseman, who was now standing in the outfield, caught the relay throw, turned, and made a strong throw to home, but it was about three feet in front of the plate, up the first base line. The catcher came out to catch the ball as Casey was still about fifteen feet away from home plate. She wasn't going to make it.

Casey had gotten the better of the catcher all game long in their verbal exchanges, as well as performing well at the plate. The frustration of this welled up inside the catcher as he caught the ball and saw Casey barreling down the third base line towards home. He gritted his teeth as he tucked the ball into his glove. He was not only going to tag her out, he was going to knock her lights out.

He saw Casey throw both her arms forward in an emphatic motion, like she was preparing to make a dramatic dive into home plate. Still three feet to the right of the plate, the catcher took two steps towards the third base line where Casey was running, and left his feet, holding his glove with the ball in front of him and hurling his whole body at Casey.

Casey knew that the catcher had the advantage, and that she could neither beat him to the plate nor knock him over. And so the move that she had made with her arms as she looked like she was going to make a big dive, was a complete decoy, and instead she simply pulled to a stop a few feet in front of the plate. The catcher, who had already left his feet and had the weight of his whole body behind him, went flying by Casey, and he madly tried to swipe at her with his glove as he flew helplessly past the play.

Casey held both her arms high in the air and sucked in her gut as much as she could, and the catcher's tag went empty as he landed with a thud on the far side of the baseline. Casey calmly walked over and stepped on home plate for the go-ahead run, as a deafening roar rose from the crowd.

"Ah Shit! Goddammit!" The catcher screamed as he contorted his body in exasperation, but was drowned out by the roar of the crowd. The scoreboard went ballistic, flashing GIRL POWER!!! as Casey's teammates swarmed around her at home plate.

"Can you believe it!" Stan Marx exclaimed into the microphone. "The Magician does it again, pulling two separate tricks on one play. That was incredible! Not only does she pull one down the line, she performs an escape routine at home plate that results in an inside-the-park home run. The woman is incredible!"

"I don't even know what to say," Gunner laughed. "Do you say 'Hasta La Baseball Baby' for an inside-the-parker? What she just did at home plate should go in every highlight film from now on. You're right, Stan. The woman is incredible."

Now the Power had a one-run lead, and all they had to do was hold Sacramento for three outs in the top of the ninth. The biggest smile on the Power bench belonged to Mooch Moran, as Casey's play had given him new life. His mood sobered a bit as he reflected on his performance from the last inning, but the other players were now coming along and smacking him on the knee, or giving him a high five, trying to bolster his confidence.

"Come on, Mooch, it's all up to you now," Crush Davis said.

Pop came over and his put a hand on Mooch's shoulders, as James Johnson made the final out for the Power. "Come on now, son, you know what you have to do. Just bear down and throw strikes."

"Sure thing, Pop," Mooch responded, as he started up the dugout steps. Butch Morris met him at the top of the stairs, and pulled him aside. He spit a big wad of tobacco on the grass, and looked at Mooch, who was now chewing bubblegum.

"All right Moran, here's the deal," Morris started. "We have a lefty coming up first, followed by two righties, so I'm not going to pull you for a left-hander. But we need you to throw strikes. Three outs and we take this thing. Okay?"

"Got it, Skip," Mooch said as he turned and walked out to the mound, his hat tilting off slightly to the right.

Casey jogged out to take her position in right field, and received a standing ovation from the folks in Casey's Corner. The scoreboard was flashing POWER STAND!!! in bright silver letters, but it couldn't match the glow that was emanating from Sue Collins' proud face. Casey caught her eye and blew her a kiss, and then turned and prepared for the start of the inning.

The first batter worked Mooch to a full count, and then to everyone's dismay, drew a walk as Mooch threw the last pitch high and outside. The crowd groaned as Sacramento now had the tying run on first with nobody out.

The next batter executed a perfect sacrifice bunt, which Scott Wilson at third fielded and threw over to Crush Davis for the first out. One down, but a runner on second base, in scoring position.

Mooch got the next batter to pop up to shallow left field, which held the base runner at second, and gave them two outs. A strike out, a ground out or a fly out and the Portland Power would win the Pacific Coast League Championship.

Mooch worked the next batter to a count of two balls and one strike. On the next pitch, he hit a hard ground ball in between the third baseman and the shortstop. Wilson dove at the ball and missed. Julio Perez, moving to his right, dove and knocked the ball down, but could not come up with it in time to throw anyone out.

The runner on second advanced to third, and now Sacramento had runners on first and third, with two outs. Mooch stood on the mound, checking the runner at first very closely. He needed to keep him from getting to second, so that if he gave up a base hit it only scored the tying run, not the go-ahead run. Mooch threw over to first twice, then threw an inside pitch to the batter for ball one. He followed that with ball two, ball three, and then, after one strike, threw ball four. Butch Morris kicked over the water cooler as the crowd groaned in dismay.

Now the pressure was intense. There was no room to move for either team. With bases loaded and two outs, down by one run, Sacramento could not afford a strike out, a ground out or a fly out. Conversely, they could score on a walk, a wild pitch, or preferably a base hit, which would most likely score two runs and give them the lead.

Mooch paced back and forth on the back of the mound, glancing out to the bullpen. No one was warming up. It was his game to win or lose. He toyed nervously with his hat as he prepared to step up to the pitching rubber, while Stan Marx narrated for the home listeners.

"Well, folks, here we are. Top of the ninth inning, two outs and bases loaded for the Sacramento Sting. All Mooch Moran and the Power need is one out and they are the Pacific Coast League Champions."

"Yeah, but he's been hot and cold tonight, Stan," added Gunner. "He needs to find a way to concentrate and throw strikes."

Stan Marx took over again. "Right, well, here we go. Moran toys with his hat for the hundredth time tonight and prepares to take the mound. He steps forward and...wait a minute, time has been called on the field. Yes, time has been called down on the field, and Casey Collins is jogging in to the pitcher's mound from right field. Apparently, she is the one who called time. Wow, I've never seen a right fielder call time like this before. Have you, Gunner?"

"No, I sure haven't Stan. I can't imagine what this could be about. Maybe she knows something about this batter, or maybe she sees something else. Heck, the way this lady plays, who knows, maybe she's going in to pitch herself."

"Well, up here in the booth, we can only speculate."

Down on the field, Casey reached the pitcher's mound as every eye in the stadium watched her, wondering what was going on. Butch Morris and Pop could only look on in wonderment. As Casey arrived, she greeted Mooch.

"Hey, Mooch," she said with a nod.

"Hey, Casey," an astonished Mooch responded.

"How're ya doing?"

Mooch looked at her. "Well, I'm kind of busy right now, you know?"

"Yeah, well. Listen Mooch, you don't need the hat routine."

"What do you mean?"

"You know what I mean. The crooked hat thing. It's distracting you more than it is the hitters."

Mooch looked at her with a frown. "You think so?"

"Yeah. Remember that day we had batting practice? You were all over the place. Once you turned your hat around straight, you threw strikes. Remember?"

Mooch's eyes went high in his head as he remembered. "Yeah, I remember. Okay." He turned his hat around straight, then looked back at Casey. "Anything else?"

Just then the home plate umpire started walking out to the pitcher's mound to break up the meeting. Casey saw him coming, and gave him a short wave, indicating the meeting was ending.

As she started to walk away from the mound, she turned to Mooch and said, "Oh, Mooch, one more thing."

Again Mooch was perplexed as he looked at her. "Yeah, what is it?"

"I love you."

"What?" he asked in shock.

"You heard me. I love you. Now throw some strikes so we can win this damn game." She turned and jogged back out to the outfield, leaving Mooch standing on the mound with a broad grin on his face.

He wound up and threw the three fastest pitches he'd ever thrown in his life, all right down the middle, and all for strikes.

Thirty-One

There was Bedlam on the field as the Portland Power players from the bench rushed out to join the players from the field, all converging on the mound in celebration. The fans roared as the scoreboard shot fireworks into the air, and "POWER PENANT!" flashed repeatedly on the screen.

The Japanese businessmen from Mitzua Motors bowed to Bud Harley, and Burt Drivers and Uncle Mike planted kisses on the cheeks of Sue Collins, as *Casey's Corner* stood and waved their GIRL POWER! signs.

Casey was somewhere in the middle of the huddle when she felt herself being hoisted in the air. James Johnson had grabbed her by one arm, and Grunt grabbed the other, as they lifted her up and onto Crush's shoulders. The big farm boy stood up straight and tall, and Casey was elevated above the other players, who were hopping and jumping around in celebration.

Swelling with pride and elation, Casey raised a fist in the air. A photographer snapped a picture, and it was featured on the front page of the next day's *Portland Times*. The caption read:

Most Valuable Player Casey Collins is hoisted on her teammate's shoulders, as the Portland Power capture their first ever Pacific Coast League Championship.

Three days later, the MVP of the championship game sat on the couch in her mother's living room back in Richmond, Washington. She had brought Mooch home with her, and he sat next to her as they enjoyed the small celebration that was being hosted by Sue Collins. They had invited a few friends, who were spread around the living room in small groups, engaged in various conversations.

Sitting there on the couch at her mother's house, Casey had a great feeling of satisfaction. As she had done throughout her entire life, she had shown that she could play with the boys.

She had proved that with speed, hustle and knowledge of the game, she could not only compete, she could excel.

As she was basking in her contentment, the phone rang, and Sue went over to answer it. "Hello? Yes. May I ask who's calling? One moment, please. Casey, it's for you."

"Who is it?" Casey asked as she looked up from the chair.

"Some guy named David Appleby. Says he's from Cincinnati."

Excerpt from… *Ninth Man II: The First Woman*

Chapter Three

This time it was Casey Collins who called the press conference. Ever since the initial phone call from the representative of the Cincinnati Reds back in October of last year, she had been caught up in a whirlwind of publicity. Once word of the offer from Cincinnati leaked out, it caused a mad scramble for Casey's services among the rest of the major league teams.

In a curious series of events, Portland had been awarded the major league franchise formerly known as the Montreal Expos. The group that was to assume ownership of the relocated franchise was the Portland Baseball Association (PBA), headed by Bud Harley, with Mitzua Motors of Japan as a silent partner. The PBA also assumed ownership of the assets of the Portland Power, which would cease to exist.

The minor league Power players that were still with the team would be reassigned to other minor league cities under the Texas Rangers organization, with which the Power had been affiliated. However, in a quirky contractual twist, since Casey Collins had only signed a 90 day contract with the Portland Power, an MLB affiliated team, and fulfilled that contract, she in effect became a free agent to the major leagues.

Every major league organization wanted to become the first to sign a woman to their roster, and Casey Collins became the first baseball player ever, man *or* woman, to receive offers from all 30 major league teams.

Tension had been building for months over speculation as to which major league team she would choose to join. For Casey's part, she had evaluated each offer with an objective eye.

First, there was the prospect of playing for the Cincinnati Reds, and honoring her father by becoming the first ever father and daughter combination to play for a major league team.

Then there was the offer from the Texas Rangers and the opportunity to play with A-Rod, the best player in the game. The California teams all offered, of course, and the prospect of playing in the warm southern weather had its appeal.

There was the offer from the Seattle Mariners, and the prospect of staying in her home state, but they had Ichiro in right field. Although it would be awesome to play on the same team as one of her idols, she wasn't about to watch him from the bench.

She even considered, albeit briefly, an offer from the Toronto Bluejays. Wouldn't it be funny if she made history by becoming the first woman to play in the majors, and it was with a Canadian team? Nah, she was an American and she would play for an American team.

Through it all there was the money. The small town girl that had been blown away less than a year ago by increasing her salary from $16,000 to $32,000, was now being offered millions. The lowest offer she had was from the Florida Marlins, and that was for $2.5 million a year for 3 years. Instant millionaire.

The second lowest offer was from the Portland Expos, for $3 million per year. Although they were fairly well financed thanks to Mitzua Motors, they had to spend money to attract some other big name free agents in order to rebuild the ex-Montreal team. But Bud Harley made it clear he wanted Casey to stay in Portland, and while it presented an opportunity to stay in a town she was now comfortable with, should she go for the big money up front, in case her career in the majors did not pan out?

And then there was "The Boss", George Steinbrenner, who's only comment was, "Whatever your best offer is, we'll add five million to it." *Wow, Babe Ruth, Mickey Mantle…Casey Collins.* It seemed unreal, but in fact all she had to do was sign her name, and it would become reality. *Casey Collins, a New York Yankee?* As she was preparing to enter this new phase of her life, why not do it on the biggest stage in the world – New York City?

As the amount of rumor and speculation grew, one thing was clear—Casey Collins would in fact become the first woman ever to play major league baseball. And the number one sports question in America had become, *which team was Casey Collins going to make history with?*

It was not an easy decision for Casey to make, but once it was made she decided to put an end to the media circus by calling a press conference to announce her decision. Only a handful of people knew the result—Casey, her lawyer/agent, Sue Collins, Mooch Moran, Anne Ross, and the representative from the organization she had chosen. All were sworn to secrecy, and it was the best kept secret since the last episode of *Survivor.*

As Casey looked around the conference room of the Royal Portland Hotel, at the audience of over 100 people, she chuckled to herself when she remembered how nervous she had been at that first press conference for the Portland Power. Now, she was definitely in control, and she was enjoying every minute of it.

She stepped to the podium as the background noise subsided, and addressed the audience, which was at full attention. "Thank you all for coming. I would first like to thank every one of the team that made a proposal, and I'd also like to say that each organization had something to offer, and that it was a difficult decision, but one that has been made. And so, I'd like to end all the speculation by announcing that my new team will be the…"

About the Author

The Ninth Man is the first full-length novel from Bill Pennabaker. A graduate of Penn State University, Bill lives with his wife Marivic in Kirkland, Washington. He is currently working on the screenplay version of The Ninth Man, as well as the sequel to the novel, called Ninth Man II: The First Woman.

Bill welcomes comments about his work at pennabaker@comcast.net

Printed in the United States
1035400003B/121-144